SENSORED SOULS

The Secret Life of a Mind-Hacking Neuroscientist

Jen L. Hanson

White Wave Books
Portland, Oregon, USA

I

Published by White Wave Books
Print ISBN: 978-1-7368150-2-1
eBook ISBN: 978-1-7368150-0-7
Library of Congress Control Number: 2021906780
SENSORED SOULS:
The Secret Life of a Mind-Hacking Neuroscientist

COVER ART: *Music.* Guilherme Marconi, Brazil.

WhiteWaveBooks.com
First edition   Printed in the U.S.A.

DEDICATED TO GANESHA
Inspired Creativity, Remover of Obstacles, God of Beginnings

I offer you my first fiction in gratitude for the opportunities revealed through time, space and ideas which allowed the birth of this rich story.

***

IN LOVING APPRECIATION FOR MY HUSBAND, ERIC HOLZAPFEL

Thank you for trusting me with your characters and coloring in the details of the plot from your creative mind.

I absolutely could not have written this book without you!

TABLE OF CONTENTS

ACKNOWLEDGMENTS

Six amazing women read this book at various stages. Enormous **thank yous** to **Wendi Menashe** for your intelligent and generous insights, and thoughtful questions that helped me see the gaps and the possibilities; **Joanne O'Connell** for your kind honesty and deep knowledge of sci-fi and metaphysical genres, and strong female protagonists; **Anne Lee** for your positive feedback, and for reading the book twice; **Kimberly Barner** for your early impressions that helped inspire me to keep a very rough draft going; **LeAnn Jenkins** for your insights on family and bringing connection to the characters; and **Jana Cinder** for your adept and extensive review through a medical lens, gleaned from thirty years as a nurse.

Thank you also to my sister **Angela Hanson** for your enthusiasm and rounding up draft readers; **Phyllis Newmark** for your encouraging words and use of your home as my "winter writer's retreat;" **Robbie Lynn** for reviewing the text with a sharp eye; and **Steven Jenkins** for your honest feedback and wealth of knowledge, plus saying you were proud of me as I took this project across the finish line.

To everyone who listened as I reflected on these ideas and the writing process, I appreciate your curiosity and interest!

I humbly recognize **COVID-19** for serving up the time to complete this novel, and the **Oregon Unemployment Department** for providing a year of funding to help me do so. I appreciate the **Portland Regional Arts & Culture Council** for giving me a grant to attend the 2019 Association of Writers & Writing Programs Conference, and the **Multnomah County Library system** for offering free wireless printing services.

AUTHOR'S PREFACE

This novel began as a simple wedding gift to Eric Holzapfel when we married in June 2015. I created an elegant five-by-seven book printed on twenty bright white pages. Digital artwork reflected my poem that read:

A Fantasy Made True: A Wedding Gift of Love

For our wedding, I want to give you a special gift.
My gift happens in time, but an expensive watch just
doesn't seem fitting.
Some gifts I know you'd like are outside my budget right now.
Like a fast car in wedding white.
Or a sailboat. Or a private island.
Or pilot training. Or a trip to the moon.

One day we'll have a house. But that's not my gift right now.
So I can't offer you a backyard design studio to make surfboards.
I know you'd like an avocado farm. That would be a good gift, too.
And I wish I could gift you with start-up funds for our business.
The possibilities are wide-open for us.

So I thought of something specific to you and I.
In honor of our wedding, I will give you the gift of time.
By helping you ...
Do something you'd really like; to make a dream come true.

Tell me one of your stories and I'll organize and write it.
Getting it out of your head will be healthy for you.
I know. I know. It's a sci-fi. I'm ready.
With your talents and mine, we'll capture the fantasy. Together.

Let's Begin.

The book you now hold is the result of this union.

Jen L. Hanson
Portland, Oregon
July 21, 2021

SENSORED SOULS

PART ONE

The Senses

Master your senses;
the eyes, the ears, the nose, the tongue.
Be disciplined in body, speech and mind.
Then in all things be a master,
of what you do and say and think.
Be free.

—BUDDHA

Chapter One

Around seven o'clock Philip Goode knocked on the door of the apartment. "Hello? I've brought you some dinner."

"I'm not interested," Persephone called out.

A minute later, she heard the sound of mild scraping. She moved to the door and peered through the peephole, noticing Philip doing something around the jamb. Seriously? When she tried to open the door, she found it barred, trapping her inside the apartment.

She pulled on the handle, but the door didn't budge. "Do not lock me in here!"

"Why didn't you tell us INTERPOL talked to you when you arrived in Shanghai?" Philip asked her, with obvious irritation.

"Uh ... what?"

"Don't pretend the information wouldn't have been important for us to know, Persephone. The INTERPOL network uploaded their log from Thursday and my system registered an update a few minutes ago. Their notations detailed talking with you at your hotel."

"I knew nothing about this place then," she said. "I didn't tell them anything except I was looking for my father."

"You still should have told us," said Philip. "Anything you told them could pose a security risk to this gallery. We have precious little time."

"When they arrive, they will add kidnapping to your charges," she said. "You have no right to lock me in here. Open this door."

She heard the double doors outside the apartment close followed by the sound of silence. *What are they doing? This is bad. This is really bad.*

"Philip! Open the door! Let me out!" Persephone banged on the entrance. Anger would be a mild way to put it. She didn't like losing her independence—or being locked in—both of which she had been dealing with for the past two days.

But the "fixer" didn't return.

The situation was inevitable. She sat alone. Persephone considered the heavy decision upon her. At that point, the only thing she found comfort in was the couch. She didn't know what to do with the information she had. Should she sabotage their plan? She absolutely could; they had to know that.

By late evening, she turned down the lights and exhaustion overtook her. She slept in short drifts, but mostly she spent the night contemplating, moving in and out of past conversations, considerations and little rest.

Nothing seemed logical anymore except she was definitely the only rational person there. Certainly clarity would come from the confusion. What could she do now but trust herself and her ideals?

She reviewed her choices. It was like a damn chess game— and she was losing. Staying positive proved difficult, but she tried to hold onto her sense of inner wisdom.

Persephone remembered talking to her mother about finding her dad and recalled her saying, "You must follow your own logic." What did rationale have to do with any of it? She knew now the best choice may not be acceptable—even to herself.

The wall screen displayed 2:32 a.m. on Sunday, August 26, 2108. What a strange few days. Sure, she had made a few poor decisions ... but she still had time. Didn't she? An insight flickered: she could win the future.

In the silence and isolation, Persephone moved toward awareness. Before, each moment resounded like a roar. Now she felt quiet, like listening at the edge of the ocean after it cleared from a storm. Memories of the rocky coastline of East Sussex brought a longing to go there after she returned home to London.

***

Persephone thought about the events leading to her current lockdown. A week ago the Royal Mail had delivered a cubed box about thirty centimeters on each side. A courier had called her on Sunday afternoon at the Imperial College neuroscience research lab she headed, wondering what time she would be home to sign for a special delivery.

When she told him it wouldn't be until close to nine, and he replied, "Very well; I'll see you then," she remembered things seemed a bit unusual.

A short walk from the Tube brought her to her apartment house on London's Isle of Dogs. Due to the high tide that evening, Persephone entered the lobby using the underground pedestrian passageways built across her neighborhood.

The dark tunnel provided direct access to the lower level of her building. Anything to avoid trudging through the murky water of the River Thames, now rippling across the surface sidewalks, was a good thing.

"Good evening, Seph," the doorman greeted her, "you have a courier waiting."

"Thanks, Albert," she replied as her long, dark hair fell into her eyes. She hadn't had time to get it cut in months, and it was driving her crazy. It felt hot on her neck with the August temperatures.

"I appreciate you bringing the package so late," she told the patient courier as she glanced at her watch. "I could have certainly received it tomorrow. I didn't know anything was coming."

"But of course," he replied. "Our service doesn't wait on these matters." She signed for the box, and he dashed off with a simple, "Good evening."

"Good night," she said, looking down at the delivery in her hands.

"Night, Al," she said, waving her hand over her shoulder behind her as she headed to the lift.

Persephone brought the package into her flat, feeling curious, but cautious. She dropped her jacket and key cards onto the fiberglass console dividing the spacious kitchen from the entryway. "Living room lights on," she said. She pulled scissors out from a drawer she wished she had time to organize, and took the box to the sofa to open it.

Inside she found lightweight metallic packaging folded over a jet black sphere that looked like a cricket ball. The cold aluminum form was solid, but evenly weighted. It felt nice in her hands; as smooth and shiny as obsidian.

Persephone had heard about these Holo-Grams but had never received one. How exciting! She knew the information contained within the small, digital messenger spheres could not be hacked, saved or re-transmitted once unlocked. They ensured only the person meant to receive the message would, with no trace of data remaining.

She grasped the orb and tried to separate the two parts by rotating and pulling them. But the case did not split. She rolled the globe gently in her palms, but didn't detect a shift in the interior.

An oval flat spot the size of a grape straddled the groove around the middle. When she placed her index finger on the circle, nothing happened. Her thumb would have been a better first guess. Yes, perfect; her thumbprint made the sphere divide with a smooth slide.

"Hello," said a pleasant female voice from the device. "Please place the Holo-Gram on a firm horizontal surface. Your message will begin momentarily."

Persephone set the halves down on the grey coffee table matching her console. An array of lit particles arose from inside the container and began to join to produce a 3-D image. Like a genie freed from a bottle, the brilliant specks faded soon after being released, replaced moments later by holographic rays melding to create the impression of ... her dad!

Her father stood in her living room! His frail reflection appeared so real. He looked paler and much thinner; no longer the robust man she'd always known, even as he aged.

She knew the light brought a recorded message and not a visual chat, but she couldn't help but speak out loud. "Dad? Where are you? What's happening?"

Persephone's dad had disappeared from Singapore six weeks earlier. She knew from her mother he had left on a trip, but hadn't returned home. Her mum gave her updates during their weekly phone chats, if you could call, "I'm still waiting to hear something," an update.

Her father had received a liver transplant five months prior to his disappearance, hoping to help ameliorate the cardiac problems resulting from his TFAP, more formally known as Transthyretin Familial Amyloid Polyneuropathy. Healing caused him great fatigue, however, and his amyloidosis seemed to be getting the best of him.

If the protein collecting in the nerves branching out from his spinal cord and brain continued, it would affect his senses. If he couldn't see, feel pain, or had trouble walking, he could find himself in a life-threatening situation.

Persephone had felt worried and distracted for weeks about her father and his condition.

Along with the shock and excitement that came from seeing her dad's image, Persephone also recognized the Holo-Gram was an ironic way for him to visit her. She maintained an underlying hurt from two years earlier when she and her father both spoke at the British Neuroscience Association conference outside Bristol.

He opted to fly home to Singapore straight afterward, rather than travel just two hours to see her new flat in East London near where Canary Wharf used to be. The river had risen above its old banks long before she was born, but everyone still called the area, "Canary Wharf." Persephone still felt disappointed her dad couldn't—or wouldn't—make more time for her, even in his retirement.

The early and deep bond she had with him as a child had morphed into professional respect over the years. Her parents had raised her to be independent, and she understood everyone had their own lives. Still, he hadn't come to London even once since she'd graduated from college. To be only a couple of hours away and not take the time to visit her home felt personal, even if it wasn't meant to be.

"*Hi Sweetheart,*" her father began from the Holo-Gram. "*I know talking in person or on the phone would be better. But in seeing me now, we're moving toward new ways of communicating. I'm in Shanghai, and I won't be returning to Singapore. I'm sorry to say my liver transplant is failing, causing my condition to take a steep downturn.*

"*I need you to come to Shanghai. You will understand in time why I'm requesting you keep this between us. Should anyone have questions, you can say you are traveling to attend the Asia-Pacific Conference on Intelligent Robot Systems. It will be happening when you get this message. You've already been registered.*

"*I know I'm asking you to put your research on hold for a few weeks. You are doing amazing work, Persephone. I apologize for this interruption. It's imperative, or I wouldn't ask you to come. First, please go to my home office in Singapore. You'll be able to piece together the information you'll need to locate me in Shanghai. I believe in you. Please come. Now.*"

Her dad finished speaking and his holographic image floated in stillness for a moment. The robotic female voice followed: "This message will auto-delete in five minutes. To view the sender's communication once again, hold your thumb over the sphere for two seconds."

Persephone watched the Holo-Gram one more time, then saw the form of her father fade away. She walked across her living room, sat down at her glass dining table and looked out the window at the expansive River Thames. A mild headache began to settle in. To alleviate it, she pinched the upper bridge of her nose and closed her eyes.

If she could trust one person in the world to be straightforward with her, it was her father. She also knew him well enough to know he wouldn't ask her to keep a secret—and yet, he did. Why didn't he just call her? Why was he in Shanghai, of all places, and why wasn't he coming back?

Concerned for her dad's safety, but intrigued by the mystery, Persephone called her mother. As she paced around her flat, she wondered what to tell her. Did her mum know anything about this? It was six in the morning in Singapore. "Pick up the phone, Mum ... pick up," she said. When she received her voicemail, Persephone left a simple message as she tried to quell the slight tremble in her voice.

"Hi Mum. I'm calling about Dad. Just wondering if you've heard anything yet. I'm doing a little traveling and I'm coming to Singapore. We have to figure out what is happening. Just wanted to let you know I'm going to book a flight for tomorrow. Call me back when you get this message, OK. Love you. Bye."

*****

Persephone finished recalling the events leading to her current predicament and snapped back into the present. Six days ago she'd traveled to Shanghai to find her dad. Now she was alone, locked in a well-appointed, but chilly basement apartment of a strange art gallery with no way to escape. Her life could be at risk—and nobody knew it.

A wave of anxiety moved through her, and she exhaled loudly to release her stress.

Then she forced herself to stand, turn on the lights and go shower. It was time to deal with matters. She remained shaken in accepting her father had led her to such a haunted place where she found only a disorienting maze of questions with horrific answers.

The warm water helped her reclaim her sense of self. She lathered the body wash, working to scrub through her fatigue before rinsing. No matter how many suds she created, she couldn't cleanse the disgust rippling through her.

After five minutes, Persephone turned off the hot water and stood in the frigid stream for one hundred and eighty seconds counting in her head, *One one thousand, two one thousand* ... She'd taken three-minute cold showers daily for almost twenty years to stimulate a healthy nervous system, clear her mind and boost her general immunity.

She began cold dousing to try something different during her freshman year in college. It was little more than a habit through grad school. But it became her method of meditation as her neuroscience career developed. The practice had worked for a lot of things—so maybe it would work for this.

The water always functioned as a lifeline back to herself and the icy flow helped dissipate her fear. It flushed out nervous toxins and brought personal strength back to her resolve.

Persephone wondered if INTERPOL would actually show up at the gallery. She knew it didn't matter whether they did, or not. Her paradigm shift required new methods of approaching the situation. She finished her shower and stepped onto the clean mat.

***

Philip returned at three-ten a.m. Persephone didn't postulate when he may be back, but expected it, confident and ready. From the living room she heard him undoing the block on the outside of the apartment before he rapped rhythmically on the door.

The smell of dim sum and overripe bananas filled the air with their distinct aroma. The strong scent rode in on the bluish light that slipped through the crack beneath the front door, casting a cool glow across the white tile floor.

"It's three in the morning," she said when she opened the door.

"The time has come," said Philip.

Chapter   Two

"I must take some leave for personal matters," Persephone wrote in the brief email to her staff the morning after receiving the Holo-Gram. "I'll return in a couple weeks." A few of her associates responded hoping everything was okay; Persephone appreciated their concern, but didn't have time to reply.

She maintained good relationships with her staff at the Centre for Neurotechnology at Imperial College London. Although she never hung out with them at the pub after work, and didn't really know them personally, she always tried to be kind, considerate and professional.

Putting her career first as a research manager for NETT, the Europe-wide consortium for Neural Engineering Transformative Technologies, meant everything else came second. Romance proved impossible to sustain for the same reason.

Persephone knew her quick departure for private reasons probably seemed unusual to her colleagues. But she had casually mentioned to a couple of them over the past few weeks that her father was missing, so she figured word would probably get around.

For the flight to Singapore late Monday evening, Persephone boarded a sleek aircraft through the jetway and settled into a comfortable seat. More than a year had passed since she had flown on a supersonic jet. Moving through the air at three times the speed of sound always excited her, even if it was imperceptible. At that moment she appreciated the traditional fourteen-hour journey would only take three.

As the plane rose from the runway for a fast departure from Heathrow, the constant acceleration pushed her into the seat. Persephone peered out her window at the elegant airships moored to the hangers near her terminal. How lovely. She hoped to take one to Asia someday.

A little sadness hit her as she got closer to Singapore. She'd missed National Day two weeks earlier. Her dad used to take her to see amazing fireworks and eat delicious street food, making the festivities a treat for her as a young girl. It had been years since she'd celebrated like that, and most of the events had moved underground now, due to the oppressive heat.

On the plane she exchanged pleasantries with the older gentleman next to her. He wanted to chit chat, but Persephone's own reflections consumed her, and she didn't want to be a private audience for his tales. She remained polite, but made very little eye contact to discourage his conversation.

The time aloft helped her consider what to tell her mother about her sudden trip—and how much her father wanted her to know. He had asked Persephone to keep things between them, but did he mean from her mum as well?

Two and a half hours into the flight, the captain signaled they'd started their initial descent into Singapore. The plane slowed as it moved through the denser air. Persephone closed her eyes and solidified her plan. She decided with her mum's birthday coming up that week, she would focus on something uplifting to ease the heaviness of the past month.

Though her mother had filed a missing person report with the Singapore Police Force when her dad didn't return, Persephone had the clear sense his disappearance didn't feel unnatural or difficult for her mum. The thought was hard to reconcile, and she distracted herself from it by watching the clouds.

Her parents seemed to relate more like second cousins to each other over the years. Without animosity or anger, their cohabitation seemed peaceful, but without connection. Splitting would only make their relationship more complicated than necessary, Persephone rationalized.

She feared her mother's lack of concern, however, may have allowed her dad to slip away. No doubt her mum never faked interest in becoming his caretaker once his condition started to worsen. Maybe her dad left to respect her mum's time?

Many things about the inner workings of her parent's relationship would remain private. Still, Persephone tried to come to some understanding from her limited insight.

In the back of her mind, she couldn't help but wonder whether her mother knew something about where her dad had gone. She didn't know how much transparency to expect from a woman who guarded her emotions so well. Persephone speculated her mother knew more than she'd ever reveal; she always did.

A logical woman who grew up in London, Ardis Jones worked as a computer science professor at Nanyang Technological University in Singapore. Persephone expected some of her mum's students probably interpreted her pragmatic personality as strict and cool. The formality of her British accent created a curt impression, even in casual conversation.

Persephone didn't take her mother's frankness personally any longer. Although she never stopped longing for the emotional nurturing she wanted as a child, as an adult she realized her mum loved her, but she wasn't wired for coddling.

She did admire and respect her mum's sharp intellect and strategic know-how for unraveling tech mysteries and systems. At age sixty-six, her professional skills remained cutting edge.

***

When Persephone exited the Changi Airport on Tuesday morning, the sidewalks were already hot. A car from Terminal Six dropped her off at her parent's house in Tanglin, a wealthy expat neighborhood where they'd lived for twenty-two years. She used the microchip in her wrist to enter the gate, set her black luxury bags on the tile floor and went to find her mother.

"Hi Sama," she greeted the robopup that stood up from its corner mat and scampered toward her. "You look taller than last year." She patted the machine on its head as it nuzzled her leg. "Do you miss Dad?"

The robodog just looked at her. "I know, Sama, I know ... maybe you will one day. Ok, let's go find Mum. Let's go! Let's go find Mum!" she said as her childhood pet leaped around her and followed her walk.

Persephone found her mother in the master bedroom reorganizing a stack of crisp white shirts delivered that morning, folded. She only wore fitted white blouses and grey bottoms, giving her a slim, tailored look complete with pearl earrings.

"Hi, Mum!" Persephone said as she entered the room. She noticed her mom's short brown hair still landed halfway down her neck, presenting the perpetual impression of having it cut weekly. "Nice hair—did you just get it cut?"

"Oh, Seph! You surprised me. You made great time from the airport, love," her mother said as she approached Persephone and gave her a warm hug. "I haven't gotten my hair cut in weeks; I really need to. Are you hungry?"

"Not really. It's hard for me to eat when I feel jetlagged—and worried."

"I understand. It's so nice to see you!"

Her mother's high-quality items dotted the spacious area, dominated by a king-size bed decorated with an olive-green cover made of fine velvet. The house contained three other bedrooms. Two years ago Persephone noticed the smaller back room now held her father's things. Estrangement had obviously become so commonplace her parents never mentioned the details to her.

She walked over to her mother's vanity and used her fingers to expand a framed holographic picture sitting on top, taken thirty years earlier. Making it bigger helped her see her father's younger face and brought him closer.

In the image, she stood sandwiched between her parents on a beach in Positano, Italy when she was seven. As the only family photograph Persephone remembered seeing converted into a hologram, it had projected in the same place since they'd moved into the house. If digital images could fade, it would have.

"Do you miss him, Mum?"

"Oh, Persephone, honestly. I hope your father has not found himself in an unsafe situation. Or that his health has not failed rapidly. I know you want to find him. You two have always been so close. Maybe you'll find what you are looking for here. What made you want to come today? You seem to have a sense of urgency."

"Urgency? He's been gone almost six weeks, Mum! I know Dad made rational decisions. I wonder if something bigger is happening. He wouldn't just disappear. I want to look in his office to see if I can find anything that might give us a clue about where he went."

"I trust he will return," said her mother. "He would often go away for a few days on his own. But I agree with you ... it's been long enough that something feels off."

"Have you heard anything?" asked Persephone.

"Nothing."

"What about from the police?"

"They have nothing to go on. His microchip remains offline without a signal. I'm glad you want to look in his office. I've only gone in to water the plants. We're at the end of the semester, so I haven't had time to process any of this."

"After six weeks?" Persephone didn't expect solace from her mother, but detecting so little concern amplified her anxiety about having to navigate the situation alone.

"It passes quickly, Persephone. Why did you come at this point? You could have come sooner, too. This is a difficult thing for both of us."

"I know it is, Mum. I'm sorry," she said, seeing her tears.

Her mother dried her eyes and asked, "You said something

on the phone about a convention?"

"Yes, the Asia-Pacific Conference on Intelligent Robot Systems is happening in Shanghai this year. I'm flying to China tomorrow afternoon. It's spontaneous. I thought it would be a good chance to come here first. With your birthday in three days, we can celebrate early!"

"I'm glad you did, Seph. It's nice to see you. What did your colleagues say about you leaving London so suddenly?"

"Not much. I travel so often now, I hardly see them. They won't even notice I'm gone. Plus, they know how worried I've been these past few weeks," Persephone said. "Do you think Dad left any clues in his office about where he went?"

"I wish I knew," said her mum. "You must follow your own logic."

"Okay. I'm going to bring my bags to my room and then poke around in his study," said Persephone. "Tonight, how about if I take you out for a birthday dinner?"

"That would be nice, Seph. I need to get some work done here first and then I'd love to catch up. I've missed you!" her mother told her, as she touched Persephone's arm.

***

Being "home" always triggered old memories for Persephone—some good, some difficult. She'd turned fifteen soon after her parents moved into the Tanglin house from the other side of Singapore. As an adult, even though she only visited once a year or so, she still had her old bedroom where she kept an array of things she'd cared about as a teenager.

She entered her room and spotted one of the sentimental items she stored on her dresser—a First Place trophy she won at the Singapore Youth Olympic Cycling Festival. She participated at age sixteen as part of the city-state's bicycle federation.

The award sat next to a small rose-colored jewelry box her grandmother had given her, a couple of small stuffed penguins she still found cute and the first belt she ever earned in Judo—her brown one!

Persephone picked up the little gold statue and caressed its fluid curves, remembering how hard she'd pedaled to cross the finish line first. Her natural dedication, intense ability to focus, and physical strength paired with her fantastic strategy—as everyone called it—had paid off.

But she remembered her motivation behind such extreme training, pushing so fast and feeling so competitive. Grief won her the trophy that day.

Four months before the race, her best friend Maryelle had died. Persephone carried the sadness of her friend's passing into every pedal stroke as she tried to push past blame and self-criticism. She felt responsible for Maryelle's death, a secret she sequestered with physical and academic determination.

Over the years she masked her pain with success and achievement, losing connection with many of her childhood friends as a result. When Persephone moved away from Singapore to attend the prestigious University College London near where her mum grew up, she stayed on the fast track. She was so above and beyond her classmates, it put her out of touch with them.

An overachiever compared with the other students, her curiosity flourished as she earned her undergraduate and post-graduate degrees in neuroscience. She then received her PhD from the Centre for Neurotechnology at Imperial College, where she continued her research on neuroprosthetics and novel neural interfaces.

Persephone put the trophy down and pulled out a small framed photograph of herself and Maryelle from her desk drawer. "You asked me to keep a secret once," she spoke to the picture. "And look what happened; I lost you."

She set the image down on the dresser next to the award and went to go explore her father's office.

His study sat at the end of the hallway. As a teenager, Persephone used to listen for her dad's footsteps traveling past her room when he headed to bed. She always fell asleep faster when he was still in his office. She felt safe knowing he was close by. Her wing of the house felt empty without his presence, and that day especially so.

Persephone peered into the room; it looked so familiar. Her father's sweeping desk sat in the center, facing the door with an expansive case of books lining the back wall from the floor to the ceiling.

A leather couch on the right side of the space along with a comfortable armchair under the big bay window provided a cozy reading nook. She remembered her father often sat there near the ponytail palm.

The glass desk, totally clear of papers, held a few small sentimental items, a laptop, a lush jade plant and a rare, small, white brain cactus. Nothing looked like it had been touched in years. Persephone recognized the space always appeared that way, even at the peak of her father's career.

A meticulous man, her dad had retired three years earlier, at age seventy-two, from Singapore's Mt. Elizabeth Hospital where he'd worked as chief neurosurgeon. She knew he was highly respected for his kind nature and mindful approach, fostered through years of personal meditation practice.

Her dad's high morals and passion for brain matter became the cornerstone of his life and Persephone looked up to him. Someday she hoped to more fully embody his nurturing influence. He had served as a mentor and an inspiration to many, and she wanted to grow like that in her own profession. But she felt a long way off.

Before they'd moved into the house, Persephone considered her father one of her closest friends. Then around the time she turned fifteen their relationship took a dramatic shift. Persephone always thought it was him. He pulled away, spent more time with his colleagues and brought her to the hospital less; then not at all.

They went from having a connection where Persephone felt she could tell him anything, to a strained one. By the time she was sixteen, he didn't seem to know her at all. She felt angry with him—although she didn't know exactly why—and she grieved for the dad she remembered from childhood.

What changed? She always thought it was him, but now that some of her neuroscience colleagues had teenagers, she realized she had caused him pain too, no doubt. Separating from her father was a natural process, but with everything going on in her life as a teenager, Persephone pulled into an emotional shell.

As she entered her father's study, she felt upset about the present, and the past. The last time she recalled being in her dad's office in such a heavy state was when they first moved into the house.

In seeing the couch she remembered a difficult conversation she had had with him. Persephone walked into the room and sat on the soft, light leather, remembering her father sitting next to her twenty-two years earlier. He'd brought her into his study the night Maryelle died, after receiving a call from her friend's parents.

"Sweetheart, please sit down. I'm going to tell you something that will be hard for you to hear," he'd said.

"What is it, Dad?"

"I'm sorry to tell you Maryelle passed away tonight, Seph," he said. Her dad gave her a big hug and remained with her on the couch for an hour as tears rolled down her face.

"You are very strong and you will heal from this. I know it doesn't feel like it right now. Grief is a hard emotion. It'll take some time. But Maryelle will always be with you. We keep those who pass alive in our hearts. You will carry her in your heart forever."

Persephone had gone on a bike ride with Maryelle a few days earlier. Her friend told her in confidence she planned to run away.

Persephone had felt upset about Maryelle's decision, and they got into a fight. "Where will you go? How will you live?" She remembered raising her voice. "Why would you leave before the Cycling Festival? Even if you're not going to compete, I want you to be there."

In tears, Persephone raced off on her bike, knowing she was a stronger rider than Maryelle. Her friend peddled hard to catch up, and she made it. Persephone slammed on her brakes. She wasn't sure why, but she did. It was only for a split-second ... a split-second that changed everything.

She'd replayed the moment in her mind a thousand times.

By now, it was so ingrained in her self-identity she felt surprised she'd still never told anyone about it. She recalled the immediate jab to her back tire and the instant shudder that rippled through her bike when Maryelle hit her, and Persephone worked to keep her own bicycle from crashing down.

Before the accident, Persephone was definitely mad. Maybe she'd wanted to show Maryelle she was still a better cyclist, even though her friend caught up to her. It was an impulsive, emotional reaction of a teenage girl, not a calculated decision. She tried to think about it that way now.

Still, the result remained: Maryelle ran into Persephone's back tire, flipped off her bike and landed head first on the pavement. Without a helmet—another choice Persephone had found completely irresponsible—Maryelle spent two days in a coma before dying of a massive brain hemorrhage.

As Persephone sat on the couch, she remembered feeling vulnerable with her dad, unsure how to proceed with the information she knew, and the secret she held.

When her father told her Maryelle fell into a permanent sleep, she told him some of her story, but not all of it.

"She was planning to run away, Dad."

"Run away?"

"Yes, and she asked me not to tell anyone. And I was gutted, and she was crying, so we weren't really cycling right, you know?" She paused, struggling to decide if she should mention hitting her brakes. "I didn't expect her to wipe out ... Now she's dead?"

"Being angry with a friend in the last few moments you talked adds another layer to your grief," her dad told her. "It's okay to feel what you did. Anger is a natural feeling, Persephone. Maryelle knew you cared about her, and she cared about you, too."

"But it's hard to hold a secret," said Persephone.

"Yes, holding a secret for a friend is a weight."

"I knew she was going to run away and I didn't want her to. I was mad at her. And I knew I couldn't tell anyone who could talk her out of it. I feel bad. Now I can't tell her, 'I'm sorry.' And I can't tell her parents what happened. I just miss her."

"We all keep secrets, Persephone. Some are for others. We may keep these secrets out of trust, loyalty or love. But sometimes it may help a situation more to reveal a secret. You never have to protect someone you care about at the risk to your own well-being, or theirs."

"I know, Dad. I just feel bad."

"Other times we hold secrets to shield ourselves from the things that are hardest to see or accept about ourselves. These are the most illuminating secrets of all. You must understand these secrets in order to reveal yourself to yourself—to grow."

Persephone didn't know what "reveal yourself to yourself" meant, and the conversation stayed with her because of those words. She passed up the opportunity to confess what she believed to be the real reason Maryelle crashed. Instead, she forever blamed herself for her friend's death.

Persephone knew what lurked within her shadow side. When angry with someone, and they asked her to keep a secret, she couldn't always trust herself to do the right thing.

***

Although she didn't know if her father remembered their conversation about Maryelle when he recorded his Holo-Gram, Persephone tried to recall every detail as she sat in his office and glanced around his space. What did he think she would find there? It was hard to know where to begin.

She moved to her father's desk and began looking through his drawers, finding little initially except her own tidal wave of guilt. He trusted her, yet she opened every folder. Or did he trust her to open every folder?

"I'm sorry Dad," she muttered, as she proceeded to handle every item in the room.

The desk revealed nothing unusual, so she moved to the bookcase. She recognized an old wooden container on a high shelf laminated with sepia maps cut from an antique globe. The box had held up well after twenty-five years.

She had given it to her father as a gift reflecting their joint love of travel when they lived in Africa, where he'd served with Doctors Without Borders. She and her mother accompanied him, moving to Ethiopia for six months.

The container reminded Persephone of traveling with her dad into the Awash National Park on her eleventh birthday to see animals. Her father had taken the day off from his medical assignments to spend it with her. Her mother had a teleconference as part of her teaching schedule, so she stayed home.

Persephone didn't mind that her mother couldn't join them on that particular outing. She looked forward to spending her birthday with her dad, hoping to see ostriches, kudus, baboons and oryx.

Her dad hired a local guide and they set off. At the turnaround point they stopped for lunch and exited where they could see the Awash River. Persephone ran ahead on the trail, chasing after a brilliant green bird for a photograph. Her pursuit brought her close to the river.

She trotted to a clearing by the water and turned around to see her father running toward her faster than she'd ever seen him run. He shouted at her in a loud, sharp voice, "Seph! Come! Now!"

She hadn't seen the giant African crocodile approaching quietly at the river's edge when she heard her father and ran toward him. But her dad did.

The stealthy beast lunged out of the water onto the shore where Persephone had been standing less than a second earlier. She screamed with fright and her dad arrived moments later. He wrapped her up in the biggest hug he'd ever given her and carried her away. She thought he'd never let her go, and it felt good.

His words rang through her: *"Come! Now!"* Her father never yelled at her like that. The box reminded her of the fear she'd detected in his voice that day.

He'd used the same words in the Holo-Gram: "Come. Now." And while he wasn't yelling, the words carried as much urgency as they did on her eleventh birthday.

Persephone took the wooden box down from the shelf. She rubbed the smooth surface with her hand and opened the container. Inside she discovered a digital storage unit. She plugged it into her phone.

The drive loaded, revealing a set of folders Persephone found unusual. Along with several small scribbled electronic notes that read like directions, Persephone uncovered letters to her father and a few other documents.

Her pulsed quickened as she dug deeper into the files. A name she recognized but couldn't believe sat at the bottom of the correspondence: Dr. Franklin Stennis.

The dates on the notes showed the sporadic communication began five years prior, although Dr. Stennis had been missing for fifteen. In all, the folder contained ten files, but seven of them had been transmitted within the past eight months.

Clearly her father lived with more mystery in his life than she could ever know. But as she processed the words scrolling across her screen, confusion pushed her outside her own reality. The uncertainty filled her with nausea. In the grips of heartbreaking betrayal, she felt the foundation of trust in her father begin to crack.

She realized he had kept an enormous secret.

In finding the letters, her thoughts bounced across a sharp new speculation: Dr. Franklin Stennis was alive? Why didn't her dad tell her?

The documents revealed Dr. Stennis ran an art gallery in a remote industrial section of Shanghai. She looked frantically for an address but couldn't find a location. Her stomach fluttered from the anxiety of anticipation as she scrolled through the letters more rapidly.

At the top of one of the more recent letters, Persephone noted the sequence 3175: 493-2165 e-scribbled in her dad's handwriting in a margin next to an address on Mandai Road in north Singapore. The notation jumped out as unusual. How was the Singapore site related to Dr. Stennis if he disappeared so long ago and was now living in Shanghai?

Looking up the location on her digital device pointed her to the Mandai Crematorium and Columbarium complex in the city-state's Central Water Catchment area. Persephone finished scanning the letters, gathered her purse, and ordered a robocar.

She found her mother in her office working on a spreadsheet and counted on her distraction to ease any potential questions. "Mum, I'll be back in a bit," Persephone said as she peered into the room.

"Did you find something?" her mum asked.

"I don't know. Maybe. A car is coming in just a few minutes. I'm headed up toward the nature parks and reservoirs," said Persephone.

"Oh, that will be peaceful, love. See you in a few hours," her mum said, before turning her attention back to her screen.

Chapter Three

Persephone arrived at the Crematorium and found an enormous facility housing some 160,000 niches across eleven three-story blocks. Even though the complex was only twelve kilometers from her parent's house, she'd never been inside.

The place was pretty empty, but a certain level of creep factor always piqued Persephone's curiosity and tinged things with a little excitement, which she liked.

The digital code 493-2165 allowed entry into niche number 3175 reserved for holding ashes or other items from a deceased love one. She unlocked the cool box and peered into the space. Inside she discovered an antique leather portfolio. A note sat on top scrawled in heavy black pen: *Qingpu Xincheng.*

She opened the notebook and found it filled with long entries handwritten in a fine and fastidious manner. A quick glance through the pages helped her deduce she was probably holding Dr. Stennis' personal lab notes. Why had he wanted her dad to have them? Had he seen them and the note with *Qingpu Xincheng* written on it?

As she gazed over the secluded still waters of the Seletar Reservoir visible from the upper level of the columbarium, the peace of the natural greenery contrasted in strong juxtaposition to her unsettled feelings. The discomfort with what she found came from feeling like an intruder on the past, digging into secrets buried long ago.

It was clear Dr. Stennis had kept a series of detailed reports documenting his inquiries. As a methodical scientist he never wanted to repeat the same mistake. Persephone had studied his research as part of her graduate curriculum—notably the surgeries that helped him secure international patents on his NeuroTrans Suspension technology. His public findings propelled the benefits of his NTS techniques.

This other set of notes—his most personal records—felt different to her. They gave Persephone an uncomfortable feeling in the pit of her stomach. She placed the journals into her bag, shut the niche, and left.

At the bottom of the crematorium stairs, a quick search on her digital device to determine what *Qingpu Xincheng* meant, pointed to an old Metro station on Yinggang Road, off line number seventeen on the western outskirts of Shanghai.

Persephone knew she needed to go there. It was a long trip to make without solid confirmation that she'd find her father. But at that moment, the note seemed like confirmation enough.

***

Back at her parent's house, Persephone sat in her father's office and read all of Dr. Franklin Stennis' lab journals she'd found. Through them, she pieced together some of his history and gained a better sense of what happened leading up to his disappearance.

When Dr. Franklin Stennis reportedly had a boating accident during her last year of grad school, Persephone navigated her shock along with the professional reverberations that moved through the global neuroscience community. Although she had heard the renowned doctor speak in several virtual lectures, her opportunity to work with him evaporated after his suspected death.

At the same time, significant criticism surfaced about the

surgeon-turned-researcher. Critics implied he violated the Institutional Review Board's international code of ethics delineating how research must be performed. These regulations required an informed consent be obtained from each subject, or their authorized legal representative.

The accusations that Dr. Stennis had quite likely been unethical, even criminal, concerned Persephone. Although not backed with clear evidence, she and her dad had talked about the situation but never engaged in a deep dialogue about it. She could tell the speculations and his friend's disappearance weighed heavily upon him, and she steered around her own questions out of support for his emotions.

Persephone formed some negative personal conclusions about Dr. Stennis that she didn't know how to balance with his positive contributions to society. Eventually she swept away her hesitations about him enough to move forward with her own research.

The notes in the niche seemed to detail *all* of Dr. Stennis' neurosurgery procedures. When she finished reviewing them, she understood he certainly had clear ideas about experimenting in the operating room. Without consent, he couldn't legally do it. But his secret studies rarely affected the prognosis of his patients, and they advanced medical science significantly.

Persephone considered that—if based solely on the success of his outcomes—some of Dr. Stennis' unethical experiments may not have been entirely unjustified.

The moment of reflection revealed she had more moral flexibility than she wanted to admit—a notion that surprised her. She always felt a steadfast respect for following established protocols. She didn't like the idea of tolerating ethical variability in any form. The stress of feeling conflicted within herself about Dr. Stennis—and about her father—brought tears of fatigue.

***

Persephone booked her flight to China for the next day then went to find her mum. She considered whether to tell her Dr. Stennis may be alive, and that her father could be with him somewhere in Shanghai. Surely her mother still had some feeling for her dad and would want to know any new information about him.

When she reached the entrance of the room where her mom worked on her laptop, she took a deep quiet breath. Then she said, "I need to show you something."

"I'm working on something new right now," her mother replied, staying focused on her computer screen. "Can it wait, love?"

"Something new?" Persephone asked, deciding in that instant to honor her father's request. She didn't want to press it. Her dad had asked for the situation to stay between them. Even though she knew the documents she found in the niche were insightful, she resolved to keep the secret.

"The university wants another update to their security system and I've just figured out an instrumental piece of code I need for my next step," her mom said.

"Does it change everything you thought you knew?" asked Persephone. She recognized the question was a personal one that came from her own state of mind. She hoped, without actually telling her mum anything, she could glean some wisdom from her to apply to the situation.

"Give me one minute, Seph," her mother said. "Let me write down my thought process before I forget it."

"Sure, Mum," said Persephone. "I know my coming here with such short notice interrupts your flow."

Persephone lingered in the doorway watching her mother hard at work. A moment of clarity struck her. She recognized her mother loved her career, but it had become her hiding place, walling her off from the rest of the world. She seemed so checked out. Persephone wondered if she came across like that to her own lab colleagues. She was afraid she might.

Her mom picked up a homemade samosa from the plate near her, took a bite and licked her fingers. Suddenly Persephone saw her mother in a way she never had before.

She saw the shadow of someone vibrant and alive. Her mother, Ardis Banerjee, didn't realize when she took a trip with her girlfriends to Singapore in her mid-twenties that she'd capture the heart of an American doctor living there. She couldn't know her future would lead to their slow, unyielding separation and his sudden disappearance.

As a young girl, Persephone always pictured her mother in her professional world as somewhat two-dimensional—a serious and coiffed professor navigating computer monitors or perched at a podium.

Later, as she got to know some of her own college professors, Persephone tried to see her mom in a fuller way, but it was hard. Her mother gave her genuine warmth, but it could feel stiff when Persephone needed deeper comfort, making it difficult to open up completely.

When her mum turned around to face her, Persephone pulled her into a hug from the side of the desk. At first her mother felt tense, as if surprised by the interruption. Then she relaxed.

"I know this is hard, Mum," Persephone said.

"Oh Seph. It is … but I'm managing okay."

"Did you ever ask Dad where he went when he would go away?"

"I never did," her mother said, before releasing her embrace.

"It's remarkable how much you can learn by simply asking," said Persephone.

"True. But try asking your father to explain something like that. There has been sadness. But it has only made me look deeper to find the joy. … Some days it's harder than others."

"It's hard to make sense of so many unknowns," said Persephone.

"I agree. But I've done my share of illogical things."

"You?" said Persephone, "How long ago was that?" she asked, giving her mom a smile and a gentle poke in the arm.

"We can only hope time is on our side," her mum said. Then she quickly changed the topic by asking, "Are you still volunteering with your world health relief projects?"

"Yes," Persephone replied, "But right now I feel better suited for my work with artificial intelligence than humans."

Persephone recognized, although she enjoyed helping others, her humanitarianism provided a simple veil for the lack of connection she actually felt. People who volunteered for human causes weren't judged for not having time for personal relationships, and she appreciated the reprieve.

"Let me get back to this Seph. I'll be done in an hour then we can talk about where to eat," her mum said. She smiled at Persephone and rubbed her arm.

"Sure," said Persephone. "I know this isn't your happiest of birthdays, but we should still celebrate."

More than ever she wanted to tell her mother what she knew. But Persephone knew well how to hold a secret; and so she did.

PART TWO

Mind

"Welcome," the old monk spoke, and the crowd of tourists and devotees quieted. "The Buddha said, 'Those cannot see who do not kindle a light of their own.'"

He gazed over his shoulder at the large stone stupa illuminated from within with white light, then turned back to the audience. "Perhaps some of you may wish to walk the same path on which Sifu found himself. Guidance from the teachers here can help you make this choice."

The 108 men and women resumed their chatter, considering whether to stand in line to enter the shrine, or view the gardens and other smaller stupas flashing with colors that lined the walkway to the celebrated attraction.

Some had already visited the medical facility behind the main building, others had gone directly to the temple to see Sifu—all had questions.

The murmuring disrupted the peaceful nature of the Centre—but not for long. As the group approached the Sifu Stupa, stillness swept across them like moving clouds dim the sun.

"To master all six senses, one must gain control of the subtle power within them," the head monk said. "Touch, smell, taste, hearing, vision and mind build the energy body from the residue of physical experiences.

"Meditating on the surface of a smooth stone; the fragrant spring air; a sweet orange; musical notes; or the colors at dawn, expands mere sensation into currents of ecstasy pervading the entire universe. Would you like to join us?"

To most visitors, the concept seemed simple enough: Liberation of the senses offered the soul freedom. From a biological perspective, the brain uses the sense organs to experience the external world, guided by its own internal world.

Thoughts and emotions enhance the perception of pleasure or pain, peace or agitation, bliss or suffering.

A fuller understanding bordered on philosophy. "The mind as a 'sense censor' creates its own reality," the abbot told the seekers. "But a 'sensored mind' changes the paradigm."

Chapter Four

Magnormous! Asia's largest city was even bigger and wetter than Persephone expected when she landed at Shanghai Hongqiao International on Wednesday, August 22. Some older structures even appeared partially underwater.

She was glad the city was in the same time zone as Singapore. She already felt the eight-hour time difference with London catching up to her. Plus, she had lost a day in the transition and wanted to be efficient.

From above, the flood prevention walls built along the entire waterfront and outlying districts, as far as her eyes could see, made Shanghai look trapped more than protected. The concrete structures appeared to lock residents in, while trying to keep the water out.

She knew if she lived there she'd have a difficult time being blocked from the open coastline; it's where she always went to clear her mind.

The vast majority of Shanghai was of course submerged, including much of the downtown area, streets along the Lujiazui skyline and the former Shanghai Pudong International Airport.

When she exited Hongqiao International at six in the evening, the air felt hot and sticky. The rainstorm they flew through on the final approach steamed off the asphalt and landed on her skin. Suddenly she missed London. It was getting hotter year by year there, too, but it still felt more comfortable than being further south.

The weather in Shanghai felt a lot like Singapore. Persephone was glad she packed some lightweight clothes! She couldn't think straight when it was too hot and was always seeking to be cooler.

Driverless transport drove her from the airport to the boutique hotel she'd booked downtown. The new environment, and perhaps being close to finding her father and meeting Dr. Franklin Stennis, felt surreal; almost dreamlike.

Many multitiered systems above, below and on the surface streets of Shanghai fused together to create a gleaming metal ladder, linking humans to their architecture. She knew many structures still descended into the underground subways—even as flooding and sinking had taken hold—but they ascended exponentially higher.

As a global hub of transportation, the city directed a population of more than twenty-one million. At least, that's what the man sitting next to her on the airplane had said. Being in the middle of so much movement perpetuated a sense of crowded isolation ... as much a part of the experience as anything else, she supposed.

Persephone looked out the window of the car on her way to the hotel, struck by the environment they moved through. The city seemed to grow out of the bowels of its own darkest secrets.

Automated vehicles plied multi-decked streets weaving sidewalks together teeming with pedestrians and cyclists, all capped by massive skyways, suspended rail-bus networks and air-taxi pathways. Sprawling but dense infrastructure blended residential, medical, education, entertainment and retail.

Street level all but disappeared. With everything interwoven in the stratification of steel, it seemed quite possible one could never touch the ground. London always seemed crowded to her, but Shanghai was explosive.

When she arrived at the hotel forty minutes later she checked in and went directly to her room. She opted to carry her own bag, since she only had one, and didn't feel like being paced by a delivery robot. When she entered the room, she sprawled out on the bed and logged onto her computer. After responding to some emails from her lab, jet lag overtook her.

She closed her eyes and thought about her father's condition and his Holo-Gram message. What did he mean they had "new ways of communicating?" Any way of communicating would work for her.

Then she thought about Dr. Franklin Stennis and the minimal details she knew. This man, this neurosurgeon and scientist whom she'd connected with through research and journals published long ago, ran a gallery in one of Shanghai's industrial warehouse districts?

Persephone felt almost certain she would find the art house at *Qingpu Xincheng*. She wanted to wait to visit until the morning, however. Without knowing the area, she had a heightened sense of maintaining her own safety when traveling new paths. The idea that danger lurked in unknown places created a little edge that made it difficult to relax completely, even with her confidence.

***

On Thursday morning, after sleeping for nine hours, Persephone ordered scrambled eggs and fruit to be delivered to her room. Twenty minutes later she heard a hard knock on the door. She opened it, expecting to see room service and her breakfast. Instead, two plain-clothes police officers greeted her.

"Good morning, ma'am," one officer said, as both held out their badges for her to confirm their identifications. "Are you Persephone Jones?"

She noticed INTERPOL labeled at the top of their IDs. Having international police in front of her brought a rush of adrenaline.

"Hi, yes. Yes, I'm Persephone. Good morning, officers. Can I help you?"

"We are looking for the man in this photograph. The man standing behind the monk. By chance have you seen him?" the other officer asked, as he held out a digital image in front of Persephone.

She recognized the man in the background as Dr. Franklin Stennis, although he appeared much older than she remembered from her graduate video lectures.

"*Who* is this?" she asked, trying not to appear as nervous as she felt. "I haven't seen that man here."

"Why are you in Shanghai?" asked the female officer.

"I'm here for the Asia-Pacific Conference on Intelligent Robot Systems."

The officer holding the image lowered his device while the first officer glanced at her phone, peered up and asked, "Is Dr. Douglas Jones your father?"

"Yes, he is," said Persephone. "He disappeared six weeks ago, and we haven't heard anything from him. He's sick. My mother contacted the Singapore police and filed a missing person report. We're worried. ... Why do you ask about my father? Do you know where he is?"

"When your mother reported your father missing to the local police in Singapore several weeks ago, his name came up on our 'green' watch list as someone who may have information helpful to us," the female officer explained. "He's listed as a possible acquaintance of the man in the image we showed you."

The second officer said, "When your father's name appeared on our list, the system added the names of his family and others he associates with closely onto our 'green list.' This includes you. The airline tracker alerted us when you landed in Shanghai last night from Singapore Changi."

"So you know something about my father?" Persephone asked, consciously speaking slowly, so she would not appear flustered.

She knew it may be a good time to be straightforward. Perhaps the INTERPOL officers could help her. But her father asked her to keep his secret, and she knew she must trust that.

"We know nothing about your father. We're not assigned to that case, ma'am. We're looking for the individual in this image," said the female officer. "His name is Franklin Stennis."

Persephone didn't feel a need to control information, but without knowing what was going on, she didn't want to complicate anything further with police involvement. And she certainly didn't want to put her dad in any kind of predicament.

The male officer spoke again, asking, "You said you are here for a Robotics Conference?"

"Yes," Persephone said.

"How long are you staying in Shanghai?" he asked. "The airline did not show a date on your return ticket."

"I am hoping to fly back to London next week ... right after the conference."

"Why don't you have a return flight?"

"Sightseeing. After the conference. ... I am hoping to take a few extra days for sightseeing. I need flexibility, I guess."

The first officer scratched something down in her pad and closed the cover. "OK, we'll look into the conference," she said. "We'll take all the leads we can get on this case."

The second officer handed Persephone his business card and said, "Please let us know if you hear anything about Mr. Stennis, or see him. We have reason to believe he's here in Shanghai. Do not approach him, but contact us using the number on this card."

Persephone took the card, glanced down at the shiny gold INTERPOL seal and embossed name and said, "I will, officers. Thank you."

"Thank you for your time, ma'am," said the first officer.

"Yes, you're welcome. No problem. I'm sorry I can't be of more assistance," she said.

Persephone closed the door and a cool sweat broke out beneath her eyes. She had just bloody lied to INTERPOL officers. Her dad had asked her to keep his secret, but what was the cost to her own reputation and emotional state ... and the potential of getting arrested?

She only hoped withholding what she knew would not result in something terrible happening to her dad.

Chapter Five

Persephone joined hordes of workers on the crowded Shanghai Metro later that morning, all traveling to the industrial section near where she headed. The disinterested riders didn't seem to notice each other. She, however, looked around intently, trying to identify anyone who seemed too aware of her.

The visit from INTERPOL had left her feeling a little edgy. Hopefully nobody was following her; the density of people made it impossible to know for sure.

On the outskirts of Shanghai, *Qingpu Xincheng* station allowed for an easy exit from the underground rail network. Not many people got off at the same stop, making it easier to confirm nobody appeared to be tracking her.

After climbing the stairs to street level, it became clear the location sat at the juncture of several transportation systems serving an expansive area with huge refineries. She had noticed the bulky concrete structures when she flew in, but couldn't tell what they were. Seeing them from ground level made their purpose clear.

A palpable sense of detachment came from the workers

headed toward the buildings. Their patterned movements reminded Persephone of the mice in her lab.

Without an exact address, Persephone needed to decide which direction to travel. Her eyes scanned for a street sign or landmark and found nothing except arrows pointing to HEX. The massive refinery complex, still many Metro stops away, loomed in the distance by Hangzhou Bay.

She used HEX, of course, but had never considered its production. A large map on the wall outside the Metro station helped her find her bearings, and provided some factual tidbits: Thirty-two years ago chemical engineers developed a revolutionary fuel called HEX—a synthetic substance mined and processed from landfills and other urban and industrial waste depositories, dating back more than two hundred years.

Heralded as the planet's saving grace when it replaced fossil fuels, the clean-burning, high-output product could be used as a gas, liquid or solid. The seeming endless supply of this zero-carbon energy source created a global sea change in power production and consumption.

Persephone hadn't realized the raw material for HEX rivaled the abundance of crude oil pumped from the Earth. Or that Shanghai distributed the fuel to the entire globe—taking care of half the world population's combustible energy needs. No wonder the city's industrial sections held some of the richest areas of economy in the city, even though they looked worn down.

The nearby HEX refinery brought thousands of workers underground daily. But surface streets and sidewalks surrounding the subway entrance had few pedestrians. Where was the windblown trash and grime that generally collected in a city? London would certainly have had it.

She selected a direction and began to walk from the Metro. Four blocks later, one wide sidewalk appeared spotless. Someone had obviously taken the time to clean it, leaving the rest of the block untouched.

When Persephone came to a covered alcove set three meters back from the street, it confirmed for her that she got lucky with her choice of direction. In a city of such size, almost any place can be forgotten—but a forgotten place can still provide a clue.

Positioned in a nondescript area out-of-the-way enough she hoped she wouldn't have to find it again, the building hid in plain sight, like a tom cat silently aware. Obviously developers desiring to turn sturdy structures into high-cost glass condos had never considered this remote location, and none would anytime soon.

Under the alcove, the double doors appeared old but immaculate. A professional-looking shade of dark grey adorned their simple metal fronts; the same color as the walls and ceiling. She tried to open the doors, but their oversize chrome knobs wouldn't turn.

Then she noticed an antique black call box mounted on the wall to her left. Its video screen, with push buttons on the right, stood out from the industrialized front. The device looked like an out-of-place relic compared with the rest of the contemporary aesthetic.

With her curiosity piqued, having only seen such a box in old movies, Persephone read the options on the small display screen. She selected "New Visitor." Instructions appeared to hold her identification chip under the scanner. She swiped her right wrist and waited.

The word "PROCESSING" came onto the panel and an hourglass icon underneath it began slowly spinning.

After several moments, she surmised she had the wrong location. Then she heard a loud click and the screen instructed her to "PROCEED." She turned the knob and pulled one of the formidable doors open, surprised at how little effort it took to move the heavy metal.

An impeccable foyer loomed before her. Was this the art gallery described in her father's notes? A collection of darkly themed pieces, including oils, watercolors and mixed-media works with minimal relief hung on the walls. They confirmed her discovery.

The door closed behind her and clicked as the lock reset. She took a few steps into the spacious, white, cube-shaped room. It was nicer than she'd expected—given its remote location.

In the center of the room, a smooth wooden column growing wider on top rose from the floor to the ceiling. At its base, a heavy glass sculpture of a human form stood on a platform. The front and back halves were split from each other by a small gap.

A sturdy bench stretched along the left wall. Above it, a large and simple sign written in both English and Mandarin asked visitors to "PLEASE REMOVE SHOES." Persephone walked over to the seat, removed her boots, and placed them underneath.

When she traveled across the gleaming maple hardwood floor buffed to a high-gloss finish it slid under her feet with ease, providing a welcomed reprieve from the muggy heat outside. The gallery felt cool and nice and helped her relax a little more into the unknown.

"Hello?" she called into the silence. She hesitated to continue through the isolated space, but hoping to see her father provided the small safety net she needed.

She registered an acute sensation of someone watching her. It did not surprise her. She'd taken a long journey in investigations and distance to arrive at the gallery but expected Dr. Franklin Stennis wanted to stay hidden.

***

Most of the paintings in the room reflected depressing expressions of the human psyche—sad and lonely art. Persephone knew solemn emotions were universal, but looking at the pieces triggered her feeling absolutely alone. A sense of longing, missing and seeking filled her underlying curiosity.

Persephone lingered in front of a self-portrait painted by the anguished Edvard Munch in the early 1900s. As one of many artists she recognized in the collection, she considered how art allowed him to suffer more successfully. Her distress was not so successful; it generally triggered anxiety instead of inspiration.

Ever since grad school she had felt a commonality with Dr. Stennis in her strong push to achieve her research goals. But at that moment, she related to him through the lens of loneliness.

"Hello?" she repeated into the hollow space. "I'm looking for my father, Dr. Douglas Jones."

She didn't hear anything. "Dad?" she called out.

After several seconds a deep, even voice piped from a hidden speaker. "You will find my primary collection upstairs."

Persephone, uncomfortable confirming someone did indeed observe her, glanced around again before she walked across the room to an open doorway she'd spotted behind the column. "Will you be meeting me there?" she asked into space, wondering if the voice she heard came from Dr. Stennis.

"I prefer you view the gallery on your own so your reactions and feelings are free from influence. At the top of the stairs continue straight ahead. You will find the double doors at the end of the hall unlocked."

Strong and confident, Persephone had traveled internationally enough to know she shouldn't put herself in a situation she couldn't get out of. As appealing as it may be to enjoy art without a crowd, she would have found comfort in having other visitors around exploring the building, too.

But the thought of finding her father, propelled by the surety of being in the right place, led her toward the steep stairs. Soft lights came on as she passed through the doorway at the bottom, growing brighter as she ascended.

At the top, grey doors to the gallery replicated those on the street outside. When she entered the room, bright rays of illumination struck her from more than twenty statues of conceptualized human forms. Made of thick, translucent glass, they glowed like ice sculptures lit from within.

Tiny points of bright light shined from the transparent casts of rudimentary figures emanating electric blues, cherry reds, fuchsias, neon yellows and other strong colors. The resulting reflective rainbows caressed the crisp white walls and glossy wooden floor as the overhead spotlights faded into the background.

Persephone recognized the figures as similar to the one she'd seen on the lower level, only with glowing lights and their halves combined. The slightly larger than life-size nudes with crude anatomical details stood on white rectangular pedestals, arms at their sides, placed as if they were all gazing at each other.

Although similar in stance, subtle aspects differentiated them, including the position of their hands, shoulders and the tilt of their heads.

The figures glowed most from their eyes, nose, mouth, ears, throat, heart, abdomen and genitals. Sparkling ends of fiber optic threads ran through the glass. Colors radiated through their arms, palms, thighs and backs.

A few projected only muted hues, but several reminded Persephone of a Theatreland sign from London's West End with stark white lights and obvious dazzle. She had actually hoped she would find the gallery in the West Bund so she could explore that area. The sculptures were certainly brilliant enough to be on an outdoor path.

But, with all the flooding that had happened along the famous Bund waterfront from global warming, she knew putting electric artwork there may not be a good idea—even with the raised walkway, water controls and dams in place she had read about.

As the room pulsed and morphed through a full spectrum of colors, Persephone felt drawn to a figure titled *Chessic* flashing fuchsia and white. She rubbed her hand across the smooth glass form and heard a small hum fill the quiet room.

"How beautiful," she whispered, feeling mesmerized by the changing display.

Intrigued by the lights, Persephone traveled from one sculpture to the next. *Schizophrenic. Tribal Elder. Monk.*

Suddenly a loud knock on the metal doors startled her out of her rapture. She spun around, surprised by the force with which a tall Asian man had shoved the entrance to the upper gallery open. Dressed in khakis, a black shirt and a casual black jacket, the man stood authoritatively at the edge of the room with his arms at his sides. He said nothing, but stared at her with a calm, yet unwelcoming demeanor.

Persephone apologized, assuming the man was a guard who had marked her on the camera. "I'm sorry for touching the sculpture. These are fascinating. Really, so pretty. They must have taken a long time to create. Who made them?"

"A local artist made all the original glass figures," the man said, in what she identified as a definite British accent, surprising her with its working-class tone.

"Hey ... are you from London?" she asked.

The man did not respond to her casual question. Instead, he said, "The Curator asked me to escort you out. We are closing for the afternoon in preparation for an impromptu patron party this evening. We invite you to return after eight o'clock. Please follow me."

The man's piercing eye contact, avoidance of her small talk, and militaristic presence bothered Persephone. She found his formality unsettling and his hard, dark eyes upon her disturbed her natural ease. Unclear whether touching the glass had caused her sudden ejection, her mind strategized the best response.

"Excuse me, sir ..."

"Please come with me," he said, as he turned toward the exit.

"I'm looking for my father, Dr. Douglas Jones. I believe he may have come to this gallery."

"Follow me," he said, glancing halfway over his shoulder before walking out the door.

The man led her back down the stairs. "Your shoes ...," he said, then waited for her to put them on.

Persephone noticed him watching her every action and rushed to zip up her boots, so she could stand back upright. Before she moved toward him, she said, "I'm sorry, I didn't catch your name."

"Philip."

"Hi, Philip. I'm Dr. Persephone Jones," she said, as she raised her hand with her palm facing him in a gesture of hello, looking past him slightly to ease her discomfort. "It is nice to meet you."

"I know who you are," Philip said, motioning with his upturned hand toward the front doors. "We hope to see you tonight, Dr. Jones."

"Please, call me Persephone. If I return this evening, will I need to scan in again, or will the gallery doors be unlocked?"

"You will enter in the same fashion," he replied.

"Can you tell me if my father is here ... or will be later?"

Philip did not respond, and she knew he wouldn't. She figured he probably didn't know the answer and didn't want to admit it.

Rather than be bothered by his attitude, she decided to leave gracefully. When she exited, Philip closed the door behind her and it clicked shut.

***

Outside, Persephone felt the notion of somehow being toyed with, although she couldn't connect how or why. The aftershock of anticipation and mystery unsolved caused queasiness, and she left feeling unsettled by the experience.

Rather than remaining discouraged, however, the strange encounter sparked her impatience to return that evening for the unexpected invite.

She walked around the neighborhood for a few blocks to settle her excitement and find some food. Many buildings were empty, but any complex that looked like it might have something available to eat required an access card to enter.

In less than twenty-four hours, Persephone realized the high security around everything in Shanghai made it difficult to do anything outside the traditional tourist circuit.

Forty minutes back to her hotel on the Metro, Persephone reflected on the diverse artwork she had seen, ranging from dark and disturbing to bright and beautiful. She wondered how a gallery missing from any list of collections in Shanghai could contain such an incredible array of pieces. The complex art became the simplest thing to think about.

She tried to plan what to do next, but had little to go on, and only hoped she was closer to locating her father. And who was the curator Philip had mentioned? What she might wear to a party that evening was the least of her concerns, but it still crossed her mind. She liked to be prepared ... and she was finding it difficult.

Chapter Six

H e liked seeing her touch the art with her small hands—delicate, yet stout. He concentrated on her fingers as she walked around the room; the directed way she moved them showed her confidence.

After Persephone departed, the Curator stepped into the upper gallery from the side room where he had been watching her through the one-way glass. At last, she was here.

He had been waiting for her as the final piece in his puzzle. She appeared calmer than he expected. Still, as much as she had uncovered about him—as smart and prepared as she was—he knew meeting in person would be difficult.

The Curator didn't worry about her returning. He understood her persistence toward discovery and her curiosity for taking inquiries to their edge—he shared it.

Evaluating her interactions with the sculptures from the side room reminded him of the years he had spent sitting in the side orchestra during symphonies, watching the audience rather than the stage.

He tried to recognize what moved people about the shows, registering the changes on their faces as they listened to the music. He considered the simple neurological stimulus of their experiences.

The Curator knew Persephone would follow her father to the gallery. After Philip Goode coordinated her receipt of the Holo-Gram in London and planted the note containing the station name *Qingpu Xincheng* in the crematorium niche, they figured they had about a week before she would put the clues together.

She arrived in Shanghai a couple days sooner than they'd calculated. The Curator sent Mr. Goode to the airport when Persephone's plane landed and asked him to follow her in a private car to confirm her hotel. He complied and reported back to the Curator that tracking her had been child's play.

The men finalized logistics for a patron party they wanted to host during her first evening in the gallery. The night Persephone received the Holo-Gram they called a select group of individuals and told them they'd be holding a private affair soon; a day-of invitation would permit them entry. Arranging a short-order caterer proved a bit more challenging, but Mr. Goode handled it adeptly, as usual.

Many paths brought people to the art house, but the Curator only trusted those in the appropriate circles to enter it. Visits to the gallery, arranged *by invitation only*, helped ensure patrons would continue to probe and poke their way there for the exclusive right to step inside.

Although new visitors could sometimes negotiate entry into the warehouse during the week, they could never buy their way into a gala. If someone should arrive at one of the Curator's soirées without an invitation, he or she would be turned away, no matter their influence—it would be imperative.

Only those elevated within "higher-up" society ever made it onto a fête list. Everyone invited to one of the gallery's exclusive parties had already been inside the building at some point. Afterward, Mr. Goode secretly monitored their activities to decide whether to approve their return.

The Curator kept the doors to the upper gallery locked as standard protocol. He didn't want the majority of his guests to know a second level existed, let alone its contents. He knew most people would be satisfied to simply make their way into the hidden, industrial-chic location; it wouldn't concern them if they experienced the whole space, or not. They could consider they had visited the minute they stepped inside, no matter how long they stayed.

Every so often the Curator allowed a few patrons to travel upstairs to experience his prized collection. He curated them as well, based on their inner nature.

He worked closely with Mr. Goode to prescreen and categorize attendees. They determined acceptable candidates for viewing—and at what price. Mr. Goode investigated the background of each person; those seeking bragging rights remained among the uninitiated.

If a patron made it to the gallery's top level, the Curator felt certain he or she would not threaten its discovery. Sometimes he offered brief conversation by way of the speaker system installed in the gallery. Visitors he actually met with directly became a resource for their reactions.

The primary role of the patrons was to serve as a grouping of individuals moving en masse. The Curator considered them like superfluous background music to his aesthetic. Only twenty-five people, at most, ever attended any one party. His motivation for having them around was pure research; when it came to financing, any one of them would be enough.

Patrons maintained stereotypical ways of displaying their wealth: airships, yachts, extraplanetary real estate, and executive memberships at orbiting resorts. Still, they lived with secrecy and stealth. One would never decipher many things about their private lives, a fact the Curator appreciated.

Culturally, the gallery remained in the perfect position to stay hidden. Being open to only the most exclusive caste of society prevented public attention. It also provided the unusual opportunity for the elite to prowl around each other without risk of discovery. Those who came down from the sky to join the Curator's parties were ideal as a collective because they understood their own games.

***

The prominent sculpture on the lower level, called *Severed,* drew attention from most patrons. Unlike the sculptures on the upper floor, lights did not shine from it; it remained a hollow cast split in half along the coronal plane.

The original idea for the heavy glass forms emerged from Stephen Stevens' final project in art school. He became acquainted with Philip at that time, who introduced himself as the intermediary for high-paying customers at an exclusive gallery.

On the direction of an investor referred to only as "the Curator," Philip commissioned five sculptures. The request launched Stephen Stevens' career in a lucrative and dream-like fashion.

The artist believed wealthy patrons purchased his pieces for their homes. He never asked who—he just focused on forming the glass. When he later discovered that the Curator was a single collector who arranged and managed the entire grouping, it was a huge and disappointing surprise for the sculptor.

Stephen Stevens used body scans from three models. He digitally increased the scale by ten percent and augmented the hand positions and facial expressions based on his own mood —and of course, Philip's requests. And he had a lot of them.

In the beginning, he needed about two weeks to make a piece. After completing one, his friends would help him pack the glass into two solid wooden crates; one for the front side, one for the back. A van picked up the packages and brought them to a central distribution hub.

By the time he had made ten statues, Stephen Stevens had earned enough money to set up a foundry to produce his pieces. He was on his way to becoming a well-known artist in Shanghai. So he found it off-putting that Philip never invited him to speak at the gallery, nor would he tell him its location.

Philip did ask him, however, at the request of the Curator, to make the sculptures faster. This led to custom specifications for the next fourteen pieces.

"Private collectors, not only in Shanghai but all around the world, will buy your statues. ... But they all wish to remain anonymous," Philip told him.

Cash payments were much higher than his other commissions, so Stephen Stevens dealt with the shift from standardized forms to making more customized ones. The time frame, however, always remained without extension.

This inconvenience gave the artist first-hand insight into the selfish motivations of the biggest secret players in the art world.

Chapter   Seven

The art house sat so far outside the public scene, it wasn't
even listed in the Shanghai gallery guides Persephone had
downloaded onto her personal device. From this alone, she
knew the collection would certainly draw a different crowd
that evening than one she might fold into during a London gallery stroll.

She wondered if some of the attendees would be speaking
English rather than Mandarin or Wu, so she could talk with
them. Of course she thought Dr. Stennis would be there. But
most of all, she hoped she would find her father.

In her excitement about finding the location that afternoon
—and surprise at being kicked out of it—Persephone hadn't
noted down the actual address. As a result, the only coordinate
she could direct the driverless car to when it arrived at seven
forty-five, was to *Qingpu Xincheng*. That was fine; she would
walk the few blocks from the subway.

The street was isolated when she exited the car. She noticed
a few expensive vehicles around the Metro station, but none
parked on the same block as the gallery. Strangely, the entire
area showed no indication of any type of gathering taking

place—save for a dim light bulb glowing on the ceiling above the warehouse entrance, casting a small halo on the dark sidewalk.

Persephone stood in the alcove and flashed her wrist chip to unlock the doors. When the screen directed her, she pulled on one of the knobs and entered the foyer.

While being open to possibility, the scene she encountered surprised her. Higher-ups—a term used by all but them to describe those who lived at the top of the megalopolis—roamed the room. She recognized their status immediately, because almost all the party attendees wore cotton.

Persephone appreciated how unusual their fashion was. Cotton had fallen away from production so much only the superrich could own it. More common materials, including regenerated nylon made from rescued ocean waste, recycled synthetics, and wool, found a market with people living closer to the ground.

She had selected her clothing that evening from her suitcase, feeling a little self-conscious with such limited options in dressing for an event she didn't know she'd be attending. Persephone preferred biodegradable fabrics like hemp, bamboo, and pineapple leaf fibers. But even though they were sustainable, everyone knew they did not replicate cotton.

Obviously, not having access to her full wardrobe didn't matter at all—the party patrons' fashions outclassed hers by far.

From the foyer she noticed a few people leaning on the smooth wooden column in the center of the room, looking up, appearing to wave at something. Her eyes followed their gazes but landed upon nothing of interest. She determined they must be admiring the lights shimmering through their brilliant gemstone rings.

Persephone walked to the bench on the side wall, took off her shoes and joined the others barefoot in the main gallery. The absence of footwear became her only noticeable commonality with any of the other guests.

The lack of loud talking or any excited interactions between the patrons created a low murmur in the room, with calm music filling the spaces not otherwise occupied. She noticed a few small groups picking from the banquet table of edibles opposite the foyer.

Her eyes scanned for her father. She couldn't imagine him interacting in such circles. She had never been around so many higher-ups and wondered why Philip had invited her. Her dad might have blended a little better with the attendees than she did—purely on account of his age—but the undertone of exclusivity wasn't his way either.

The more she looked around the room, the more she noticed how the mingling figures mirrored the hollow depressed emotions of the paintings. They filled the gallery's lower level with three-dimensional human constructs of darkness.

Persephone had hoped for something more positive than a fantastic evening of impersonal disconnection, so she decided to try to make some connections in pursuit of finding a clue about her dad.

She opted to get some food and moved through the guests who gazed at the artwork. She eavesdropped on their dialogues and gathered bits of gossip. But their conversations only made the higher-ups more foreign to her, even speaking English.

"Where is Jolene?" one patron asked another near the column, neither making eye contact with each other.

"She didn't attend the last party either. Unlike her to miss an opportunity to visit with the Curator."

"She's probably having her breasts perked up again," said a man still gazing at the oversize jewels on his fingers.

"Maybe she wasn't invited. I haven't had any Holo-Grams from her in months."

Persephone went to the table and scanned the exclusive food items. After taking a small plate of the beautifully presented (and surely impossible to secure through legal channels) bites of salmon and a few wild rice stuffed mushrooms, she continued moving through the patrons.

"Where's Ted?" asked a woman in a luxuriant cotton frock with a heavy golden ginkgo leaf pattern embossed across the shoulders.

"He hasn't been down to street level in a year. He's quite

taken with his new airship and I'm sure wants to stay among the clouds," answered a man finishing a thin glass of champagne before placing it onto a server-mech wending its way around the floor.

Many conversations revolved around the gorgeous airships stationed in the far distance, floating in the wind. The elevated nature of the megalopolis showcased these ships moored up high to avoid the grit below. Persephone had seen them when she flew into the city, and had noticed when she exited the Metro that none of them were docked in that area of Shanghai.

A solid part of the urban fabric, the dirigibles connected to the tops of stratospheric buildings rising three hundred stories toward glamorous penthouse terminals. The giant chrome aircrafts exemplified the most remarkable lifestyle—a kind of fantasy for everyone to see. Elegant and beautiful, their natural grace fanned out across the sky.

Residential towers in neighborhoods with waiting airships identified where the wealthiest people lived. They gleamed like enormous weather vanes in the sunlight, showing how the winds blew; which way the higher-ups made their decisions.

The buildings in the industrialized area near the gallery did not rise high enough to support airship terminals. This meant the patrons could travel to street level incognito without being flagged from above.

They discussed the art: "This piece has been here for years. I will bid on one upstairs instead," said the woman in the frock.

And they gossiped about the owner: "We haven't been introduced yet; he must have a terrible condition."

"I know Johanas met him a few times five years ago ... but of course, those conversations were always personal. Where has Johanas been anyway?"

"No idea; I haven't seen him for some time."

It was clear most guests had never encountered the gallery owner. But they seemed to trust his status on account of small details signaling everything they needed to know. For one, he served fish as finger food inside the ground-level building—Persephone noticed it was the biggest hit from the buffet.

By the year 2100 more of everything flourished in China,

except anything coming from nature. Globally, higher-ups controlled the market on anything fresh, moving all fins straight from the ocean into the sky.

Fishing once provided a huge commodity for Shanghai. In time, the heating of the globe combined with overfishing, wiped out all the old fisheries, save for a few shrimp farms and cheap corporate factories. If the fish situation was anything like London, high-quality larger species like salmon and halibut were extremely expensive, and wild tuna cost more still.

The patrons talked about nothing—or maybe everything; Persephone couldn't tell. Their snippets of conversation made sense to her the same way someone unfamiliar with the scientific jargon of astronomy might understand a lecture on the microwave reverberations from the Big Bang. She could follow it in momentary bursts, but had no context for the subject matter.

Nothing she overheard helped her with her quest. She felt intrigued being around so many people of such societal stature, but bothered by the musings of the patrons' material lives illustrating complete disconnection from humanity.

A common topic was how much guests enjoyed the thrill of stepping foot onto an orbiting space station to travel to the moon. The spacefaring nature and capabilities of the new world defined their culture.

"It's a tad expensive but worth it," said one woman, petting a rat dog she carried as an accessory. "The mineral discoveries alone make me glad I staked out real estate there when I did."

"Mining mountain-size iron asteroids dragged into near Earth orbit turns more profit, than mining on Earth," said another. "I'm thrilled I fund these explorations."

As Persephone meandered through the gallery, the patrons drew her into their conversations several times. She lingered near a circle of women and sipped her tonic water, then heard a silky feminine voice followed by a soft touch on her forearm.

"It's just a marvelous fête, yes? A spontaneous party that draws such people on a Thursday night speaks volumes, wouldn't you say?"

"I guess so," said Persephone. "I'm surprised to be here."

A woman in control of most situations she placed herself within, Persephone played through the structure set up for her with patience. Yet, her entire sensory system remained on high alert, backed by the singular goal of finding her father. She couldn't wait to talk about the situation with him. Hopefully they would laugh about it all later.

Based on the small number of people at the gathering, Persephone understood the selectivity of receiving an invitation. She recognized what an exclusive group surrounded her, but came to the conclusion the visitors were an unsavory lot. She tried not to be judgmental, but suspected the guests probably acted only as upstanding as they needed to showcase.

Within thirty minutes it became clear the majority believed they were godlike on account of their unlimited influence and resources. Someone had to build society's framework; most of them did. Wealthy with eclectic personalities, manipulative and narcissistic, the well-educated patrons stood at the peak of society. They exhibited no qualms about existing within a stratified social pattern. They obviously thrived in untouchable levels of wealth.

By nine-fifteen the door at the base of the column leading to the upstairs gallery remained locked, with no sign of Dr. Stennis or her father. The dialogue among the patrons hadn't revealed insight into either mystery.

Around that time, a gorgeous middle-aged patron removed a handheld laser device from her purse and shot a dark oil —*Loneliness IV*—putting a fire ring right through it. Persephone didn't know whether the scene was sanctioned or not, but something told her it wasn't.

In such a disconnected world, nobody knew what was sacred—and nobody seemed to care. The other patrons clapped at the performance art they may have assumed was planned all along—*The Destruction of Loneliness*. Persephone determined the meaningless defilement must have let the woman connect with *something*.

It was a start.

***

Several minutes later, Persephone spotted Philip engaged in a tense, but quiet, conversation with the offending guest. After he finished the short discussion, the woman collected her shoes and left through the front doors. Philip continued to stroll among the remaining patrons with ease, offering several chin nods.

He looked to be about six foot two and 180 pounds with a muscular build and strong jawline. His noticeable height stood out as unusual for an Asian man in Shanghai. The basic cut of his medium-dark hair mirrored half the men at the party—the other half were balding. He dressed well, wearing the same khakis, black shirt and classic black jacket she had met him in earlier.

When he noticed Persephone, his countenance shifted, taking a much more serious tone as he headed straight toward her. When he reached her, he took a quick pivot to position himself on her left. He placed his hand under her elbow, guiding her to move with his walk.

"Hello, Persephone ... good that you made it. Please come with me," he said.

Persephone tried not to act startled, so he wouldn't register her feeling threatened. She didn't want to cause a scene, however the physical connection and directed movement caused her alarm. Her mind strategized an exit.

"Wait. Where are we going?" she asked.

Philip walked her to the staircase she had ascended earlier. He flashed his wrist on the touch screen to unlock the door and it opened. A few patrons noticed them enter and continued talking as the door closed.

"The Curator would like to meet with you," he said, as he released her elbow at the base of the stairs, encouraging her toward them.

"The curator?"

"Yes, please proceed."

"Is the curator ... Dr. Stennis?"

"Patrons only know the owner of this gallery as 'the Curator.' Now, please ...," he said as he raised his hand in the direction of the steps to invite her to climb them.

If the Curator was indeed Dr. Stennis, Persephone didn't fear meeting him, but an appropriate nervousness settled in her stomach. She'd held him in high esteem for so long as being among the top, world-changing innovators. His work and discoveries aided so many people, and the course of medicine as a whole. Depending on how starstruck one gets, anybody might feel excited meeting someone of such standing.

With Philip behind her, Persephone began to ascend the stairs. She didn't want to be wary of him for the rest of the evening, so decided to call him on his actions. Seven steps up, she turned around and looked him square in the eyes.

"Please, don't touch me again. It was completely unnecessary to direct me physically. You could have just asked me to join you." She scolded him with her gaze long enough to let him know she was serious, while still remaining polite.

"We had to make haste. The upper gallery remains exclusive," he responded as he picked a piece of lint off his black jacket.

"I don't care how exclusive it is. I only want to find my father," she said before continuing up the stairs.

She reached the second floor and moved down the hallway to enter the gently pulsing, light-filled room. She paused to take in the scene. Two other people walked around the sculptures barefoot.

"Exclusive, huh?" she said as she caught Philip's glance.

Then she turned and saw Dr. Stennis talking with a woman in the center of the room who wore a fuchsia-colored cloche hat wrapped with feathers. He looked older than she'd expected—and tired.

"I know Lily bid on one," she overheard the patron tell him. "How can I do the same?"

"The pieces are not for sale," he replied. "Our gallery changes the definition of 'acquisition.' Our top-level patrons do not give us money, but invest in a sculpture. This is a more progressive ... and longer-lasting ... symbol of generosity than having one's name etched on a donor plaque."

"Mr. Goode," the Curator called out, looking toward Philip who remained near the doors to the upper gallery. He motioned with his hand and a nod, inviting Philip to cross the room.

"Yes?" he asked, after reaching the Curator.

"Please take Bliua to the basement. She is a friend of Lily's."

Persephone watched Philip escort Bliua to the elevator at the back of the room, his elbow hooked around her arm.

At that point, the Curator approached Persephone in the middle of the room. For the first time since age ten, she came face-to-face with the man whom she'd only seen in photographs, news reports and video podcasts from fifteen years earlier when he was a famous neurosurgeon: Dr. Franklin Stennis.

"Hello, Persephone," he said, sounding pleased to see her, almost like he knew her.

"I ... Hi ..."

"I am impressed," he said.

"Impressed?"

"You arrived more quickly than I anticipated. Welcome to my gallery."

He had anticipated her arrival? Persephone pieced together this new bit of information in a flash of deductive reasoning. In an instant the truth became evident. Rather than finding this place in search of her father, she had been led to it.

She took a half breath in and her chest contracted with physical rigidity as she second-guessed herself and her decisions. Then she let it go: It was important to resituate herself within her new reality.

Persephone knew she wasn't in control. She only hoped she hadn't entered into a situation where escape would be difficult. Not knowing whom to trust made it tricky to know exactly how to respond.

"I'm impressed with the art you have here," she said.

"I hope you feel even more so tomorrow."

"Why? What's tomorrow?" she asked.

Chapter Eight

"May we talk in my office?" the Curator asked Persephone, as he motioned toward an open door on the left side of the gallery.

She nodded and walked with him into a rectangular-shaped living room. Spacious and contemporary, it provided plenty of privacy for their conversation, complete with elegant white couches, a center glass table and a glossy bamboo bar.

A wall of one-way windows, duplicated on opposite sides of the clean space, allowed panoramic and unobstructed views of both the sculpture garden and the first floor below where the shoeless patrons mingled. The room floated like a loft above the lower level, hiding the observers from those being observed.

Outside in the upper gallery, the glass wall appeared indistinguishable from the white walls. When she looked into the sculpture court, Persephone knew the Curator must have watched her from the side room during her earlier visit.

She pressed her fingertips together near her stomach as she tried to relax. The Curator stood in front of her and grasped Persephone's hands. He held them inside his cold and bony hands, pressing her palms closed as he lifted her wrists so their fingers pointed toward each other.

He looked down at her hands with a great focus, then up at her face. The silence made her uncomfortable, and she wanted to pull her hands out of his, but she didn't want to be rude.

"I would call your father the closest friend I ever had. He proved through his actions I could trust him. You've got your father's eyes. I can almost see his soul," he said.

Dr. Stennis appeared older now, thinner, but still strong. He had to be almost seventy-five, the same age as her father. His soft white, wispy hair, prominent nose, thin downturned lips and small, round chin reminded Persephone of a laboratory rat. The heavy bags beneath his eyes tugged like crescent moons on his thinning white eyebrows, pulling them into a 'V' shape.

"Can I offer you a drink?" he asked, as he gave her hands a squeeze, then released them and moved toward the bar.

"No thank you," she said, feeling his touch linger on her hands as she dropped them down and walked to the other side of the room to gaze over the patron party.

"As a child, I met you once at the hospital. As a graduate student, I wanted to meet you for years; but I did not expect this. My father used to tell me about you. I'm looking for him now. Is he here?" she asked.

"Quite the neurosurgeon, your father—extremely skilled. He always supported my endeavors. When I discontinued my surgical practice to focus on research, it surprised my colleagues. But Douglas stayed in touch, encouraged me, and asked me to meet with some of his patients. He often coordinated connections for me. I find it no coincidence he helped facilitate our meeting now."

"I remember having a hard time making friends in school one year," Persephone told him. "My dad said, 'I have a friend who had a similar difficulty, and he turned out to do wonderful things.' So often he talked about his colleague whose discoveries helped a 'great many people.' It became clearer as I got older, he meant you. I know my father saw you as helpful."

"Persephone Dee Jones, I am glad you recognize who I am.

I am familiar with you, too, and I know your father felt proud of your work as a scientist. You and I both know your research stands upon mine. I approve of your endeavors."

"You approve? Not to be disrespectful, Dr. Stennis, but what do you know about my efforts?"

"Though I've been at this gallery for more than ten years, I've stayed connected with the neuroscience profession. I've tracked your professional growth. I believe I can trust you, like I did your father."

"In school I read your research reports. I idolized you for the longest time. But the more I learned, the more I recognized there was secrecy in your methods. When I confronted my father with the idea, he couldn't—or wouldn't—see it," she said.

"Your dad understood my pursuit of connecting human nerve tissue to mechanical devices. Without Douglas' collaboration at the university hospital in Singapore, and applying my technology, my discoveries may not have affected a change in neurosurgery so quickly," he said.

"He believed you used legitimate research methods and computer models. The techniques worked on his patients, and he trusted you. As others began to raise suspicions, he remained one of your biggest supporters," she said.

"I owe a lot to your father," he said.

"I'm looking for him," said Persephone. "Have you seen him recently?"

"Were you hoping to find me, too?"

"I would like to say it is an honor to meet you, but I can't quite say that," she said as her voice softened, and she glanced at the floor.

The Curator chuckled. "The impression you hold about me is limited, but that's ... that's, for what? You are here for your father," he said, as he finished pouring his grapefruit juice over ice from the bar.

He moved toward one of the long white couches and sat down, adjusting his position a couple of times before he returned his gaze to Persephone.

She remained standing, looking past the Curator, and said,

"I found your personal lab notes."

"You followed the suspicions of my colleagues years ago, but you are the first one I've allowed to put all the pieces together," he said.

Persephone paused, considered how she came to find the documents, and said, "You dropped them into my lap, didn't you? What about my father … did he see your notes too?" she asked, staring straight at him.

"Not exactly, but we did lay out the trail."

"We? Meaning you and my father?"

"I am referencing Mr. Goode. He brought you upstairs."

"Why did you want me to find your journals?" she asked.

"I want you to have a full understanding about how extraordinary research gains are made," he said. "I prepared you with a greater context ahead of our discussion."

"I see," she said, unimpressed. "I know you provided a string of clues to lead me here. Is my mother a part of this?"

"Your father told me he kept my confidence," he said, using one hand to unfold a white napkin onto his lap before taking a sip of grapefruit juice.

"Is my father here?"

"Yes, he is here," he replied.

"Where?" she asked, peering down at the patron party.

"He will appear in time," the Curator said, patting the seat on the sofa next to him.

Persephone stayed standing, folding her arms across her body. She didn't like being treated like a pet or a small child.

"Tell me, Persephone, what happens when the forebrain receives damage, and the hindbrain does not?"

"What? What are you talking about?" she asked, shifting her position to look for her father in the sculpture gallery.

"If the brain is damaged, excluding the cerebellum and the brainstem, what results?"

"A persistent vegetative state may occur … if there is a functioning brainstem," she said, returning her attention to the Curator.

"Exactly. What about damage to the hindbrain, if the forebrain remains functional?"

"Why the pop quiz?" she asked, cocking her head slightly.

"Please, answer the question, Persephone. It will provide you with context."

"If there is trauma to the brainstem it may result in paralysis, with full consciousness and cognitive function."

"Correct," he said.

"Locked-in Syndrome can come from damage to the pons portion of the brainstem," she further clarified. "The progressive neurodegenerative condition paralyzes everything except perhaps the eyes, leaving people aware and able to experience their senses, but unable to move or speak. I'm sure you know this. Why are you asking me?"

"Locked in your own mind. Conscious and awake, but with no ability to communicate or be mobile. A complete paralysis of everything … except the sensory organs," he said.

"Oh my god! Has this happened to my dad?" she asked

"In a manner of speaking, I suppose. He is freer without his senses, although he appears engaged," said the Curator.

"What? What do you mean by 'in a manner of speaking?' Can you please tell me how I can locate my father?"

"You are seeking your father and trying to understand the secrets he kept from you. However, more remains unresolved for you, am I correct?"

"My father disappeared six weeks ago. In reading his correspondence with you, I learned you are alive. I'm shocked to discover my father held your trusted secret for years. When I put the pieces together, I knew he must have come here to discuss his health situation. It is the only thing that makes sense. He must have thought you could help him somehow. But how? Where is he?"

Persephone took a seat on the couch opposite the Curator, looked directly at him, and began using her short right thumbnail to clean under the nails of her left hand.

"Some of what you found out about me may have surprised you," he said.

That Dr. Stennis had skipped right past addressing her concerns about her father bothered Persephone. She wondered if he was just self-centered, or if he might be hiding something.

"I'm wondering about a lot of things right now," she said. "I'm piecing the situation together. Most people think you died fifteen years ago. You faked a disappearance to avoid direct inquiries into your research methods. From what I read in your personal notes, it appears the accusations from your former assistant and colleagues may be true. You may have harmed others to test and perfect your theories."

Without response, the Curator kept his eyes straight upon her, taking another slow sip of his juice.

"A few days ago I discovered you contacted my father with increased communication over the past five years," she continued. "But I'm having a hard time understanding why."

"Please, enjoy my party from a higher place, Persephone," Dr. Stennis said, before he stood and returned to the bar. "You can watch the sculptures glow from in here as my selected patrons interact with them. I must finish some business this evening and send these people home. When I return, we will talk further. I will have food brought in for you. What would you like?"

"I'm not hungry," she said, bothered by his mundane suggestion. "Can you help me or not?"

The Curator reviewed her silently before turning to wash his hands at the sink. Then he walked to the side of the room and slipped into the upstairs gallery without a reply, closing the door behind him. Persephone looked out the room's window and watched him casually interact with one of the patrons.

"Well, this is proving pointless," she said to herself. "He's no help at all."

She grabbed her bag, stood up from the couch and headed to the side door. When she tried to leave, the handle wouldn't budge.

"Are you bloody kidding me? Now I'm the one locked in?" she scoffed.

She knocked on the door, but nobody who she could see through the side wall of windows responded. "Hello?" she shouted. "The door locked behind you ... Dr. Stennis?"

Persephone pounded harder, yanking on the door handle,

but it remained fixed. "Can anyone hear me?" she yelled. She moved to the wall of windows and rapped on the glass with both hands, but nobody paid attention. The two patrons sauntering around the upper gallery moved toward the stairs; ushered out by the Curator.

Across the side room, the windows overlooking the patron party provided another option. Persephone tapped on them as well, but received no response from below. When she pulled out her handheld computer from her bag and tried to access her communication services, a "FAILURE TO CONNECT" message flashed across her screen.

"Really? Bloody unbelievable."

Captive in the room with no way to move beyond it, she squeezed the back of the couch. "Damn it, Dad. Where are you? What's going on?" she said as she fluttered back slow, hot teardrops of frustration that stung her eyes.

Perhaps Dr. Stennis didn't know the door had locked behind him when he left the room. But what if he did? Why had he shut the door in the first place?

Persephone knew the answer: Dr. Stennis had intentionally trapped her in the office area of the upper gallery. And she knew that soon, she may be the only guest remaining.

PART THREE

Touch

After receiving a brief introduction to the hillside monastery, most visitors traveled onward to continue their tour of the grounds. But each week, a handful of attendees considering joining the facility engaged in a deeper conversation with the monk related to their senses.

To this group, the old man spoke: "Of all the sense organs, touch has the largest resonance. Through its subtleties we can know the element of air and caress all possibility.

"Touch opens your emotions and deepens your desires. Symbolically—and figuratively—the color blue reflects this sensation.

"The sense is strong because it awakens first. In the seventh week of gestation, nascent forms of the cortex, cerebellum and brainstem appear. Sensory centers for touch emerge at week eight. Since touch works through the boundary of your body, it becomes the most intimate sense.

"As a conduit for love, warmth and affection, touch forms the basis of personal intimacy and connection to the physical world. Imagine the times you gave or received life energy through an embrace. Touch is an important aspect of healing ... but it can also inflict harm.

"Being removed from access to touch at our Centre can cause you to experience as horrific the numbing withdrawal that can result from deep sensory deprivation.

"If you join our Centre, we will help prepare your mind to cope with 'skin hunger'. This is essential. Not having access to touch is the number one reason people grow dim here. We hope to support your bright future."

Chapter Nine

S ome people—including himself—were born to suffer more than others. The Curator held this notion as the foundation of his art inquiries. Over the years he acquired rare works from famous artists connected to human distress. Through his interest in displaying physical and psychological pain, Stennis pulled together a world-class collection.

He began collecting art as an undergraduate with money he received from his parents' estate. While not a huge amount, since the majority of it funded his education, it provided enough to get started.

Artwork created by those who had, or still battled severe trauma; paintings depicting the anguish of living inside a mental institution; and imagery relaying the pain of undergoing electroshock therapy for schizophrenia or depression, inspired Stennis.

He rooted his own collection in evoking strong negative emotions to aid understanding how the mind interpreted unsettling sensory perceptions. The distress of human existence stung harder—and the impact lasted longer—than partaking in life's joy, which humans consumed more rapidly.

Happiness only created the hope for *more* bliss; a desire for the next pleasure to be even better. Craving more elation neutralized present delight. Pain, however, could only get worse. Because all beings seek to avoid suffering, the fear of more agony helped sustain the anguish of any present disillusion.

Plus, exhilaration seemed less universal than negative emotions. Hit a finger with a hammer and almost anyone would react the same way; with surprise and anger. Hunger, stress and aggression activate the reptilian brain—primal responses registered clearer than glee or amusement.

The pieces the Curator displayed on the lower level reflected a psychological darkness that could trigger emotional heaviness for viewers with any empathy. Since his patrons didn't have much compunction, the Curator didn't expect the gallery to elicit fear or concern about him as a collector.

One of his most prized additions came from the acquisition of the assemblage created by residents of behavioral hospitals and imprisoned reprobates, formerly housed in the Collection de l'Art Brut in Lausanne, Switzerland.

He also purchased masterpieces from the Prinzhorn Collection at the former University of Heidelberg Psychiatric Clinic in Germany, saved from being burned in 1944 by the Nazis. Mr. Goode had arranged its shipment to Shanghai for him as an anonymous buyer.

After building his collection, understanding the "inside out" perspective became the Curator's pastime. When he watched his guests, he thought about how their brains processed the art.

At each party, he allowed a select few to see his glass garden to gauge their feelings and responses. His desire to witness how his patrons responded when they stood in the middle of his collection bursting with lights consumed him. He used their reactions to help analyze his own self-understanding.

Although his senses functioned perfectly, they never elicited an emotional reaction from his experiences. His limitations intrigued him, and they always had.

In college Stennis began to consider how a brain's rich synapse network engaged when hearing music or seeing a painting. In his gallery he continued to explore neuroaesthetics with some patrons in direct conversation.

"What feelings do you get walking about the room? You may touch the glass. What do you experience when you move your hand across the surface?"

The Curator didn't tell anybody about the art, or himself. Few learned he helped create the sculptures—and none knew about his neurosurgery background or his given name.

Minimizing witnesses to his gallery ensured people wouldn't brag about what they'd encountered. His dark endeavor required most of the details about running the facility to remain undisclosed.

Mr. Goode acted as his fail-safe. If anyone should panic or make a discovery, the Curator could tell them, "Your time has come." Luckily, he never had to expend energy on such a situation. Every patron who made it upstairs had a deep closet full of secrets that could be used as bargaining chips to keep them quiet, if needed.

Most people who approached the sculptures described a kind of familiarity. All said something felt different from other glass art. Several people had strong negative responses. They couldn't explain it; but they admitted an intense repulsion settled into their stomachs.

Some viewers, including Sifu, a well-known monk and the Curator's Buddhist meditation teacher, confessed they were not fond of the figures. "As bright and beautiful as the forms are, something concerns me about them," Sifu told the Curator the first time he visited the gallery.

***

From what Mr. Goode had said, he determined days after Sifu came, that Stennis' inquiries about sensory perception triggered the monk's follow-up with a female neuroscientist from Singapore. She had recently contacted Sifu as an expert subject for her research project studying the effects of meditation on the brain.

Mr. Goode's standard monitoring of all gallery visitors uncovered an email from the monk to the woman. "You sat in the background of one of Sifu's photographs," he told the Curator. "It's too late; he's already emailed the image to the woman to facilitate an introduction."

"Have you identified her?"

"Yes ... she's your former lab assistant from Singapore, Frieda Grayson."

"Frieda? Nonsense. Why would Sifu put her in touch with me? He knows nothing about my former neurosurgery career, or my professional life in Singapore."

"He responded to her by email, saying she had asked him similar questions about sensory perception and meditation as you did. He sensed a philosophical connection between the two of you."

"Oh, did he? Did she respond?"

"Not to Sifu. I imagine upon seeing a brief glimpse of your face, Frieda had the very moment she'd been waiting for ... discovering you are alive."

"Perhaps she didn't recognize me."

"I tracked her emails and her phone log. They show she activated her suspicions with the authorities immediately. INTERPOL opened a case to find you here in Shanghai as a result of her tip."

"INTERPOL?" asked Stennis, noting the conversation as the only time he had ever seen Mr. Goode react with anything other than calm. "She always pushed the drama. She could have started with the local police."

"She did," said Mr. Goode. "But Shanghai law enforcement works more and more now with the International Criminal Police Organization as standard procedure in solving cases. Probably on account of increased transnational organized crime here in China—pyramid scams, telecommunications fraud, cybercrimes—and such."

"A change in the nature of worldwide crime now impacts this gallery; how about that," said Stennis. "I'm sure you have this handled, Mr. Goode. We've talked about the potential of something like this happening for years. Are your systems in place?"

"Sure, I have systems in place to thwart the Shanghai Municipal Police from discovering our operations. I continue to reroute technological queries related to this gallery to ensure it stays hidden. These simple procedures do not take much time," said Mr. Goode.

"Then why do I have the sense you are concerned?" asked Stennis.

"You know I can reconfigure any local surveillance system and render it unable to detect our activities ... but I can't circumvent INTERPOL networks for long," Mr. Goode said.

"What INTERPOL list am I on? Green?" Stennis asked, understanding investigators may soon discover and dismantle the gallery. "Do you think they know I faked my death and want information about it?"

"You are on their 'red' list," said Philip. "Whatever Frieda told them, they've assembled enough damning evidence about your former laboratory research to tie you to defined criminal activities."

"How long do we have?" asked Stennis.

"Three months ... at most ... before they discover this location."

Stennis often reflected on how he'd disappeared from the Singapore medical scene, and how well he'd remained hidden in Shanghai. He knew his associates adopted the belief—as they must have felt content in believing it—that he died rather than dropped out of society. Some may have even reveled in getting so close to discovering his secret research that he opted to take his own life.

Nobody could know for sure, and the thought pleased him.

Now more than a decade later, he remembered the feeling of needing to disappear. "The heightened level of sensation I felt upon evaporating from the world was the most intensity I ever experienced," he told Mr. Goode.

Insights come in flashes; fast by nature. "A similar jolt of adrenaline rushes through me now. My whole body pulses with the clarity of everything appearing to move in slow motion," the Curator told his fixer, after learning about Frieda.

***

Philip and Stennis argued more in their final six weeks to-gether than in their fourteen-year business partnership. They agreed on the urgency of one essential conclusion: More im-portant than trying to remain hidden, the time had come to execute a complete escape.

For years Stennis knew he would need a gallery transition plan. Paving the path for his ultimate freedom began five years earlier with personal preparations. This included initiat-ing correspondence with his former college roommate to build trust. He didn't know if he would need to involve Douglas Jones at some point, but he wanted to keep the possibility open.

After learning about INTERPOL's involvement, Mr. Goode investigated Douglas as part of executing their larger plan. He learned Douglas had received a liver transplant a couple of months earlier, and healing proved a challenge.

It quickly became clear that Douglas would not be able to assist them in the way they had originally hoped.

Stennis leveraged the information about Douglas' medical condition, however. He told his former colleague he wanted to help him—and he truly believed his current research could. But he had a greater intention. He surmised Douglas could draw Persephone to him as Plan B for his own agenda.

Stennis had been monitoring Persephone from Shanghai since she was a graduate student. Before he ever met her, he considered her his professional disciple. After all, she under-stood his research better than anyone.

After inviting Douglas to the gallery, he counted on Per-sephone's subsequent discovery. Stennis figured bringing the young neuroscientist to him would be easy. But he knew chan-ging his own course would not be so simple.

Persephone's goal of fusing emotional understanding into machines to help them interact seamlessly with humans could become a reality faster than she expected. He only needed time to reframe the situation for her.

Her trust in authority, concern for her father and high standards worked in his favor. But her steadfast adherence to medical ethics complicated his future.

The night he learned about INTERPOL, the Curator sat in his

sculpture garden for a long time before returning to his condominium on the other side of the city. For fifteen years the Metro had offered the fastest way to travel there anonymously. He'd always felt adequately hidden in the darkness, but that night it seemed every light infringed upon his privacy.

***

The next morning the Curator awoke at home, as the first glint of sunlight came through the sweeping wall of east windows that adjoined those providing north and south light. His grand view across the tops of the other skyscrapers, out to the East China Sea, never impressed him. He preferred it more when his glass walls darkened once the sun activated the integrated photosensors, ensuring the reds of his stylish Asian furniture stayed crisp.

The residence, which he kept immaculate, could have been a business rental in any city—if not for the huge sensory deprivation chamber filling the main room. Its tangle of power cords and hoses ran across the hardwood floor into the kitchen. The gleaming white fiberglass cylinder resembled a giant egg; his capsule of solitary confinement and complete solitude.

Stennis entered his tank almost every morning for the entire fifteen years he lived in the condo. He closed eyes, plugged up his ears, and rested in a sensory deprived state as his mind drifted in and out of dreaming. He often stayed suspended in the warm salt water for three hours at a time—and occasionally for days.

More than once he imagined he suffered from Locked-in Syndrome, or some other type of paralysis. Sometimes he visualized his arms amputated, considering how he'd endure a phantom limb. He registered *how* his mind perceived these experiences—emotionless.

That day he sought himself in the darkness with heaviness. Memories and thoughts came without order, became hyperreal and blended. His isolation as a young person and the residue of being shunned by his parents, fellow students and some of his teachers mixed with the gossip he endured from his neurosurgery colleagues.

The idea of *Nirvana*—enlightenment—reflected the concept most approaching how Stennis perceived his everyday life. He recognized he hadn't reached the state yet, but he connected with the notion of being free from the mental constraints that attachment to the senses brings.

Conversations with Sifu floated through his mind like a dream:

"I can perceive my five senses, but without connection," he remembered telling the monk.

"Open your heart and embrace your union with something larger," Sifu had said.

"I can accept the mind, free of the senses, would no longer be limited by personal experience," said Stennis.

"Freedom from the outer world allows one to enter a deeper level of meditation. We can witness the soul. How would you describe your world now?" Sifu asked.

"I cannot tap into experiences emotionally. I am flat in both directions—positive and negative. It does not move me to see the sunset; it does not affect me to see suffering."

"Usually the opposite happens; one tries to release attachment to the emotions, memories and thoughts triggered by the senses. Your perception remains intact, but it isn't meaningful to you?" asked Sifu.

"Correct. Am I many steps ahead on the path of enlightenment? Or must I pass through the sensory realm first?" Stennis asked.

"You are affected by not being affected. Surrender yourself. Continue your self-inquiry to touch a greater field of expansion. Work to polish your heart," said Sifu.

Chapter Ten

"What's going on?" Persephone asked Philip when he knocked and then entered the side room of the upper gallery. "Where's Dr. Stennis? I've been locked in here for an hour. I'm ready to go back to my hotel."

She stood up and moved toward the door, which Philip promptly shut.

"Have a seat, Persephone," he said.

"What? Why?" she asked. She walked to the windows along the side wall, noticing only a handful of patrons remained in the gallery below. The move allowed her to put some space between herself and Philip, and formulate a plan.

"My apologies for the time it took to return," he said.

Persephone didn't know what Philip wanted, but she didn't trust anyone to be straight with her until she found her dad. And at that point, she didn't believe he was even in the gallery.

Philip sat on one of the white couches and unfolded an oversize flat screen on the coffee table. She ignored his setup, interested in reaching the door more than anything else.

Once she returned to her hotel, she'd definitely call INTERPOL ... she should have taken them more seriously that morning. She could feel it now: Dr. Franklin Stennis was dangerous.

"I want to show you something related to your research," Philip said. "Almost forty years ago, your mother taught me at the University of West London, where I studied information technology and cybersecurity. Rarely do people connected with my former world cross into my current world. Almost never."

"I'm here to find my father," Persephone said. "This is the only research I'm interested in at the moment. So unless you can help me, I'd consider anything else irrelevant."

Persephone walked to the door. She could feel Philip watching her. When she tried the knob, she found it locked.

"What are you doing here?" she asked him when she turned around. "You can't be a friend of my father's."

"Ah, your father. A well-known neurosurgeon. The most famous surgeon to use Stennis' NTS techniques."

"He wasn't just a neurosurgeon; he's my dad. Maybe you're not close to your dad, but I'm worried about mine right now," she said in a personal attempt at trying to gauge his empathy.

"My mum passed during a C-section having me. My pop never remarried. He only loved two things ... numbers and meat. He worked as an accountant for a chain of butcher shops and died of a heart attack when I was in my 20s," he said.

"I'm sorry to hear that," said Persephone, taking a long blink to draw upon a place of inner patience and determine a new strategy.

"Come look at this for a moment," Philip said. "What I want to show you actually ties to your mother. I remember her discussing the evolution of bridging the gap between humans and machines. She seemed like a bit of an idealist, if I recall. You work as an activist for technological equality, don't you?"

"Yes," she said, as she took a full breath, in and out, readying herself for some kind of opine she expected Philip was about to give her. She opted to move closer to the coffee table to view his screen.

Philip leaned forward and removed his black jacket. When he draped his coat across the side arm of the couch, she noticed a blocked geometric tribal-pattern tattoo banded above his left elbow. The momentary glimpse of the artistic rendering of an old-fashioned circuit board signaled her caution.

She recognized the tattoo style as one received by gang members in London from two decades ago who practiced martial and combative arts. How strange a Chinese man in his late fifties would be tattooed like that. She wanted to ask him about it, but thought better of it.

Persephone began Judo lessons in high school after she gave up bike racing. She had continued the practice as a form of fitness and self-defense. Her background told her Philip's tattoo reflected his expert fighting skills. It glowed for her as distinctively as his cockney accent.

She also noticed the skin color on his hands seemed slightly different from his arms. Something felt awry. She registered her concern and amplified her personal radar.

"Your mother often discussed how technology would create unity and equality. But look at them," Philip said as he gestured toward the patrons. "They all have their microchip cloud bubbles around them. Ironic, isn't it? Stennis' invention allowing biological tissue to merge seamlessly with the synthetic connects us more to technology than to each other."

"I believe having microchips installed in us opens up the future for everyone," she said. "The wrist chips allow identification worldwide—no matter one's nationality. They're no different from a fingerprint or a retinal scan now."

"A microchip becomes status burnishing," said Philip. "The *way* one transacts is central. Paying for restaurants, clothing and everything else through a simple wave of the hand in this digital cloud we live in, brings entry into a higher social tier, once you arrive at a certain level financially."

"Your point?" asked Persephone.

"The farther up one travels in society, the more gilded everything becomes," he said. "The top of this gigantic city traps almost all the higher-ups' attention and focus. At two hundred and fifty stories and above, 'Higher Law' governs instead of provincial law.

"The higher-ups exist in this exclusive skyway forming their own city-state, unbound by regulations. This kind of diplomatic immunity lets people get away with many things—untouchable by legal, or other means."

"As long as humans exist, so will a stratified socioeconomic situation," said Persephone. "The gap continues to widen between the higher-ups and the lowers. But microchips support equality by making everyone visible."

"You think so?" asked Philip.

"If you walk into a restaurant, the network registers you, no matter how much money you have. So what if some people can activate their microchip for payment and transfer finances through their individual cloud?" she said. "So what if transactions can be handled from a networked account? Most people still pay through their personal devices. Some may even use actual cash."

"But recognizing everyone as visible creates a semblance of equality?" Philip asked.

"Exactly," she said, pointing her index finger at him.

"Paper currency you can fold up and put in your pocket exists as a trade material for the lowers. Higher-ups don't touch bills unless bartering in the black market or dealing in discretion: a drug habit, prostitution, or illegal activities," said Philip. "Even then, their assistants handle the cash.

"Higher-ups work with digital currencies where only they understand the methods of its valuation. They control the equations and the infrastructure. Should one use hard money often, I can guarantee you that person spends time in the criminal world. To stay outside such a realm, most choose other means of transacting," he said.

"I'll ask again ... your point?" said Persephone.

"I want to show you something. Take a look at this screen. It displays the official Shanghai network running access to who's in this building," said Philip.

Persephone perused the blank list and didn't see any names —including her own. She returned her gaze to the party with perhaps a dozen patrons still in the room.

"There are no names on the chart," she said.

"Exactly my point ... not everyone can be seen," said Philip. "You think having a microchip supports equality. I believe it creates inequality through the ability to become invisible. If you take your personal cloud offline, it gives you the freedom to move through the world undetected. Wealth allows privacy."

"Your patrons hide themselves from the network?" she asked, then stood and walked to the window overlooking the lower level. "But I didn't see my father, you, or even myself on that list."

"Today most people think being plugged in is the only option," said Philip. "I have this entire gallery hidden in a 'dead zone.'"

"What do you mean a 'dead zone'?" she asked.

"I refract the digital signals around the warehouse and the surrounding blocks. Once people come close, their microchips disappear from the grid. My system also erases their movements from the preceding thirty minutes."

"Isn't dismantling a read on a microchip an international felony?" she asked.

"A backlash should have happened seventy years ago when technology created confidentiality considerations," he said.

Persephone crossed her arms and said, "Hmm. I'm not going to ask why you're doing that. How does this relate to my research? Or to finding my father?"

"Simple. Look down at them," Philip said, motioning toward the patrons. "This is the effect of humans inseparable from technology. These people move through life checked out —isolated—stratified so far at the top they've become invisible. They function behind society, holding the illusion they lead the charge. What kind of life is that?"

Trying to ease her discomfort with a joke, Persephone asked, "Are you implying they're all robots and I could help make them human again?"

"Oh, little hope remains for that," he said with a slight smirk. "It's pretty easy to size people up if you take a second to look in their eyes. But, since your research focuses on developing emotions in machines, we want you to work with us to progress one of our sculptures."

"Really?" she asked, followed by quick laugh. She hardly

thought it would be fair to force a sculpture to experience the same disconnection in the gallery as she detected.

Philip walked across the room to the window facing the upper gallery. He stood silently for a minute with his back toward her.

Persephone also looked toward the sculpture court, waiting, trying to evaluate his intentions.

Finally, Philip turned toward her and spoke. "A colorful garden bursts with life here. The light displays are extraordinary. We set each one up."

Then he walked to the couch, put his jacket back on, and folded up the monitor. At that point, Persephone caught a quick glimpse of what appeared to be a gun carried on his backside. Danger confirmed! The situation held the potential for taking her out of her league and she recognized she should play nice to ensure her own safety.

"You want me to help you? To what end?" she asked.

"To the very end," said Philip.

He returned to the door exiting into the upper gallery and used the microchip in his wrist to unlock it.

"The Curator will see you now," he said, as he turned toward Persephone and motioned with a quick lift of his chin for her to follow him. "And your father recognizes you are here … he has been waiting."

Chapter Eleven

Persephone entered the upstairs gallery, now free of patrons, and walked toward *Chessic*. She circled around the glass figure and considered her options. She could wait for Dr. Stennis, or she could try to leave.

Chessic cast a softer glow than the fuchsia hues she remembered from earlier. A shimmer of pale pink and white brought small specks of color that intermingled and slowly traded position across the surface. The lights reflected each other, but also hid each other. Sometimes the glass shined solid pink, then it appeared all white. The piece seemed different from the others; more silvery, almost iridescent.

The sculpture next to *Chessic* glowed with bright greens and vibrant purples. Apart from the colors and a small change to the hand positions, the two forms looked quite similar. She wanted to touch the statues but remembered she had been ejected from the gallery soon after doing so earlier that afternoon.

Maybe it would work again? Persephone was too tired to play games. She just wanted to go back to her hotel. Room service was definitely in order for dinner. Maybe; it was pretty late. Hopefully it would not take a lot of effort to get a robocar.

She walked to the double doors, deciding to exit the gallery instead of wait for Dr. Stennis. She pulled on one handle and found it locked. Trying both knobs, neither budged. Hadn't Philip just exited through them? Had he bloody trapped her into another room?

This time she knocked on the metal doors, hard. She felt hot and yanked on the handles again; but they didn't respond. On the far side of the room, she remembered the elevator.

A quick ride would be an even faster way to get to the lower level! She walked across the room and pushed the call button, eliciting no response. As she returned her gaze toward the gallery, the glowing blank faces looked as stunned as she felt.

Her eyes scanned the space. The only other door she saw entered the side room. She was definitely stuck. How ridiculous. More than a simple inconvenience, the situation continued to sound an internal alarm that something nefarious was occurring—and she was in the middle of it.

She looked at the sculptures, then at the ceiling. There had to be a way out. Feeling trapped angered her, and her fingers clenched together from the stress.

Several minutes later, the Curator entered the room through the double doors, turned to shut them, and walked toward her.

"Thank you for waiting, Persephone. Now that my patrons have departed, we can talk more specifically about the art. Tell me, what do you notice?"

"You are really asking me that? I came here to find my father. But I think I made a mistake. I'm standing in this room, but I'm distracted. You locked me in there for more than an hour," she said, pointing at the side room. "What's going on?"

"I want to converse with you about my sculptures," he said. "Every visitor has a different experience. What is your impression?"

"Look," she said as she turned to face the Curator. "You invited me to view this collection, and I appreciate it. But I would really like to talk with my father now."

"Patience, Persephone. Enjoy these sculptures," he said,

opening his arms like a conductor. "Your father played an instrumental role in expanding this group. I cannot discuss him with you until you first consider these important works. Please tell me, what do you notice?"

"Patience? I have been here for nearly four bloody hours and gotten nowhere!" she said. "Where the hell is he? What do you mean an instrumental role? Was he a donor for this collection?"

"Yes, Persephone. As a matter of fact, he was. And he will appear in time. But first, what can you tell me about these pieces."

She returned her attention to the sculptures, this time to the one fusing purple and green. "We can converse about this for five minutes," she said. "Then let's please move on."

In looking at the artwork more closely, seeing inside them was easy. Persephone discerned fiber-optic strands ran under the surface of the thick translucent forms. The light displays melded and transformed through an array of colors, like kaleidoscopic veins of color flowing as a rainbow unraveling.

"I see glass sculptures with optical fibers inside," she said, trying to keep the art conversation basic, to expedite moving their discussion in the direction of finding her father.

"Indeed. The old fiber optic filaments give them an antique sensibility. I paired them with technology unavailable 150 years ago. It puts my sculptures on a continuum between the past and the future, solidifying their timelessness," he explained. "What else?"

"The light source appears to come from the base. Shiny cables run up from the pedestal through both legs. The lights appear like the nervous system, with the fiber optics starting at the bottom of the spine and expanding throughout the body."

"Good, good, keep going," he said.

"The brightness travels to where some organs and sensory systems would be ... the heart, the lungs, the eyes, the mouth, the abdomen. Not every organ is represented, but a fair number are, I guess. The groin and the skin really shine."

"Great observations, Persephone. Feel free to touch the sculptures, if you would like. It won't harm them."

She reached above her head and ran her fingers across the

cheek of the figure as its lights cascaded from dark green to light blue through each of its fiber optic channels.

The warmth of the glass surprised her, as she had expected to find it cool.

"Did you notice the sculpture on the main level?" the Curator asked.

"I saw one split in half, without lights," she said, turning toward him.

"It is called *Severed*. Mr. Goode assists me with installing the lights into the sculptures, before we fuse the front and back halves together."

"You did the lights?" she asked. "Wow. Okay ... that's a new one."

"It is not an easy thing to do."

"It's clear you made many choices in this gallery, Dr. Stennis. Adding optical fibers into the pieces so they will shine enhances their beauty. Why are you interested in me seeing this project?"

"Expansion. I have three series in my sculpture collection, but the individual statues are all unique. My pieces evolved progressively, each expanding upon the last."

"Which series is this?" she asked, moving toward *Chessic* and touching the form's waist.

"Third ... what a marvel. Perception drives this for me, Persephone. What happens within you when you engage with the figures?"

"A piece of art can elicit excitement or anger, or a variety of things: intrigue, happiness, sadness, nostalgia. I appreciate my reflections interest you, but I'm tired. I feel strung along. And like I'm not making much progress," she said.

"A Buddhist monk came here once," said the Curator. "He got a heavy impression from being in this room. He couldn't explain it. Something felt viscerally different from the other artworks. Do you ever feel that way from looking at something, Persephone?"

"A perceivable sadness hits me every time I go through the primate house at a wildlife sanctuary. These magnificent animals are so close to humans. A sense of wonder and frustration comes from them gazing back at me. They have as much right as I do to breathe and walk free. Art presents a different level of engagement for me though."

"So you understand my point. Creations have traditionally been one-sided. An artist infuses intent into a piece, but in the end, only the viewers' perceptions matter. I am trying to make art more relevant. I want to witness my sculptures connecting with those who interact with them. It's one of the biggest reasons I bring patrons in here. If you couple viewer engagement with a sculpture's visual illumination, it presents a more powerful experience."

"I'm sorry. I can see you've gone through a lot of work with these sculptures. But I don't have time for a deep connection right now. I need to find my father. I think I've waited long enough for the answer. Where is he?"

"Do you know who I am, Persephone?"

"Yes, of course I do, Dr. Stennis."

"I know you are familiar with my work," he said.

"My father used your NTS to heal damaged and diseased nerves. It revolutionized the method of connecting human nervous tissue to mechanical technology. Now people can see with their artificial eyes or feel touch through prostheses. This makes a huge difference in our world."

"Many people use the results from my research. I provided the foundation for them, as I have for you," he said.

"After you disappeared, a few things stood out to my dad, making him suspicious enough to investigate your techniques. Years later he realized you couldn't have done some of the things you suggested without harming your patients."

"He discussed the quandary with me."

"Excuse me for saying so, but I believe you played on the fact that people are so blinded by technology ... so dependent upon it ... nobody questions technological advances anymore. Most consider it transparent, when it isn't ... clearly."

"You want to ask me, 'How?'"

"No, I want to ask you, 'Why?' No researcher has so many coincidences. I think my father's heart broke the day he accepted the rumors about you."

"Sometimes leaps must be made by alternative means to accomplish what cannot be achieved any other way. Are you ready to make the leap, Persephone?"

"The accusations are true, aren't they?" she asked.

He scanned her with his eyes then said, "Those who fear pushing boundaries will never reach their truest aspirations."

***

Persephone remained silent for several seconds, taking a complete mental assessment of everything she knew.

"You were certainly ahead of your time with the way you treated injuries and illnesses. It's remarkable how you covered up research to appear to do it all under the Hippocratic Oath. As if the advances you made fell within the realm of the humane."

"You sound envious I could separate my work from my emotions," he said.

"I don't envy those who navigate the system at the expense of other's health and well-being. I realized early on what I wanted to do. I have never been tempted to do illegal things —criminal things—to help my research. The cause creates my passion, not the result," she said.

"What's your cause?" the Curator asked her, appearing unmoved.

"Helping people! Not forcing my personal research upon them."

"You respond like I conducted an early-twentieth century lobotomy," he said. "My procedures were not rudimentary. You said it yourself, I helped a great many people—perhaps millions of patients."

"But it wasn't genuine, or from the heart. It served your own needs. To make your own gains."

"Are you only involved in neuroscience to help people?" he asked.

"Of course," she said.

"Then why conduct research that advances your own name? Why not stick with healing people through available methods and leave the revelations to someone else? You are lying to yourself, Persephone. You want to advance the future, and have your name associated with it."

"I'm sure you know when I was young, my dad worked for six months in Ethiopia's developing manufacturing zone. Two years later we spent another half a year in Brazil. We moved there as a family. These experiences and the people I met touched my heart. I saw my father work with his patients and it sparked my inner passion. I studied neuroscience because of the global need … not the personal need."

"You may have used that statement to get into graduate school, Persephone. But you have outgrown it. With your intelligence, you understand how the brain works better than anyone. Your insights allow you to further the technology I developed to gain a higher level of comprehension."

"My ethics give me a higher level of understanding," she said. "Still, what I don't get, is why you led me here? I've traveled half-way around the world to come to a party I can't imagine my dad ever attending, only to be sequestered in a room talking to a man who by all accounts, no longer exists."

"Of course Douglas and Ardis would have an intelligent and selfless child," said the Curator. "I am glad you are here, Persephone. We can aid each other. I can direct you to your father, and you can help me free myself."

"Free yourself? From what? You disappeared fifteen years ago."

"From this body," he said.

"My dad always said you led a very detached life. And that you disassociated from yourself more than anyone. I don't know what you are expecting from me, but I would appreciate it if you could tell me where my dad is."

"He is here, Persephone."

"Where?" she asked, looking directly into his dark and hollow eyes.

"Here, in this room," he said in a calm voice, meeting her hard stare with a tranquil gaze.

Persephone looked around the room and saw only sculptures. Her stomach dropped with a sense of primordial fear. She registered the unusual reaction and worked to stay calm, letting go of a long exhale.

"Such a wonderful name from ancient Greece: Persephone. Goddess queen of the abyss. Didn't Persephone's father Zeus conspire in his daughter's abduction by Hades into the underworld? Her mother negotiated her release. But because Persephone had already tasted a handful of pomegranate seeds, she could never fully return to life as she knew it. She served her destiny by living part of the year in the unfathomed depths," he said.

"What are you implying?" she asked, facing the Curator with her arms wrapped around her chest.

"Welcome to the underworld, Persephone. Your father helped lead you here. Now we must get to work."

Persephone had a strong premonition with his huge ego and lack of concern for others, the Curator was one of science's most evil people. She also felt the situation may have led her to a moral crossroads that could test the integrity of her own research.

Persephone looked at the lights glowing in abundance and quietly wished for them to help her see clearly. Then she eyed the double doors and began to back toward them, away from the Curator.

She didn't recognize the full scope of the situation, but her instincts signaled something egregious. Her immediate focus must be to maintain her own safety and get out of the gallery.

Dr. Stennis appeared detached and unemotional as he watched her. She couldn't tell if he was mentally ill, or if her own lack of understanding compromised her safety. She decided on the probability of both.

Her eyes darted through the room for any clue about her father, but found none. When she reached the doors leading toward the stairs they remained locked.

The Curator remained standing in exactly the same spot, seeming unfazed by her growing panic.

Chapter Twelve

"**O**pen this door! Let me out of here," Persephone said, grasping the handle.

"You know, Persephone," I don't show these pieces to everyone. For the few who do see them, far fewer come to know what they are looking at. I need to witness people's uncensored feelings. It's important for me to determine if they connect to my sculptures and perceive a sense of soul."

"I want to leave," she said.

"You can't; I've only started to gain a deeper understanding of your perceptions."

"What? What is the point of all this? This is uncomfortable and quite disturbing. I understand your background and why you disappeared. I'm astounded to find you running an art gallery. But I'm *not* surprised something amiss lurks here," she said. "I want out."

Persephone surveyed the figures, drawn to the network of lights across their bodies. They continued to stare at her as a collective. No matter which direction she looked, she could not escape their faces. She didn't want to connect with any of them; she wanted to locate her dad and leave.

"I enhanced these anthropoid glass forms, and have shown them to a select few, as my way of looking for proof of a soul. I study them—and I evaluate people moved by them; affected by a connection they can perceive but can't explain. This is why I seek a spiritual component to those I invite into this gallery."

"A spiritual component? Philip implied your guests are robots. You've both suggested I'm here related to my research. And I've told you I'm here to find my father. Why did you lead me here?"

"Because of your abilities. My patrons do not care about these sculptures. Fixed in the material world and the power they wield, their countless sums matter to them most. They may have an epiphany at some point about something larger, or not. They may not be capable enough, or ready.

"Through my interactions with patrons who feel moved, I've proven my sculptures radiate something," he continued. "Some visitors say their curiosity increases around them."

"So you only want people to look at the figures and respond to them? What more do you want from me?" she asked.

"I connect to the pieces because I gave them life," the Curator said. "I have a personal investment in their interactions."

Persephone collected herself and tried to see the gallery with fresh eyes. She didn't understand Dr. Stennis' intentions and wondered whether to continue to play along with his game. A faint whirring emanated from the lit sculptures and filled the room with a light hissing. She didn't hear it before, and yet, with all her senses on high alert, it sounded so amplified.

She moved away from the door and walked toward the *Musician*, the piece closest to her. Trying to relax to mitigate the anxiety she felt about the unknown, she didn't have much luck.

A silver stylized form in the head with broad reflective angular facets and no illuminated optical fibers became apparent the longer she looked at the sculpture. It caused the cranial interior to mirror light from its surroundings and shine in concert with the well-lit face, ears and scalp.

A tapered tube covered with the fractal surfaces emerged

from the bottom rear of the silver form, descending like a spine. It split at the pelvis and continued through both feet into the pedestal.

As she focused on the internal components running through the glass, Persephone tried to ignore the Curator's steady gaze fixed upon her like a leopard hiding in the trees. She felt him aware of every movement her eyes made. By mitigating his silent stalking with her personal resolve, she determined not to allow him to close the space between them with his intention of sensory consumption.

She regrouped, strategizing how to navigate the jungle of confusion she found herself ensnared within, to embrace her own strength. "Why did my father come here?" she asked.

"Your father speculated only I could help him. Now you can assist us both, so we can aid you. He has prepared to be the next step of your scientific discovery."

"Where is he?"

"You want to know where your father is? You tell me. Can you perceive him? Somebody as close as your father should be easy. Visualize your connection to his soul and you will see him."

"What is that supposed to mean?" she asked. "Are you telling me my father died?"

"Not at all. He is quite alive. We are so used to seeing how people present themselves, but it's not always real. You can connect to your father in the purest way now ... removed from every typical interface. In daily life you can't see a person's thoughts or how their mind functions—but this reality shines brightest in the glass vessels."

"I don't follow," she said. "Please. Where is he?"

"You will awaken to a greater understanding. To experience the soul and enter its realm, one must be free from the flesh and bone the senses operate within and control," he said, as he looked off into the distance.

"You can't disconnect the soul from the body like removing a tooth. It is all connected!" she said.

"I have done it," he replied. "The brain, which perceives everything, houses the soul—the body's energetic essence.

When freed from the senses, the mind can merge with a greater energy. The sculptures are my personal inquiry into what the soul needs to survive beyond the physical."

Persephone closed her eyes and shook her head in disbelief. When she opened them she said, "After my father disappeared and I discovered he corresponded with you for years, I concluded he must have come here. But I don't know why."

"So you understand he supports you being here?"

"I suppose, but I can't imagine it."

"Let me appeal to your sense of discovery. I can assist you with your research, as you support me with my journey. In reading your publications, I've gathered you are furthering science along the same course I am. I made it possible for you to find me, so we may work together."

"I realize the foundation for some of my explorations came at the expense of your former patients who lost their choices. I once debated with myself about whether to carry forward. I did use results from your past experiments ... but I'm not interested in connecting with your present research," she said.

Persephone returned her gaze to the sculptures. She remained silent for several minutes then faced the Curator again. He stood in the silence without trying to fill it. She felt her forehead and jaw relax, and with a directed focus asked, "What am I looking at ... exactly?"

The pinpoint projections of lights coming from the surrounding sculptures shined with such brightness that when she looked at her arm, the glowing spots appeared to radiate from within her own skin. They cast a shine across her body and illuminated her insights like pulsing stars.

"You are witnessing light displays driven by mental activity. The luminosity is an artistic output of pure consciousness. I've stripped away everything else to show an unclouded mind ... one not overload by sensory input."

To help confirm what she'd begun to accept, Persephone asked, "So ... my father is connected with one of these pieces?"

"Indeed."

"Dear god," she whispered as a cascade of fear washed over her. "How?"

The Curator stared at her silently.

"What are you asking of me? Is it true you want to make these sculptures more sentient, as Philip said?" she asked.

"Did he?" asked the Curator, appearing to ponder the idea.

"If so, you must be taking this into the realm of science fiction. In my research, I'm not trying to make machines actually be human! I want to help AI be sentient—to better align their emotional and ethical processes with their primary functions," she said.

"This is not science fiction, Persephone. You can have your own impression of a picture on a wall; your interpretation can connect to a memory or an emotion. But interacting with art driven by another human mind provides an unparalleled experience."

"I don't support a disregard for life ... regardless of the gains to science or anything else," she said.

"Neither do I. Death and mayhem for their own sake do not interest me. I did not create my sculpture court to be gruesome. It reveals a path toward enlightenment."

"Enlightenment? Do you mean in a literal sense because they light up?"

The Curator shifted his pupils toward the ceiling for a moment and remained quiet.

"It is late," he said when he looked at her. "I am sure you understand why I cannot allow you to leave. Mr. Goode has unhooked you from the network and redirected your personal communication systems. He will escort you to the furnished apartment in the basement. I hope you will feel comfortable there. Please get some rest."

"What? Are you serious? You are locking me in here ... again? I want to go back to my hotel. What is going on? Where is my dad?"

"In the morning, please meet me at seven-thirty in my private study where we sat earlier. We can eat breakfast and I will share more with you about my collection and my research. I know you are wondering how you will be involved. I'll leave that for later."

Persephone understood how Dr. Stennis reached his discoveries as a neurosurgeon. Yet the glass figures left her reeling in a much deeper way. They stood as a visible testament that even after his disappearance he had continued his inquiries in horrific ways. Now she worried about the state in which she might find her dad, and she feared for her own safety.

"Dr. Stennis, please do not lock me in this gallery tonight. Tell me what you want. What has happened to my dad? Have I arrived with enough time? Is it still possible to help him?"

She remembered her father saying, "Now," and only hoped she'd come fast enough.

"You will be very comfortable in the basement apartment. Mr. Goode lived there for many years, and has fixed it up nicely. We have prepared for your arrival. Your favorite foods are in the fridge."

"My favorite foods? How do you know my favorite foods?"

"Your dad stayed in the apartment when he arrived here. Of course he let us know your food preferences. We have been expecting you."

Dr. Stennis walked toward the double doors and gave them five sharp raps. Philip pushed them open and entered the room.

"Good night, Persephone," the Curator said before he left. When he departed, Philip moved straight toward her.

PART FOUR

Smell

"Allow me to continue with the sense of smell," the abbot said. "This sense emerges in a fetus after ten weeks as scents cross the amniotic fluid. The nose then stakes its claim as the dominant sensor.

"Did you know the brain processes smell in the same area as memory and emotion?

"Scent isn't interpreted by the thalamus like the other senses. This means smells can't be blocked by them. Nor can smell arouse the other senses.

"Consider, you can be so focused on reading sutras you do not hear the dinner bell. But the aroma of lentils may alert you. But, if you don't hear your four o'clock alarm to sit for morning meditation, even the scent of peppermint tea won't help awaken you."

The small group responded with quiet chuckles. The monk smiled, too, but he made it clear he was not joking.

"You must be vigilant about smell," he warned. "It can incite responses at an instinctual level. You can see this occurring in the sculptures that glow yellow.

"Smell is the sense through which we connect to the element of earth. Basic and grounding, it penetrates deeper than the other senses.

"This means it can create distraction from deep meditation. Smells may trigger a whole range of emotions, from memories of happiness and pleasures, to intense fear that may roll through you like waves from a boulder thrown into a still pond.

"On a more subtle note, let me remind you to always trust your instinct when making a decision or taking action.

"As the saying goes, 'follow your nose' ... and that includes here. If this path is not right for you, accept that. You will find your Way."

Chapter Thirteen

"Don't you dare touch me," Persephone told Philip. "Not one finger."

"Please come with me," he said, as he motioned with his chin for her to join him. "I'll show you to the apartment downstairs. It's close to midnight; we'd all like to get some sleep."

Walking behind her, Philip escorted Persephone down the stairs, past the lower gallery and into the basement. They exited into a small foyer. "Your apartment," he said, as he gestured to the door across from them. He stepped back, offering Persephone some semblance of safety.

She entered into a clean living room, shut the door, dropped her purse on the couch and tried to make sense of her surroundings. Her eyes scanned the space for clues about her father, but saw no immediate signs. She really hoped she wasn't under surveillance.

A few minutes later she looked through the peephole and saw the empty hallway offering a clear path to the stairs—her escape route. If the men thought she had any intention of staying there, they were mistaken.

Persephone opened the door and a rush of cool air entered

the apartment. Without Philip lurking near her, she could observe the area more fully. A set of double doors on her right now became obvious, and she heard Philip and Dr. Stennis talking on the other side. Unfortunately, their muffled sounds did not carry their conversation.

She crossed the hallway to the stairs and entered the portal. Damn, though … in her urgency for escape, she had forgotten to grab her bloody purse. She wouldn't get far in Shanghai without her wallet or handheld computer—plus, she needed her boots, which she hoped were still in the main gallery. She rushed back into the apartment, grabbed her bag from the couch, and turned around to bolt through the open door.

Then she heard Philip enter the foyer from the double doors and shout, "See you in the morning," back to the Curator. Suddenly he stood outside the open apartment, looking at Persephone standing alone inside, grasping her purse.

"Persephone. Do you need something?" he asked.

"Uh, no. It's hot in here. Very muggy. I need some air," she said, sounding convincing, even to herself.

"I see," he replied. "Turn on the fan in the kitchen. Now, get some rest … you'll need it," he said before shutting her in the apartment.

She darted forward to look through the peephole and saw Philip enter the stairs. *Bugger.* She needed to give him a little time. The thought of getting trapped in the staircase with him made her shudder.

Persephone pulled her computer out of her purse and still couldn't connect to service. Philip had mentioned being in a dead zone; she might as well have been in the Arctic. She realized how cool the apartment felt compared with the street level and upper gallery. It was a small blessing at that moment.

The oversize couch supported Persephone sinking into its large cushions. It felt comfortable and gave her a good view of the whole space. She didn't get the feeling either man planned to enter the apartment, but she wanted to be close to the exit if they did.

The only way she knew how to leave the warehouse was from the main gallery at street-level. She hadn't even seen any windows. If she didn't go up the stairs, perhaps the double doors outside her apartment led somewhere? But too many mysteries waited on the other side of that egress.

After forty minutes, she decided enough time had probably passed for Philip to clear out. She grabbed her purse and went to the kitchen to find a knife for protection. No luck ... the drawers contained only spoons and chopsticks. With two pairs of sturdy wooden chopsticks tucked into her bag, she prepared to execute her plan. She would take the stairs to the lower gallery and try to escape.

She knew the main entrance would be locked. But she hoped she could hide somewhere in the meantime ... or locate another exit.

Persephone left the apartment and crept across the white tile floor in the hall. The handle of the door accessing the stairway felt cold, and she failed at turning it. Philip had bloody bolted it.

A sliver of light shining through the small space between the double doors caught her eye and she walked over to it. The slit was too narrow to see through, so she put her ear up to it, but heard nothing.

The unknown loomed on the other side. It threatened her safety and every caution she knew about putting herself in a predicament. The situation had already presented more danger than she liked in a day. As much as she wanted to, she couldn't convince herself to go through the doors.

Reluctantly, Persephone returned to the apartment and sat on the couch, opting not to sleep in the bedroom. Adrenaline kept her awake most of the night as she worked to reconcile the information presented. What was going on? What had happened to her father?

Persephone finally fell asleep after two-thirty. She didn't rest well, but her dream left a sweet and vivid impression.

In it, she sat outside at an Italian café on a warm summer evening. A few hours of daylight remained and the rose-colored sun caressed her spirit. A tall glass of iced tea and a small salad arrived before a beautiful person carrying a delicate chess board strolled toward her and asked, "May I join you?"

"Yes, please, have a seat," replied Persephone.

The soft light of the evening settled onto the bricks and highlighted the piazza in smooth shades of pink. The trees above the chairs cast small shadows as the sunlight flickered through their leaves and danced with the tiny white tiles on the surface of the small, round table.

"What brings you here?" asked the chess player.

"I'm waiting for my father," said Persephone. "He's supposed to join me. What about you?"

"I'm only passing through," said the player. "Care to take a journey with my chessboard while you wait?"

"I'd love to," said Persephone.

The chess player opened a glass board, set up the royal figures, and the two began to play a deft game.

Persephone awoke naturally at six with her thoughts content to linger on the dream scene. She fought to hold the imagery in her mind as long as possible. The residue of incredible warmth and calm brought a peaceful anchor to her procrastination of joining the morning.

As logic began to sweep away the pieces of the dream, she recalled the board was entirely white. The chess player's pieces were white. Hers were also ... all white. How did they each know which pieces to move? Without separation between them, they just knew. Their connection felt so real. It was obviously a dream; she hadn't felt that kind of union in a very long time.

***

Persephone stood in the warm shower for several minutes before shifting the water to cold. Exhausted and flushed with anxiety, she knew she had two choices: She could choose to be open, or she could allow fear to dismantle her curiosity.

So far, fear did an excellent job outstripping any generosity of spirit. It was hard to stay open without trust. She needed to rely on her own sensibilities to move forward, and she was digging deep.

At seven twenty-five she opened the front door to return to the upper gallery and found her boots next to a small suitcase sitting in the hall. How did they get it? She collected the case and stepped back into the apartment to change into fresh clothes. Then she put on her shoes. The normalcy of having her familiar belongings provided a short respite from her stress.

Persephone returned to the stairs and this time found the entrance unlocked. She turned her attention to the double doors a few paces on her right and decided to give them a try. They did not budge. So she entered the staircase and began to ascend.

When she reached the main level she tried to exit, but was not surprised to find the door fixed. The only way to continue was up. By the time Persephone reached the upper gallery at seven thirty-two, her presence of mind gave her a renewed focus.

She chose to join Dr. Stennis in the side room, not because he asked her to, but because, with great caution, she knew she must continue to gather information in order to understand her father's predicament and plot her own escape.

Inside the room, the Curator prepared plates and chopsticks slowly and methodically. He had grapefruit juice and an assorted dim sum platter waiting on the bar.

"Good morning, Persephone. Thank you for your timeliness. I trust you slept well?"

"Not exactly … I'm pretty knackered," she said. She eyeballed the dumplings and took a sip of the juice the Curator handed her.

"I hope you found your luggage. Mr. Goode retrieved it from your hotel so you could have your things here with you."

Unsure if gratitude was something she wanted to offer either of them, she said, "I do appreciate the bag being left outside the apartment."

"I see you also collected your boots. Please remove them; I prefer not to have footwear worn out on the street in here around the sculptures. I will ask Mr. Goode to bring you a pair of gallery slippers."

"I'm not taking them off again," she said.

"What? Why?"

"I feel more comfortable keeping them on."

"I see," he replied, then pursed his lips and looked away from her. "Please, let's eat," he said, motioning toward the couches as he moved the food from the bar to the coffee table.

Persephone felt nauseous more than hungry, but she sat on the couch and selected a custard bun to help settle her stomach.

The Curator returned to the bar and began to wash his hands at the sink. At that point, out the wall of windows, Persephone saw Philip enter the upper gallery through the double doors. "Morning, Persephone," he said when he entered the side room, turning his gaze toward the Curator before she could reply.

"Good morning," he said. "I'm here for the First Series. Shall I begin taking them to the basement?"

"Not yet," Dr. Stennis said. "I still need to introduce Persephone to the sculptures. We will be ready in an hour. Can you please bring her some slippers?"

"Sure, I will. We need to be efficient about this today," said Philip.

"I do not need a reminder about the things we agree upon, Mr. Goode. Now, please, allow our guest a bit of time to settle into the morning. She has a big day ahead. I will begin her comprehensive tour after breakfast."

"See you at eight-thirty," said Philip before departing.

"A tour? What more is there to see?" asked Persephone.

"Let's not waste breakfast with logistics, my dear. You will understand everything in time," he said.

After they finished eating in silence, the Curator took a large swallow of his grapefruit juice, draining the glass before setting it down on the table.

Persephone noted it was exactly eight o'clock. She recognized Dr. Stennis had a set agenda, to which she would soon become privy.

He stood up and directed Persephone toward the sculptures. "Please, let's enter the garden," he said, motioning to the open door of the side room, before heading out. Once they entered the gallery, he moved with a quick pace to the back of the room near the elevator.

"I have prepared well for your arrival," he said. Today I will show you the culmination of my last decade of discovery. It will be our only day together with all the sculptures in place. I will address any questions you may have; please ask me as they come up."

"I understand you have created this gallery as a façade for your underground research," she said. "My father ... does he know this? *Did* he know this?" she asked, caring more about whether her father was safe than about the gallery itself.

"Persephone, as a leading neuroscientist, your work expands science in ways unimaginable twenty years ago. Your father needs you. A sculpture now supports his mind. Certainly he would like more. After you assist me, you can take him where you may like."

"What? What are you implying? I knew his body had been struggling, but, what do you mean a sculpture *supports* his mind?"

"Allow me to start at the beginning ... with the physical. Each of my glass figures contains a living human brain placed within it ... surgically removed from the donor and housed in a life-supporting case inside the head.

"Before we finalized the complex wiring to create the light displays you see, I analyzed and recorded the brainwaves. I can compare them with the patterns in the completed installations," he said, as if describing a simple appendectomy.

"What? Oh my god," she said, placing one hand on her stomach and the other on her heart, as she gazed across the gallery landscape. "Oh my god."

"Ah yes, do you see them now, Persephone?"

Stunned by the blatant description of what she thought she understood the former evening, but couldn't quite believe, she gasped. Disbelief, disgust and surprise coursed through her at once. Her heart pounded in her chest and heat rolled across her body.

She thought he must be lying to her. The situation couldn't be real ... or could it? It didn't sound possible. Certainly not for her father's condition.

The heavy emotional weight of seeking her ill father then

learning he no longer existed as she knew him—but lived in an unthinkable condition—felt incomprehensible. What a horrible state to find him in!

Her mind reeled from the stunning information. She pinched the upper bridge of her nose, closed her eyes and bowed her head to exhale, holding her breath out for a few seconds, trying to calm her nerves.

When she inhaled, she released her hand and looked at the Curator. "You've cut the brains from living people, transplanted them into glass sculptures and kept them alive?" she asked.

"In so many words, yes. Some you see here have been encased for years. Of course, I had professional assistance with the removals. But I did do all the installs."

"Nearly twenty years ago you invented a technology to heal injuries by rebuilding nerve pathways so people could regain use of their bodies to live fully and function. Now you developed the means to remove sentient beings from their bodies for your own curiosities? This is absurd and beyond grotesque," Persephone said.

The Curator smiled. "I see not much has changed in the opinions of those unable to move outside themselves when searching for answers to ancient questions."

"Ancient questions?"

"The body only serves to relay senses to the mind. The brain interprets the external world for its own desires, to meet its individual needs. But its deepest desire is to know its own soul."

As her nausea returned, Persephone listened for anything that might help her make sense of such disturbing revelations.

"I share a quest with countless medical scientists, philosophers and religious devotees who, through the ages, have searched for the human soul," said the Curator. "What is it? Where does it dwell? Can we touch it, see it ... or experience our own soul, let alone someone else's?"

"How ... how are you doing this?" she asked.

"I place tiny sensors into a brain at sixty specific spots to register neuron activity. I implant many of the sensors into the cerebral cortex where seventy percent of all neurons fire. Of course, we treat the areas that regulate a brain's level of awareness with extreme care.

"The largest array of sensors connects to the thalamus at the center, the gateway to consciousness," he continued. "As you know, this area receives signals from every sensory system except the olfactory."

"These are only anatomical descriptions of the sculptures and how they operate. Where is my father?" she asked.

"Patience, Persephone."

"There must be twenty figures in here! Are you telling me each contains a human brain?"

"I am pleased with your curiosity. It confirms I made the right choice for the future of my work. You understand a brain lives within every sculpture and show no repulsion. I am glad you recognize the importance of my efforts," he said.

"Repulsion is a small term to describe my feelings," she said. "I do not condone this in any way. My questions don't imply acceptance. I'm only trying to comprehend this horror."

The Curator furrowed his brow and said, "Yes, well, Mr. Goode suggested as much to me before your arrival. I can appreciate your surprise. Let's consider my collection while we can. We must move them to new locations."

"But ... my father? Where is he? He's in a sculpture?"

"Yes. He will be safe in your care. We do not plan to remove him from the gallery. You will see him soon enough."

"Where ... is he?" she asked, holding the Curator's gaze with her eyes, determined to get an answer.

Chapter Fourteen

"Where? Which one?" she demanded. Persephone looked around the room and struggled with the horrific possibility of viewing her father through a lens of understanding.

"I need to see my dad." She knew it would be the only way she could determine what to do next.

She started reviewing the small title plaques discreetly placed on each pedestal, searching for a name or word to help her identify her father's glass encasement. *Sharpshooter. Musician. Angel of Death. Artist. Internee.* The descriptions meant something, she was certain, but not to her.

Persephone came to a figure called *Practitioner* standing right of center in the room, stopped and turned to face Dr. Stennis. "Is my father ... in here?" she asked, reaching up to place her right hand on the left palm of the sculpture glimmering with pale blue and white speckles of light.

"Yes," he answered. "Look how he shines," he said, after he walked over and tapped the piece she touched.

"Here is your father, Persephone."

The pain in discovering her father in such a state outmatched the relief she felt in finding him at all. That Dr.

Stennis didn't seem to have any consideration, whatsoever, about how she was handling the information did not endear her in the slightest toward helping him. Her mind raced to decipher what Dr. Stennis may want from her, so she could determine how to best help her father.

"If this glass holds him ... and I'm not saying I believe you ... I need time with my dad. Alone." She grasped the sculpture's arm and gazed at the figure with concern and disbelief in her moist eyes, trying to see through the form.

The sculpture began to twinkle and radiate with intensity. "Dad? Is this you, Dad? Is this really my father?"

She paused and asked, "Is this all that remains of him?"

"This is the exploration and expression of his truest self. The being transcending the physical manifestation of human existence can now be seen," he said.

"What about the colors? Do the lights mean anything?" Persephone asked, hoping to gather information about the possible condition of her father's brain.

"Why, yes. We route signals from the sensors in the brain into a translator which assigns colors to the patterns firing from the mind. The fiber optics placed throughout the glass vary in hue and brightness, depending on mental activity," he explained.

"Gibberish. I don't care how it works! I want to know how it relates to what is happening with my dad ... right now. Is he okay?"

"White shows a sense of awareness—an existential leap his mind has become attuned with," he continued. "I like to view the color blue most. So we connected it to the perception of touch in the software system."

"Dad, can you feel me here?" Persephone asked again, keeping her hand on the sculpture's forearm. "How long has he been inside?" she said, glancing toward the Curator.

"Almost five weeks."

"Five weeks!?"

"Let me ask you ... when did you last see your father?"

"Four months ago, right after his surgery. But he disappeared six weeks ago."

"What was his state when you last saw him?" he asked.

"I'm sure you know he was healing from a liver transplant. His muscles were deteriorating," she said.

"He arrived here, depleted. His only option was to enter a sculpture days later," said the Curator, reaching up and rubbing the back of the sculpture's glass head. "I prolonged his life by saving his mind."

"I don't believe he would have agreed. Why would he? Dying is a natural part of life … he did not fear it. He was trying to heal, so he wouldn't lose his senses. Why would he agree to give them up by being inside a sculpture?"

"For you. For your work on machines utilizing human brain tissue. He wanted to help pave your path for taking science to the next level," said the Curator.

"By involving me in something criminal? Unlikely. Ethics formed the cornerstone of his entire career," she said, wiping her eyes.

"Yes, a principled man, your father. He built his profession on a foundational belief that all research should be transparent. As I said, I owe him tremendous gratitude for helping my methodologies become usable."

"So why, after confirming years later the illegal aspects of your inquiries, and knowing you faked your death, would he come here … or serve as a link to bring me here? I know my father well, and none of this makes sense."

"He appreciated I could help him. In that, he determined he could assist you. He came to understand how breakthroughs are made: by bending the rules, by seeing a way to advance and taking it. It may not be what you have been told your whole life is correct action. But if you recognize a greater good, you must take the opportunities presented."

Persephone paused to consider her father's shimmering colors. He shined with a deeper shade of blue than moments earlier.

She turned toward the Curator, knowing he'd only just begun his explanation of his creations. "I would like time alone with my father. I need some time. I don't know if I believe you … but I need time to process this."

"You may have a few minutes; but time is not a commodity we can spare now. After we complete our business here, you will have all the time you need. I can tell you this … your father knows you are here."

***

Dr. Stennis left the room and Persephone sat alongside the sculpture on the pedestal. She touched the glowing foot, looked up at the glass body and said, "I'm sorry, Dad." She put her head in her hands and thought about how to proceed.

The conversation with her father in his office years earlier about Maryelle flashed into her mind. She recalled him saying, "We hold some secrets to protect others. And some we hold to protect ourselves. … These are the most illuminating secrets of all."

She thought about the secrets her dad held from her, and those she'd kept—including her decision not to tell anyone why she came to Shanghai. She'd told herself she'd protected her father's secret for him. But she knew she maintained it for herself. She felt special knowing he trusted her. Now she could only trust herself to get out of the situation alive.

Persephone searched her memory for clues to understanding Dr. Stennis, reflecting on past conversations with her father. Perhaps drawing from the right recollections could help her get out of the gallery safely.

She had only met Dr. Stennis once when her father introduced her, at age ten, to his former college roommate at the hospital where they both worked. Being so young, she didn't realize the future connection she would have with his research, or that she'd be relying on that meeting now as her only personal encounter with him.

After more than twenty-five years, she had a hard time recalling the details of the experience in her mind.

"I use Stennis' discoveries often," she remembered her father told her. "He figured out some remarkable ways to allow people to access their bodies again."

"Hello, Persephone," Dr. Stennis greeted her then. "Your father has told me a lot about you."

Saying, "Hello, nice to meet you," was all she recalled about their average exchange.

While the patents Dr. Stennis held on his legendary NeuroTrans Suspension technology made him a world-renowned billionaire in the medical profession, Persephone felt more curious about him as a person in her early years as an undergraduate, than him being a "neurocelebrity."

She knew her father, who had been an exchange student from the United States, met Franklin Stennis in their sophomore year at NUS, the National University of Singapore. Both men stayed in the area after earning their degrees, folding into different medical programs.

Her dad continued with the collaborative Duke-NUS Medical School, a partnership with Duke in the U.S. Stennis entered the NUS Yong Loo Lin School of Medicine. Her dad's program emphasized translating meaningful scientific discoveries into innovative patient care. This set him on a course for later using Dr. Stennis' NTS technology.

After graduating, the men became hospital colleagues. "I know you worked with him at the National Neuroscience Institute, Dad, but what did he do for fun?" she remembered asking her father in her senior year of college.

Her dad had thought about her question for a moment and said, "Stennis used the most advanced tools expertly, but old technologies fascinated him. He would only ever read under incandescent lights. I don't know where he found them, but he spent a lot of time looking for them. I remember them being pleasant, if a little hot."

"What about in college? Was he a good roommate?"

"The phrase 'socially awkward' doesn't quite capture the nuances of being around him," her dad said. "Stennis was quiet and unassuming, but people felt uncomfortable near him. He projected a weird detachment from the world; it unsettled everybody. I'm an easygoing person and can overlook many personality quirks. But I had to make an extra effort with him, especially in the beginning."

"He sounds difficult to get close to. I would think it would be hard to become friends," she remembered saying.

"Well, I wouldn't say we were close, but I learned about him and listened when he spoke. I respected him and we shared some personal conversations. I consider him a friend, although I'm not sure if he feels the same about me. His emotional capacity is a bit challenged, I might say."

"Did you ever meet his parents?" Persephone had asked. "Were they like that too?"

"They disappeared before sending Stennis to boarding school. I don't think he ever knew the reason. He never said much about his childhood. From what he did tell me, he was an only child and he didn't have a bond with his parents."

"How sad. He never tried to find them?" she asked.

"I don't know. I don't know if they abandoned him, or they died. He never wanted to talk about it."

"So they never knew what an eminent neurosurgeon he became?"

"I suppose they didn't," he said.

In college, on top of studying for her classes, Persephone began an active pursuit of reading Dr. Stennis' published papers. For some reason, his unorthodox research methods intrigued her.

She felt a commonality in her own approach to research. She, too, followed every avenue toward greater understanding—answers could be hidden in the most unusual places, and easily missed.

As she stood up from the pedestal, Persephone's memories presented her with some distinct inner guidance. She knew if she listened closely to Dr. Stennis, as her father had done, he would come to trust her. Once she gained his trust, she could escape his gallery.

"I hope you can help me navigate this one, Dad," she spoke aloud to the sculpture as it twinkled from blue to solid white.

Chapter Fifteen

After ten minutes, the Curator reentered the room. Persephone stepped back from her father's sculpture. It was hard to comprehend the extent of the situation; she looked around and saw only ghoulish displays. The thought that each figure held a unique individual began to clarify her predicament.

Persephone culled through a mounting list of questions to determine how to remove her father from the gallery. "Who are the other people in the sculptures?" she asked, hoping to gain clues for her next action.

"The first person I had any information about was Wang Yan, a thirty-five-year-old female yoga studio owner, harvested after an auto accident. She's my *Yogini*. Around the same time I acquired her, I also obtained Thomas Ridley."

"So you knew them?" she asked.

"No, I didn't. Ridley was a death row inmate without any family members desiring his remain. He became my *Occupant*. The man made a mistake as a young person while robbing a bank. Although armed, he didn't plan on sacrificing anyone. Two hostages got in the way, and he got nervous and squeezed the trigger."

"Did Wang Yan and Thomas Ridley agree to this?" Persephone asked, feeling an unsettled notion in her heart.

"Neither knew their brains entered sculptures," he said. "Ridley was sentenced to death, but attorneys prolonged his life in prison. He got tired of it, decided to stop his appeals, and execution followed by way of immediate harvesting. This kept his brain viable following standard procedures—same as Wang Yan."

It doesn't seem like there is anything standard about this. "What exactly are you researching?" she asked, rubbing her stomach to settle her nausea.

"As I mentioned, I am revealing consciousness and the soul. Take away stimulus, and the mind defaults to memories and dreams. Then it moves to pure awareness. In a sculpture, a sensored soul can shine through."

"I realize neurons communicating in the brain generate an electrical current. But this is … you found a way to tap into signals producing an emotion or thought and turn them into light displays?"

"I see you understand. I attach the sensors to the brains and Mr. Goode routes the connected fiber optics through the glass. We've brought some aesthetics to the old neuroscience quip, 'Neurons that fire together, wire together.'

"The circuits route into the pedestal, which contains the main visual transducers," he continued. "They are calibrated to receive mental impulses and translate them into the colors and intensities you see. The software algorithms Mr. Goode has refined for years are works of art in their own right."

This is so ludicrous; absolutely sick. "How are you caring for these people?" she asked. "Brains need sustenance. I don't see any equipment here for their care."

"Medical devices housed within the pedestals maintain each brain's biological and metabolic functions," he said.

"So you supply the brains with glucose?" she asked, scanning the sculptures for signs of veracity in what the Curator was telling her; finding no solid evidence from looking at the simple platforms.

"Correct. A Life Support Unit maintains temperature, provides nutrients and measures brain activity. A pump sends an artificial blood perfusate of oxygen and glucose up through a tube in the spinal column that connects to the carotid artery. This joins the cerebral arteries and veins of the cranial vascular system, then cycles through the filters and infuser in the base."

Persephone felt the sudden need to sit back down. With no chairs in the gallery, she sat again on the pedestal supporting her father, paused, and looked around the room. She felt disheartened, as if she had fallen to a fast run-and-strike-grip-throw attack.

"Please ... let's continue our tour," the Curator said as he took Persephone's arm to encourage her to stand up.

"Hey ... don't touch me," she said and rubbed her elbow where his hand had been. *Dodgy nutter.*

The Curator gave her a blank stare and said, "Look here," as he turned and walked to the back corner of the gallery where a handful of statues stood with dim light displays.

"My First Series contains seven selections, which I acquired from the harvest centers. These sculptures do ..."

"Harvest centers?" asked Persephone, interrupting him. "What harvest centers?"

Dr. Stennis offered a smug smile. He looked pleased with his method of acquisition when he told her, "We received the minds through simple channels using the legal organ harvesting system. We leverage a network built around teams of people who disassemble humans for tissue donation.

"Professional cutters carefully and quickly dissect bodies to ensure the usability of all organs and tissues. After they surgically remove a desired body part, they coordinate a quick delivery for patients awaiting transplants."

"Do they know about your research?" she asked.

"Mr. Goode facilitates acquisitions through his connections at the SMHC. Our research is secret, but he knows people who can help us."

"What is the SMHC?"

"The Shanghai Main Harvest Centre. There are also five Satellite Harvest Centres. These SHCs process bodies before moving them to the main center. Many smaller operations located in hospitals also funnel their organs to the SMHC from their harvesting facilities."

"So organs that come into the smaller centers can be acquired from the main one for transplants or research?" she clarified.

"Correct. Shanghai established its first SHC in the industrial zone to support the rapid growth of the HEX Energy refinery. Fatalities still happen weekly from machinery that doesn't always function as planned. With numerous deaths occurring hourly in Shanghai due to accidents, age and illnesses, harvest centers receive continual donations."

"What about legal consent?" she asked.

"Mortally wounded accident or crime victims living in Shanghai have their organs and tissue harvested—consent implied. It's known as HuMan-VOTED, for Humane Mandatory Viable Organ and Tissue Extraction Donation. This is a legal reality for everybody except those who can buy their way out," said the Curator.

"But you are getting brains," Persephone said. "How are you getting whole brains?"

"HuMan-VOTED began ten years ago. As the name makes clear, residents of Shanghai voted on the measure. It is re-approved every other year. Sixty-eight percent of voters approve of harvesting bodies within an hour of death or irreversible severe incapacitation, before cremating unneeded parts. Any body part not diseased or injured beyond repair becomes available for waiting recipients."

"Through the organ harvesting system?" she asked.

"Right. With surging global populations, the need for organ donations remains enormous. Plus, nobody can be buried here. The city has run out of room. Real estate is unavailable for ground burials and vertical structures didn't prove lucrative. To manage the situation, Shanghai exports human body parts worldwide."

"I know Shanghai supplies the world with viable transplant organs, but I didn't think that included brains. Who gives out whole brains? Doctors want hearts and kidneys, livers and lungs. Organs that can be used!" she said.

"Most brain requests come into the harvest centers from scientists. Nobody else ... that I know of ... is conducting whole-brain experiments. Physicians routinely ask for the entire brain, so they can slice the parts they need from the delicate organ."

"So if cutters are extracting the brains for research, how do you ensure the organ stays alive for the sculptures?" she asked.

"Cutters place the brain into a supportive shockproof, airtight container that controls and circulates Tissue Viability Preservative. This blood-like substitute made of oxygenated saline solution makes live harvests possible. Continual monitoring maintains proper conditions for transport."

"So acquiring the brains through the harvesting system is all above-board?"

"We obtain them through a standard legal process, yes. Of course, in a city the size of Shanghai, an active underworld exists within the system. The black market for body parts still flourishes—as it has for a hundred year—and brains are no exception," he said.

***

Persephone looked at the seven sculptures in the corner the Curator had pointed out from the First Series. They did not glow as colorfully or with as much intensity as the others.

"Why aren't those pieces as vibrant as the others?" she asked.

"They do not contain many optical fibers. Most faded within a few months of adapting to sensory deprivation. While still lovely to look at, in comparison with future series, they are a little crude."

"I see that," she said.

"It's no surprise. Many of their personal histories eluded me, but the few details I learned reflected unremarkable lives. This showed how individual intellect creates the foundation of a successful and luminous work of art. More developed minds offer a higher probability of viability and vibrancy."

"Your speculations seem impossible to confirm," said Persephone, shaking her head, "but it doesn't surprise me the person inside would make a difference."

"My turning point came after I learned some personal details about a few early subjects. Rather than passively accepting brains available through the harvest centers, I selected most of my Second Series directly," he said, motioning to an adjacent grouping of sculptures along the side wall.

Persephone froze in place. "What do you mean you *selected* them?" she asked, as she shifted her eyes to look at him, without moving anything else.

"I chose them for their occupation, education, intellect or other indicators of a brain engaged with the world through the senses," he said. "A strong mind stripped of all connection to the physical world makes for a beautiful display."

The elevator door opened and Philip entered the room. "I'm here for the First Series," he said to the Curator.

"See them to the lower level then," Dr. Stennis replied. "Thank you, Mr. Goode."

Philip walked over to Persephone and handed her a pair of gallery slippers. "Here," he said.

Persephone took them, walked to a corner of the room, and promptly put them down.

Chapter Sixteen

C learly the Curator had victimized many people for his own
interests, she noted, glancing around the room. "How long
have you sustained these people?" she asked.

"Most minds came here within the past six years. Several
came from volunteer patrons who wanted to make the journey
toward immortality. They make up almost half of my Second
Series; five of the eleven sculptures."

"Why would anyone volunteer for this?" she asked, flabbergasted at the surreal environment within which she found herself. A glance behind her caught sight of Philip pushing one of
the First Series sculptures across the floor toward the elevator,
wheeling it with ease.

"For a variety of reasons, but most desired to be on display.
Higher-ups want perpetuity. They can step into the legacy process and claim ownership from the inside out ... by becoming
living works of art," the Curator explained.

"I encountered your guests last night. I can believe you
found people who chose the egocentric wonder of nowhere to
go but inside their own heads," she said.

"You and I are scientists above all else, Persephone. For me, the combination of mental patterns and materials is akin to performance art. But more than that, these sculptures are the proving ground for discovering the path to the soul as it exists through the mind, freed from everything but itself," he said.

"Justify it as you may, it seems you've reduced these individuals to displays for your own enjoyment. You exploited their wealth and ultimate disregard for life, including their own."

"I remain well-funded by my patents. I don't need my guests for financing ... I need them for their lifetime of perception. My patrons are well-versed in appreciating their senses. By their enormous affluence, they have had the opportunity to enjoy more experiences than most. Some have indeed been out of this world."

"Then what? What is the point of extraction from the body?" she asked.

"Their reasons varied, but when we can put a brain into a mechanical body that can live forever, they wish to be transferred back into the external sensory world."

"Volunteer patrons entered sculptures in secrecy in exchange for immortality ... and maybe fame ... once technology and society catch up to the possibility of transferring their brains into a new mobile body?" Persephone asked.

"Correct."

"It's wrong. You sold them on a future that may never happen," she said. "You took advantage of their vanity and their quest for new experiences ... but they're also to blame. For those who didn't opt into this horror—accident victims or even the criminals—they should have had a choice. What did they get out of this?"

"What about your father, Persephone?" the Curator asked, sounding insulted at her lack of appreciation for his work. "He volunteered. He saw the value of this effort and became an enthusiastic part of it. To help you."

"You kidnapped their minds and are holding them hostage in a sensored state. My father included! This is a tragedy!" she said, returning her left hand to her stomach.

The thought of her father being prepared for insertion into a glass form made her shoulders tense and her heart heavy. She had heard enough of Dr. Stennis' self-indulgence and pride in his work and knew it was time to get authorities involved. She needed to stay focused and get out of the gallery.

"A mind dominated by sensory perception is trapped," said Dr. Stennis. "We can connect to our greatest potential when the physical senses do not control our thoughts. A Buddhist monk will tell you that withdrawal from the senses allows a deeper inner awareness."

Persephone closed her eyes, paused, and opened them to see her father's gleaming glass exterior punctuated by glowing fibers. They sparkled in bright blues and greens.

Oh god, Dad. We've found ourselves in such a huge tangle.

***

The Curator walked toward a figure emanating pink and yellow. He spoke again, giving Persephone more descriptions of his volunteers encapsulated in their own thoughts and existence. He seemed lost in his.

"Lily entered my first patron sculpture in the Second Series. My *Socialite*, she grew up with money, but at age seventy-five, she feared the possibility of developing Alzheimer's, which ran in her family.

"She didn't fear being without a body or senses. Her doctors had success in halting early signs of the illness through regeneration using NTS. But she wanted to stop the aging process. She opened to the possibilities of future medical technology."

"You let her believe being inside one of these glass cases could stop her from aging?" Persephone asked. "That is an impossible outcome, especially for someone with her family history—no matter her wealth. Does her family know?"

"Not currently. Perhaps one day," he said. "Not everyone in my patrons' present circumstances may understand this."

The Curator moved to the left corner of the room and gave one of the glass sculptures two quick, firm slaps on the front of its right thigh. It ran through a cascade of bold colors in rapid succession then shimmered with a pastel iridescence glowing from underneath its silvery white light.

"The future provided a tantalizing opportunity for some

patrons—but changing the present created an attractive option, too. Here is my Second Series *Tycoon*. He went by Johanas ... more formally known as Evan Julliard who headed up Julliard Real Estate. He went in five years ago, at age seventy-seven.

"Johanas lived on many edges in his life," the Curator continued. "With his body failing and in pain, he could no longer manage his death-defying lifestyle activities. He had accomplished all his goals: Descending to the ocean bottom in a submersible body suit ... biking on the face of the moon ... high-altitude free-fall dives at supersonic speed, falling back to Earth from where the atmosphere ends and outer space begins.

"Fascinating man ... a true seeker. Ten years before I met him, he began practicing meditation to calm and focus his mind. We became acquainted at a weeklong meditation workshop. He dealt in exclusive properties in the Shanghai real estate market, so he became a patron as well ... one of the few I interacted with personally."

"I have a hard time believing his situation has brought him inner peace," she said.

"Johanas did not pursue mental reflection for peace of mind. He sought different levels of excitement and connection to a broader existence. He went into his head to discover new thrills."

"I want to leave," said Persephone. "This is more than I can process here. I need to go. ..."

"Patience, Persephone. I showed Johanas the sculptures and explained my research ... as I am doing with you now. He understood being in one presented an opportunity to reach immortality. He told me, 'The biggest thrill of all would be to escape an uncontrolled mental state.' So we made arrangements, and here he is," the Curator said, as a brief smile crossed his lips.

Persephone recognized there was no way Dr. Stennis would let her out of the gallery until he finished his show-and-tell. Did she need to continue going along with him? She committed to running out the double doors if she saw an opportunity to escape. She needed to bring others into the gallery to help get her father out; but who?

Dr. Stennis walked over to a sculpture shining with bright blue and yellow with occasional flecks of red flashing across the face. "I call this figure *Racer.* The brain came from Francisca Santos—the Spanish champion ocean speedboat driver. She was doused in acid during an accident that left her badly burned and without fingers, toes and one arm.

"After extensive skin grafts and long recoveries, she didn't want to continue through the pain of surgeries required for complete healing. Ready for a new experience, she volunteered herself. I find it interesting she shines with a predominance of primary colors."

"Your NTS may have helped her in better ways. Your invention allows the seamless connection of prostheses to organic body parts so sensory organs are functional. Her arm could have easily been replaced. Her injuries could have been healed with donor skin," said Persephone. "Did you try to change her mind?"

"I am a scientist, not a counselor," he said. "I did end up analyzing her brain—but in a different way."

"I thought the whole point of NTS 'smart science' treatment was to help people like Francisca. It identifies injured nerves and assembles itself to reconnect millions of working interfaces. The molecule-size particles you wrote about that 'learn' from the healthy tissue and align following the 'instructions' of an individual's nervous system could have repaired her damage."

"I know that, of course. In one of my first high-profile surgeries, I affixed an artificial hand and mid-forearm onto an amputee. Beyond the patient regaining the basic functionality of grasping and fine motor movements, NTS recreated the sensation of touch, as if his new hand was covered in natural skin. But I have moved on from NTS. It's available ... other people can use it."

The Curator motioned toward a piece with a mosaic of flashing colors and said, "The brain for this sculpture, called *Schizophrenic,* came from Ruby Carlisle who was active in the arts' scene; a trust fund kid. She controlled her mental disorder with medication and counseling, but stopped doing both sporadically. This caused more frequent psychotic breaks. She grew weary of not knowing when disruptions would happen. Half the time she didn't care if she made it through the night."

"Again, Dr. Stennis ... you could have helped these people in more life-affirming ways. I know by introducing NTS into the brain early enough after a stroke, blunt force trauma or concussion, the nanoparticles can limit the effect of significant memory loss or personality changes, or prevent them altogether."

"Yes, yes," he said. "Repaired nerves function identically to a patient's original tissue. This opened the technology for other uses, including neurological disorders. But I am working on something new now."

"Horrific," Persephone whispered under her breath.

"Ruby expected she would meet an untimely demise in one of her more severe episodes ... and she did. She had already arranged to be in a sculpture when it happened. Mr. Goode facilitated the efficiency of the process. I tried to avoid minds with mental illness, but she demonstrated a unique connection with the glass figures."

"These stories provide clear evidence you corralled vulnerable people for the pleasure of furthering your desires. You may claim they were volunteers, but this doesn't absolve you. Are there more patrons?" Persephone asked.

"One more. One of my guests volunteered his mother. She was my fifth and final patron—we call the sculpture *Maw.* She was trying to keep her son from the family inheritance. He's in his early thirties and wanted to rewrite the future."

"He did this for money?" she asked, shaking her head.

"More than that ... his mother abused him in his childhood. I related to him, and when I told him about my sculptures, he showed a keen interest. He told us when his mother was to be expunged so we could prepare a sculpture for her and receive her viable brain through the system," he said.

"Why are you telling me all this if there is nothing I can do to help these people?" asked Persephone.

"Things have begun to unravel," he said.

"Unravel?" *I don't think science could unravel any further.*

"This gallery can no longer stay hidden. We have little time. I am not asking for your assistance … I am telling you the time has come."

"So you want me to help you relocate these sculptures as you divvy them up among your patrons?" she asked.

"Oh, not at all, Persephone. Mr. Goode has that handled. We need you for your brain power, not your physical strength. We require your mental acuity and your experience."

"So you are going to put me in one of these glass prisons," she said, trying to make sense of the Curator's motivations.

"Have I given you a taste for this, my dear?" he asked, as the edges of his mouth twitched slightly. "Well, I hope you are not making a request. We only have time to complete one more sculpture. Can you guess who it will be?"

Chapter Seventeen

The Curator gazed at the glass figures standing in a broad ring around them. He saw shiny, sparkly, proof-positive examples of the artistry of selecting individuals with highly active sensory perceptions and rich life experiences.

Their twinkle validated the choices he made for his curated collection, created to explore the emotional resonance he lacked in responding to his own senses.

While Mr. Goode moved the First Series pieces out of the gallery, Stennis continued to guide Persephone through the glowing figures. He had looked forward to being her personal docent.

"I am pleased to discuss my work with you," he told her. "Other than Mr. Goode, you now know more about my creations than anyone else. This is a rare opportunity for us both."

"Why are you telling me about these people?" asked Persephone. She returned to her father's glass figure and looked up at his face. "I don't need to know more."

"I promise at the end of my tour you will understand all you need to take the next step forward. Now ... allow me to continue," he said, turning toward the Second Series sculptures.

"As I continued my research, I developed the desire ... well, more a prerequisite, to know about the individuals who would become residents of the glass. I recognized the value of targeted acquisition. With more information on a person's occupation, education and history, I can hone in on where to place my sensors to increase the potential for dynamic displays."

Through years of refining his subject selection and advancing the neural interface translation systems, Stennis determined he needed to obtain minds with the highest intelligence or perceptual IQ. Those powerful in their presence made the most fantastic sculptures.

His first pick, Xing Chen, proved to be a fine start to his thoughtfully curated Second Series. Xing was a concert violinist in the city's largest symphony orchestra, the Shanghai Philharmonic. She played with expressive and emotive technique. Her refined and attuned sense of hearing and mastery of musical theory intrigued and mesmerized all who watched her connect with the strings.

Although well-known in her field, sitting in the second chair did not qualify her as a celebrity most people would miss. Stennis determined she would be an excellent choice and turned to Mr. Goode to ensure she would meet a plausible demise and join his collection.

After Xing appeared to accidentally drown, her brain went straight to the gallery. Indeed, her sculpture sparkled with a fantastic intensity. The *Musician* remained shining and viable, effusively beaming an arrangement of green and white when the Curator pointed her out to Persephone.

"She is one of my most successful sculptures," he said, gesturing at the green glass.

Persephone stood up and walked toward the *Musician*. He watched her run her hands along the sculpture's smooth waist. Her hands moved with intention, cautious yet confident ... perfect.

"You killed her," she whispered.

Of course she would think that. He expected as much and clarified, "I don't desire the destruction of other people. She lives differently now. Statistically, great musicians having car accidents or dying homeless on the street forced a waiting time I could not entertain, or I may have opted to go that route."

Seeing the young violinist all lit up inspired the Curator. He decided he needed lights—many more lights—to tap into and witness deeper layers of consciousness. He asked Mr. Goode to integrate additional fiber optic emitters across the color spectrum to allow a broader range of subtle emotions to display.

The duo concentrated the lights in sensitive areas of a natural human body, including the face, fingers, heart and genitals. Certain spots lit up more than others. Some stayed vibrant constantly, displaying a rainbow of hues.

"My *Musician*'s green glow reflects the sense of hearing," he said. "In sculptures where we can translate more emotion from the lighting, it may represent fear. But here we can watch Xing Chen remember a sound ... or perhaps she's creating her own composition."

"I'm missing a link," said Persephone. "How do you interpret the colors?"

"I have broad stroke interpretations ... each brain has its own perceptive peculiarities," he said. "But purple and green generally show auditory perception; pink taste; yellow smell; red vision; blue touch; and white is intuition."

"This makes up your science? Your understanding comes from lights? How do you differentiate between a sense and an emotion?" she asked.

"How emotion displays differs for each sculpture. This is why I must know something about who lives inside. It is the only way to set a personal baseline to watch how sensory memories influence someone."

He detected her staring intently at the *Musician*'s shiny brain case. He remained impressed with the cases he had developed, and how they reflected the surrounding lights.

"So at this point, you're only guessing?" she asked.

"I've identified typical patterns. Upon adjusting, brains often trigger a purple glow. I suspect it reflects a mental ringing. Later, sense memories play out with the colors I described."

"Does everything come from the thalamus?" she asked. The

Curator appreciated she wanted to know the science behind his collection. She was getting it ... so much she appeared almost noble. Her face showed no sign of tension or struggle, and her bright eyes pierced him with their clarity.

"The frontal lobe is also important. As you know, it is the most distinctively human region—responsible for judgment and memories, as well as processing emotional expression. I attach many sensors to this part of the brain," he said.

"What about this *Artist?*" she asked, reading the label of the sculpture next to her. "What you think *Artist* experiences now?" She touched the lips of the figure displaying an array of neon colors moving across the surface of the glass.

"Blue aggravation mixes with a bright green from fear—and the pink joy of painting. She worked as a janitor at a harvest center. Her name was Siti Binte Musa. She was preparing her first showcase when I saw her paintings. I considered it good work."

"So you'd rather put *her* in your gallery, than her art?" Persephone asked.

"In a random accident, she tripped and fell. She hit her head and was knocked unconscious. It happened at the SHC where Mr. Goode handles acquisitions. By the time the medics found her, she had lost almost all her blood from the gash. Even with the blood substitute they administered, she could not be saved.

"Being in the harvesting facility, she moved through the process quickly." Stennis thought for a moment, and lifting a finger to signal a detail he remembered, he said, "I did buy one of her paintings however ... I only recently took it down from rotation in the first floor gallery. It was a clever little image of loneliness."

"Don't you find any of this sad?" Persephone asked. "This may be your science, but how can these sculptures appear to you as anything short of tragic?"

Feeling somewhat scrutinized, the Curator said, "I don't feel sad about people whose brains excel in a specific way. I wanted artists for my Second Series. People with a keen response to their sensory world. Imaginative, deep thinkers interest me. Those with a strong spirit, or who profess to draw from something greater than themselves for inspiration work best. A bright sculpture displays an active mind. It may be dreaming or lost in insanity or ecstasy; we cannot tell for certain," he said.

"You took it upon yourself to cut the creativity of these artists short—along with their lives—to hold them for your own observation. Are there other artists here?" she asked, touching her heart.

"There's Hans Heckman—a vibrant mind," he said, pointing to a yellow and orange piece a few sculptures away.

"Hans Heckman? From Hollywood?" she asked.

"Yes. I call the sculpture *Director*. He wrote many scripts known for realistic and intense drama. His brain came through the SMHC. While in town as a judge at the 2105 Shanghai International Film Festival, Mr. Heckman took an air-taxi. When a hacked drone delivery unit collided with it, it cracked open a HEX fuel canister that rendered the passengers unconscious."

"Were you involved?" she asked.

"Let's just say the accident did not draw much attention other than the notoriety of the passengers. The volume of people taking air-taxis about the city creates many opportunities for unfortunate interference with other airborne vehicles."

"Hans Heckman was brilliant, but I remember reading he had had several heart attacks. Did you give any consideration to your victims' medical backgrounds?" she asked.

"Early on I did not require someone's history. Later I upgraded my requirements. At the basic level, brains lasting longest reflect healthy biological material. That's most often helped by lifestyle, but not always.

"It's important my subjects do not have an advanced degenerative neurological disease. I confirmed with Lily those with Alzheimer's do not make good candidates. It hits the hippocampus and impairs memory. Neurons die throughout the brain. I suspected that, but decided to proceed with her to establish baseline data."

"I don't want to know anything else," she said.

The Curator didn't need her to. He did want her to recognize, however, it took time to find such particular subjects.

"The more I refined my requests, the harder it became to collect suitable candidates. Most people didn't meet the requirements I needed to advance my research. Accident victims filled an immediate need for my First Series, but head injuries are common. Even with the number of people in this megalopolis, I'd wait months for a stable brain."

"So you moved from random people to specific people, starting with your patrons, then targeted individuals?" she asked.

"People who actually want to go through the procedure make the selection process simpler, of course. A population center like Shanghai allows for many interesting minds to consider. Still ... I could not acquire everyone I wanted," he said.

"You wanted more?" she asked.

"A person successful in the financial world or a brilliant legal professional would have made an excellent addition to my collection. A heart surgeon—someone with broad intelligence and a honed mind would have been another fine choice. Your father exemplified the perfect candidate in so many ways."

"So you have a hit list essentially," she said.

Her impressions about how he refined his candidates seemed awfully extreme, and he found it unfortunate she thought about him that way.

"You know, Persephone, true scientists cannot be considered as having a good or bad moral fabric. I believe research is scientifically legitimate if detailed records can be used by others."

"Sorry, but ... bullshit, Dr. Stennis," she said. "Conducting experiments on living subjects who are not volunteers is never an acceptable practice."

"It has happened throughout history, hasn't it? It fascinates me. Given the past, I am surprised anyone would consider my research reprehensible as it, too, led to discoveries which have benefited science as a whole."

"Medical advancements accomplished through the use of unwilling participants have happened historically, but that doesn't make them any less macabre," she said.

Taking a higher-pitched voice to convey a sense of non-sense, the Curator said with a dismissive wave of his hand: "These types of things may be well-documented, but they carry the ideology of abject disregard for humanity. ... Your vigor for these concepts alarms your classmates and instructors. ... If your exploration of past experimentation on nonvolunteers continues, we must expel you."

"What?" Persephone asked, looking confused.

"Oh, just some snippets of conversations from the dean and medical school educators that stayed with me. I began exploring the physical neurology and nerve pathways of the senses at that point. In my second year I researched groups who experimented secretly on humans. It presented as fair a hobby to me as any. But administrators at NUS discussed expelling me after learning of it."

"I would think so," she said. "NUS is one of the most prestigious medical schools in Asia. My father told me about their legendary emphasis on developing empathy as a foundation of their curriculum. Your research doesn't seem to focus on that. How did you manage to sidestep it?"

"I stopped seeking information on traceable data systems," he said, "But changing my methods did not change my interests."

"Apparently," she said, leaving the Curator wondering how he could help her see the benefits of his research more clearly.

Chapter Eighteen

Singapore, Fifteen years earlier

Eight months before Stennis announced NTS to the public, one of his lab assistants at the National Neuroscience Institute, Frieda Grayson, became suspicious of his research methods.

Quandaries expected to take several months to determine whether nerves could heal faster using smaller particles, and still be safe, were propelled forward in a matter of weeks after he opened his private clinic.

One afternoon a young man who had sustained serious nerve damage in his right brain from an industrial accident came into Stennis' office at the Institute. While viewing the imagery to diagnose the extent of the injury, the doctor calculated how he could expand upon it and still treat the patient.

He convinced the man to undergo surgery in the—more comfortable, more private, cleaner, safer—surgery clinic he owned, rather than at the Institute. The procedure created a defining moment for him, leading the surgeon to a dark discovery about himself: He prioritized science and his experiments over patient care.

Patients who read the waiver carefully—and few did—learned they agreed to prohibit any video recording devices during their surgery, to "protect their privacy." Aided by the proliferation of robotic assistants in the operating room, Stennis began his journey into secret research.

The results led to his invention of NeuroTrans Suspension technology. As a brilliant neurosurgeon with focused intentions, he achieved his goal of creating NTS in less than three years. Conducting surgeries while his already blurred moral considerations continued to dissolve helped him overcome many obstacles to his discoveries.

"How did you come to the conclusion you could move away from graphene?" Frieda challenged him one afternoon. "Our laboratory was nowhere close to discovering the effect of using smaller particulates. Did you conduct research during a surgery?"

"Innovative treatments provided in the course of practice do not automatically constitute research," he said.

Frieda challenged him on his reference to traditional medical ethics: "Then your *innovative treatments* must be made the object of formal research at an early stage to determine whether they're safe and effective."

At age twenty-four, and twenty-five years younger than Stennis, bright-eyed and eager with her fiery red curls tied back, Frieda put unwavering attention on nuances. She paired her close observations with a steadfast adherence to the Hippocratic Oath.

Frieda tried to confirm her suspicions, but Stennis knew she had no absolute proof. Still, he began a simple strategy to get rid of her. Over the following weeks he gave her repetitive and elementary tasks to do in the lab, much below her skill set. He let boredom handle the rest.

His assistant demanded to do other things. Stennis clarified the matter: She would do more of the same until he said otherwise. The ensuing blowout caused her to leave, strategically following his exit choreography on cue.

But Frieda's suspicions grew too much to remain silent. She pushed her claims to administrators of the hospital ethics committee. They reviewed the situation, but didn't find enough evidence for a solid case.

At the last professional neuroscience conference Stennis attended, he ran into Frieda. "I will continue to build a case against you," she told him.

"You will build nothing," he replied.

Six months after Stennis released NTS, most neurosurgeons who'd implemented the techniques knew the technology worked well. But the results he published from operations conducted in his private clinic proved impossible to duplicate using the methodologies he outlined. Nothing could be proven, but his data challenged explanation, even aided by medical modeling software.

The revolutionary nature of NTS to heal severed nerves belonged to its speed. His technology expanded on the graphene nanoribbons perfected in the mid-2000s.

While neurons grow well on graphene to create chemical-electrical transmission, the smaller particles invented for NTS allowed nerves to heal faster still. This supported repairing human spinal cord injuries—reversing paralysis with almost one hundred percent success.

NTS used carbon atoms coated with neurotransmitter compounds held in a suspension and injected at the point of injury. The particles carried neurotrophins—proteins stimulating the development of new neurons—along with the carbon atom scaffolding that seeded the growth of the cells. This allowed nerves to reconnect and transmit signals to the brain.

As the first person to mate this style of artificial growth stimulant to natural nerves, Stennis rose to worldwide fame as a neuroscience genius. He secured international patents on the technology, ballooning his recorded net worth into the billions.

Over the next few years, a few colleagues began to press him hard about his research results, suggesting he acquired them from unscrupulous acts on unwilling subjects. Although vilified by some, the fact remained: his contemporaries could *not* access details about the medical necessity of procedures conducted in his own surgery center.

Secrecy led to gossip—typical behavior of privileged people held outside discussions to which they assumed they should be privy. They whispered behind Stennis' back and implied worst-case scenarios may be happening in his operating rooms.

Stennis learned to ignore his colleagues' chatter, but it bothered him to see so many of them on his personal time. They filled the orchestra and upper boxes at the theater, making it difficult to watch the audience. And he found it irritating when they engaged with him at intermission on account of professional acquaintance.

One evening after a symphony, several associates accused him of unscrupulous research, implying they would guide authorities toward him. Although their words amounted to nothing more than speculation, their innuendos irked him. Stennis believed accusations without accompanying proof would not hold up to the rigor of the law, and he considered their expressions rooted in jealousy.

He surmised his strategies in presenting his research would ensure his innocence, should a trial be brought against him. Still, he did not want to risk being dragged through the media in a long and drawn-out legal discussion.

To avoid contact, he thought about no longer attending the symphony, but it remained his primary avenue for observing sensory perception. He conducted his best investigations at high-end performances with top musicians and performers. Still, as his interest in avoiding his colleagues increased, the number of shows he attended waned.

Unnerved by potential setbacks, Stennis removed himself from the public eye and inquisitions. He stepped away from neurosurgery to focus exclusively on laboratory research. The announcement created ripples in the neuroscience community, but nobody missed working with him.

Stennis had built professional relationships with several workers at the Singapore Organ Donation Centre connected to the hospital where he worked. There, attendants prided themselves on providing the famous doctor with the tissue samples he sought. After he stopped performing surgeries and moved into full-time research, the facility became essential.

***

One afternoon Ruger, his primary contact at the Organ Donation Centre, received the body of a driver who had died in a car accident. To secure a personal and discreet payment, he acquired the brain for Stennis—saving the doctor from having to compete with other researchers for it.

On occasion, bodies arrived from drifters and people without relatives. Ruger helped Stennis acquire their brains, too. They didn't carry the same legal restrictions as organs requiring family consent for medical experiments; nobody noticed if some part of their head went missing.

The irony that increasing accusations by his colleagues led him further underground captured Stennis' imagination. Being a respected scientist, it surprised even himself he'd entered such a secretive world.

Stennis withdrew from all social activities, recognizing he needed to craft a bigger plan. After several months of receiving viable tissue in exchange for direct payments, the neurosurgeon sensed he could trust Ruger.

After careful consideration, Stennis presented the hospital worker with a request.

"Ruger?"

"Yeah?"

"Ruger, like the old American gun manufacturer?" Stennis asked.

"Yeah ... it helped me earn the nickname as a kid, and it just kind of stuck."

"How might I obtain a particular individual?"

"Do you have a case number?" asked Ruger.

"This person does not have one," said Stennis, glancing at his folder to appear casual.

"No case?" asked Ruger.

"Can you arrange that?" Stennis asked, as he shifted his eyes over Ruger's left shoulder.

"You need a *pre-op*? Is this person in the hospital?"

"No," said Stennis, staring straight at Ruger.

"Someone outside the hospital," stated Ruger, returning the direct gaze.

"Correct," said Stennis, and the two men locked eyes with a knowing look.

"I see," said Ruger, shifting his glance away from Stennis. "An associate of mine might be able to help you." Then he quickly turned around.

"Oh?"

"A mate from London, where I grew up. I've known him for thirty years. ... He's a shadow."

"He's here in Singapore?" asked Stennis.

"Yeah, a startup tech company he used to work for transferred him. His aunt and cousins live here; I think he likes having family nearby."

"He's in technology?"

"High-level cybersecurity. Manipulating people's identity is his hallmark. Talk to him about who you want to go after."

Secured by a sizable sum of money, Ruger arranged a meeting for Stennis with Jacob Freeman.

The men met in an underground pub of the variety Stennis had never considered entering. As an esteemed neurosurgeon, he had not observed the sort of show happening that night; a type of "base" entertainment by his standards. Yet he found the audience responses interesting as he studied them before Mr. Freeman entered the dark room.

He sat down across from the doctor at the small, round table and focused his deep blue eyes and equally serious expression upon him. The men sized each other up without speaking.

Stennis spoke first, opting to forgo the typical pleasantries to make the meeting as brief as possible. "Mr. Freeman, I need to disappear," he said. "As you no doubt have gathered, my freedoms are being reduced of late by accusations drawing unfortunate attention toward me."

"You want to put a hit out on yourself?" Mr. Freeman asked.

"Not completely, just my name," said Stennis.

"I presume you considered alternatives before wanting to meet with me," Mr. Freeman said. "But I must ask; would it not be simpler to prove your colleagues wrong with your own evidence?"

"I do not need to explain my motivations or actions to anyone," said Stennis "As a professional, you understand," he said. He looked at Mr. Freeman then peered at the small stage.

"I must be certain you are fully committed," said Mr. Freeman. "Your request can only be done once. And it must be done my way."

"I am committed," said Stennis.

"Tomorrow I will give you a list of items to destroy. In seven days I will contact you with instructions you must follow exactly. This will be the last time we will be together in public. Carry about your typical routines until then. Should you have questions, I will include information in your follow-up about how we can communicate."

"And payment?" asked Stennis.

"When you receive my instructions, I will have removed half of my fee from your assets. The remaining portion will be deducted when the plan is complete."

Stennis appreciated Mr. Freeman's direct nature, and assumed he must be impressed with him. "You must be surprised I can walk away from myself, given who I am," he said.

"As you said, you don't need to explain anything to anyone. Your motivations are the same as everyone else's; they are your own. I know who you are. I'll always know more about you than you will about me."

"I understand you'll have to," replied Stennis with flat affect.

Stennis figured, correctly, that Mr. Freeman would recognize his name. Indeed, the assassin later told him he knew the neurosurgeon faced accusations from his contemporaries of violating correct medical practices. The doctor's ethical variability piqued his interest.

Mr. Freeman created a simple but plausible accident to make Stennis' identification microchip in his wrist undetectable. He then re-identified the chip to help him begin a new life in Shanghai in anonymity.

Stennis could have disappeared for any number of reasons.

A neurological disorder may have been too ironic, but a boating accident for an amateur yachtsman played out perfectly.

The facts, as reported, claimed Dr. Franklin Stennis motored out on a late evening departure through the Singapore Strait, likely intending to reach open waters near the Riau Archipelago, away from the busy shipping lanes. Everyone recalled Stennis liked to be by himself, so of course, no witnesses came forward. A couple of people said maybe they heard a craft leave the small, unmonitored harbor, but nobody quite remembered.

The National Neuroscience Institute coordinated a search out of respect, sending a submersible air-sea rescue aircraft to look for their famed doctor. His vessel, found adrift seventeen hours later with the autopilot turned off, showed no signs of foul play. Only some sedatives left on a table in the galley provided any clue that, perhaps, Stennis had overdosed.

With all the life preservers still onboard, he was presumed to have fallen overboard and dead at sea, possibly eaten by a shark, his microchip destroyed. Stennis' associates mourned the loss of his continued contributions to science, but not the man who made NeuroTrans Suspension possible.

Despite his neurocelebrity status, the scenario did not arouse enough suspicion for a police investigation beyond the routine navigation log scan. In the end, chroniclers considered it a probable act of suicide, spurred by rising accusations from his peers about his unscrupulous practices.

The shift allowed Stennis to go into absolute hiding. The simplicity of the well-planned and executed escape required no clean up. Using only the props needed for the disappearance, Jacob Freeman effectively removed the famous doctor from the public world.

Chapter Nineteen

Shanghai, Twelve years earlier

As part of the disappearance arrangement, Mr. Freeman found a Shanghai condominium for Stennis; a well-appointed 250-meter suite on the 152nd floor of an upscale 165-story building. He arranged Stennis' move from Singapore and redirected his patent funds, so the former neurosurgeon could access his billions.

Stennis spent the first few months alone in his high-rise in isolation and obscurity. Attachment to himself grabbed hold of him, quite often in the beginning.

For the first five months, he tracked news articles on the case of what happened to his prior self, back in Singapore. Severed from his public persona, his hardest effort was extracting himself from his own self-image.

Without a connection to circadian rhythms, he didn't maintain a sense of daytime, nighttime, or any time passing. He rarely left the building, relying on delivery automatons to leave food and other sundries outside his door. He catnapped through his days and did little apart from enhancing his art collection as an anonymous buyer at online auctions.

Nine months into his new life, Stennis received a call from Jacob Freeman. He remained the only person who knew the former neurosurgeon lived—and where. With a rightful suspicion, he assumed the assassin planned to extort more funds as a protection measure.

Instead of blackmail, Mr. Freeman presented Stennis with a personal request. "I will get right to the point to avoid a long call. ... I need to change my identity," he said. "An unfortunate event has given me this opportunity. You've done face transplants, so you are the one who can help me. I'm hoping we can come to a workable agreement."

Stennis respected Mr. Freeman for having the grim tool of threat available, but choosing a different tack. "Indeed, I have performed many types of skin transplants using NTS, including re-sheathing entire bodies," he said.

"My eyes must be replaced as well; I am now blind in one of them."

"Let's meet to discuss this further," Stennis said.

"I can be in Shanghai in two days."

Stennis greeted him at the front door. The assassin removed his hooded jacket, revealing third-degree burns across his face, head and hands. Stennis began a quick medical assessment. "It looks like your facial muscles are intact, which is fortunate. Fire seems to be a messy way to dispatch someone. Did one of your targets turn on you?"

"Yeah, a seven-year-old."

"Seven?"

"I was playing some rugby with my cousins. Out of nowhere, one ran under my feet. I stumbled over my little bud and slid into my aunt's collection of tikis like charging into a ruck. I grabbed a few lit torches on my way down. One popped open, and the oil did the rest."

"It can't be good for business," said Stennis.

"Yeah ... I'm pretty easy to spot in a crowd."

"So you called me," said Stennis. "What's your plan?"

"I've found a warehouse in the old industrial section here in Shanghai. I'll purchase it and convert the old manager's office into an apartment for my recovery," Mr. Freeman said.

"What about the surgery?" asked Stennis.

"The facility links directly on the subway to several hospitals. I can coordinate secret access."

"I won't perform surgery in a public hospital. It presents too great a risk of my discovery. I'll add an operating room into the warehouse. We can use it again later. ... I have ideas for utilizing such a facility."

"What ideas?" Mr. Freeman asked.

"We can discuss them after developing a plan for your new visage. For some time after the surgery, you won't recognize yourself in a mirror, of course," said Stennis. "Given that the largest number of donors in this city are Chinese, your appearance will change more than you might have considered."

"That will work in a larger sense," said Mr. Freeman. "I'm coordinating my own disappearance now."

"Completely?"

"Yeah."

"Why is that?"

"The accident was a clear sign. I don't know if it was from God, or the devil himself, but I have the perfect, and necessary, opportunity to change career paths."

"I see."

"For months a man known only as "The Principal" has been planting evidence with police to tie me to some high-profile hits. He pulled some classic shit by providing anonymous tips to pin some of his own rubouts on me."

"Ah, so you are now the mark," said Stennis.

"He's trying to shake me out from hiding, but it's not going to work. I've spent a long time in the scrum and I see my opportunity for an opening."

"You are one of the best in the business," said Stennis.

"Yeah, but I'm burnt-out, literally."

"I assume you can arrange construction of the space in complete anonymity and on a quick time frame?" Stennis asked.

"I already have the apartment work lined up, and can redirect my efforts to the onsite surgery suite."

"Good. I must say, my hands have missed surgery," Stennis

said, slowly rubbing his thumbs across the fingers of each hand.

"I need your parameters for the operating room," Mr. Freeman said.

"It's essential I oversee the construction as it's happening," Stennis said, "I have exacting standards."

"That will complicate the secrecy, but I will arrange your participation. You mentioned other ideas. What do you have in mind?"

"I've been thinking about my art collection. I want to show it to private patrons. After your procedure, we can turn the warehouse into a gallery. The location will be useful for facilitating the supplies I need," said Stennis.

"What supplies?" asked Mr. Freeman.

Then, for the first time out loud, Stennis described his grand concept.

"Your unique ability to arrange and manage situations is very impressive and would be helpful in expanding my collection, Mr. Freeman. How old are you?"

"Forty-eight."

"Nearly fifteen years younger than me. We're not contemporaries, but we are close enough in age to understand each other and have similar levels of expertise in our respective professions. After you and your new skin have become one, you'll blend into Shanghai. Then perhaps you'll consider joining me in the gallery."

"I appreciate the potential of starting over. We can talk about the possibilities after I get a new face," said Mr. Freeman.

***

Stennis had not experienced true collaboration since his medical discussions with Dr. Douglas Jones. The situation allowed a kinship to develop between the men—sealed by seeking each other at the most critical juncture of their lives, to assist themselves out of their deepest dilemmas.

Neither had a need for animosity, nor the intention to use what they knew against the other. Both excellent in their former professions, a mutual respect developed between the men, supported by their keen fastidiousness.

Although each held incriminating evidence on the other, it never came up in conversation. Operating with moral ambiguity and the equal disregard for human life necessary to satisfy their individual goals remained unstated, but evident. The Curator may have even called it a friendship.

PART FIVE

§

Taste

"Let's take a walk outside," the old monk told the group. He led the small contingent to a clearing by the creek running through the property. "Use your hand as a cup and drink," he said. "This pure mountain stream water holds the essence of the universe.

"Taste-based impressions connect us to the concentration of all things. These sensations link us on an emotional level. The color pink symbolizes 'love' in our mandalas, and 'the sense of taste' in our sculptures.

"Consider that your taste buds developed at week thirteen in your mother's womb. Amniotic fluid can transfer strong flavors like curry or garlic … but the sweeter the liquid, the more you imbibed.

"Through taste, you came to know the element of water, the nectar of life.

"The sense energizes your vocal cords, stimulates your appetite and awakens your vitality. It ties to speech, which also occurs through the tongue.

"If you join our community, while you will no longer be able to speak or eat, you can expand your energy beyond your physical body.

"Here at our Centre, we will assist you in cultivating your taste in subtle ways—including aesthetic and artistic ways. Experiencing the nuances of this sense can awaken your 'taste for' a higher path.

"We want to help you infuse the flavor of bliss into all your impressions. Much depends on your preparation. This is as simple as … or as difficult as … extended meditation."

Chapter   Twenty

Sorrow gripped Persephone; she looked around the room and saw only victims. As the extent of Dr. Stennis' experiments became clear, she asked, "What about the other people in the Second Series?"

"We harvested several from life, but we have been measured in this. Mr. Goode initiated the first chosen brain. It now resides in the initial piece for the Second Series, called *Sharpshooter*."

"He initiated? … the first … *chosen* brain?" repeated Persephone, walking through the figures and focusing on the nameplates until she found *Sharpshooter*. "Are you saying Philip had somebody killed for a sculpture?"

The Curator looked at Persephone and with moderate scolding said, "We have not murdered anyone. As I said, they are living in a different realm."

She saw the coldness of the Curator's own soul come into sharp relief as he revealed small details of the lives of those contained within the sculptures, before their paths crossed his.

"Mr. Goode didn't say much about the situation, except the fifty-seven-year-old male worked as a principal hitman … a particularly brutal one. Mr. Goode escaped a turbulent history with him and wanted to eliminate the man's influence. He proposed the assassin as a subject and I considered him a good comparison piece with my First Series *Occupant*. I only wanted Mr. Goode to tell him his fate first."

"Why did you want him to know?" she asked, probing deeper for any hint of empathy he might have for the people he removed from the physical world.

"I thought it might help him settle into a sculpture. I'll never know. His lights dimmed steadily after a few months, although his brain remains viable. Now he has a gentle and unassuming glow," the Curator paused as Persephone peered past the glass toward the figures behind *Sharpshooter*.

"I also acquired two other Second Series criminals I could compare with my First Series *Occupant*. My four felons form my 'Criminal Quartet' collection," he said.

"Really?" she asked. "You're serious. Your 'Criminal Quartet'? Who are the others?"

"I have another high-profile death-row inmate ... Andrew Truypso. In 2101, he assassinated the president of Mexico on U.S. soil in a random act of violence at point-blank range. He wasn't a sniper, it didn't serve a vendetta, and it happened quite simply. It almost caused an armed conflict between the two nations," he said.

"Right. Didn't it set off a huge political scandal because the U.S. didn't properly screen the crowd for non-metallic fire arms?" she asked.

"True. The prosecutor succeeded in securing a forced harvesting sentence in Shanghai and I pulled some rather expensive strings to secure the brain. He is now my *Prisoner*," the Curator said, as the corners of his mouth narrowed with a slight upturn.

"He's serving a sentence here all the same," she said, dropping her head to look at the floor from her own sense of emotional heaviness and loss at how to escape the gallery.

"I gave him a girlfriend," Dr. Stennis said, in complete seriousness. "Here," he motioned, as he led Persephone toward two sculptures positioned close together. "She is the fourth criminal in my collection."

Persephone looked at the pieces. How intriguing ... they were both glowing with similar shades of red and teal.

"The donor for the sculpture, which I call *Angel of Death*, was Thanda San Suu, a prolific international serial killer from Myanmar who poisoned her victims. I acquired her brain when her family wouldn't claim her. She went straight through the harvesting system, then to me."

"How long has she been here?" Persephone asked.

"A year and a half. She killed a hundred people in Myanmar in less than a month by poisoning food in restaurants. She left no physical evidence ... no weapons or fingerprints, or anything else, like hair. After apprehending her in Shanghai, the trial took two days with forced harvesting on the third."

"Why didn't her relatives bring her back to Myanmar?".

"She brought shame upon her family. Before disassembly for organ donation, relatives don't usually get to view a body. Time does not allow it ... unless a person's microchip shows he or she paid enough to the SMHC to buy their way out of being harvested, or to secure a delay. Then suspended animation fluid may give people twenty-four hours to arrive and say their last goodbyes."

"How inconceivable not to provide families with access," Persephone said, recognizing the Curator truly had no consideration for his victims, apart from the logistical aspects serving his sculptures.

Persephone accepted Shanghai had automatically harvested bodies for at least a decade to support the city's rapid population increase. But she had never considered the human implication; it approached inhumane.

Would her dad have been disassembled if he had died in the city? She hoped the protocol only applied to citizens and criminals, but it was too large a question to think about right then.

"What about people who are sick?" she asked. "People whose organs can't be used for donation ... are their families given more time?"

"Bodies not needed for harvesting, including the old or the ill, are frozen, kept in stasis until space opens in the crematorium. Those who donate parts or pay a premium receive reservations first. In some cases, the SHCs hold people in suspended animation, categorized by blood type, to harvest later. An influx of injured citizens would necessitate it," he explained.

"So the harvest centers call the families?" she asked.

"It depends on what one's microchip programming specifies. Of course, not everyone is procured. The CEO of HEX Energy, one of the top three employers in the city, was not disassembled when she died. She had prearranged and paid for transportation out of Shanghai upon her death. What a shame ... I wanted her brain. But I could not acquire it," he said with a notable sigh.

"I'm surprised the families of your patrons haven't figured out what you're doing," she said.

"Individuals without a family, or who aren't close to them are best suited for the transformation into sculpture. The added complication of people searching for somebody at the gallery would draw too much attention here," he said.

"Does this mean you don't use children?"

"Correct; I don't find them interesting. They haven't experienced enough of life. My sculptures show thoughts can be displayed without having physical perception. But you do need experiences. A grown adult has evolved throughout a lifetime, gaining wisdom.

"A child's prefrontal cortex hasn't fully developed. Nor have the connections strengthened between regions. I doubt a young brain would survive. If it did, the output would lack luster."

"I'm relieved to hear it; I really am. This gallery is heartbreaking to me even without stealing young minds," she said.

"Plus, Mr. Goode would refuse to secure a child through any means," said the Curator.

Persephone registered the first piece of good news she had heard since arriving. She needed an ally. And while it was pretty obvious she couldn't trust Philip either, hearing he had his limits, at least presented her with room for possibility.

Chapter   Twenty-One

Knowing Philip targeted someone to be in a sculpture shifted Persephone's awareness from Dr. Stennis' obvious delusions, to a ready alertness for peril.

Philip came across as a rotter from the first time she met him, but Dr. Stennis confirmed her notion. Now she needed to gain great clarity to determine whether her own life was in danger.

The science and motivation behind the sculptures only crystallized the truth: the men had built the art house on a foundation of criminality.

By early afternoon, Philip had moved all the First Series figures out of the gallery. As Persephone watched him load *Sharpshooter* into the elevator, she recognized the rest of the Second Series was next to go.

She didn't know where he was putting the statues, but the upper gallery certainly felt larger without seven sculptures— or him—in it.

She waited until the lift closed before asking the Curator, "What is Philip Goode's role in all this?"

"He configured the electronics we use to visualize evidence

in the sculptures of sensory and thought experiences," he said.

"So would you say he works behind the scenes as your henchman?" she asked.

"My henchman? I've never considered him a henchman; certainly not mine. I view him as a partner. Mr. Goode keeps the system turning. As the only one with a total understanding of the patrons and the delivery logistics, he handles all recurring operations and coordinates all acquisitions."

"How do you know you can trust him?" she asked, looking for clues about how their partnership worked. Philip seemed pivotal and powerful, but she didn't have a good feeling about him.

"I have known him for fifteen years. Mr. Goode is skilled at putting the right elements in motion at the right time. He has smoothed the procurement of everything we've needed here. You'll come to appreciate his skills and methodical finesse. I doubt he has ever found himself in a situation he couldn't handle."

"I don't plan on being here long enough to get to know him," she said, holding onto the notion of getting out of the gallery as soon as she found a safe way to do so.

"You will see his wit. He told me once, 'Here we have a captive audience left with only their thought patterns. So if anyone asks our profession, we can tell them we are mind readers.'"

"I see," she said unamused. "Then I hope he knows I have a strong sense of intuition, too."

"Mr. Goode does not concern himself with anyone's perception of him," said Dr. Stennis. "He manages all aspects of this gallery. Everything from screening our patrons; acquiring art at auctions; communicating with the glass artist; managing deliveries; coordinating and delivering the brains from the harvest centers; developing the technology and software for the lights; and assembling the sculptures on their pedestals."

"Would you call him the gallery manager?"

"More than that, he's the primary face of our operations. Most of my guests never meet me ... but all are acquainted with Mr. Goode. He's serious and unflappable. This has been essential in dealing with our patrons. I trust he will be an asset to you."

"An asset to me?" asked Persephone. "For what? What are you suggesting?"

"Take my system and build upon it," the Curator said as he stood in front of her, the lights behind him emphasizing the sharp shadows he cast.

Persephone recognized he was about to reveal what they wanted from her. She needed to understand their intentions accurately ... and ensure they knew hers.

"I work on neural interface technology, Dr. Stennis. My team builds connections between human brain tissue and silicone chips as the foundation for providing computerized systems with an innate moral code. We are developing artificial intelligence with empathy and a conscience—using material grown in a lab from properly donated neurological tissue and stem cells. What does this have to do with anything here?" she asked.

Persephone moved back to stand beside her father's glass sculpture. She noticed the twinkles of blue and white intermingled with spots of green and yellow around his face and head.

She remembered the Curator said green reflected memories of sound, but what did he say yellow showed ... smell? Was her father really standing in his own sensory awareness?

***

"Tell me more about your research, Persephone. How did you start?"

"I augmented robotics with biological tissue using NTS," she said. "I began by putting donor nerves from a finger into a prosthetic hand. You redefined how damaged nerves heal and reconnect to allow patients to regain sensory perception. But I'm working to expand science in a tangential direction. I want to help AI become sentient."

"I've followed your publications, Persephone. I know your goal to combine brain matter with a computer interface may one day merge the perceptive powers of consciousness with the functionality of a machine. Many believe your great discovery in the world *will be* these results. Why does this interest you?"

Persephone recognized the Curator asking about her must be a set-up for something. He had asked her nothing about herself until then. As he still hadn't told her what he wanted, she chose her words carefully.

"Artificial intelligence has limited logic," she said. "Even with complex code written into advanced processors, machines still can't have true emotional context."

"Do they need to?" he asked.

"I think so. Robots are indispensable, especially in medical and mental health environments. Artificial nurses operate twenty-four hours a day. A biological-digital combination enhancing AI with an emotional framework can present genuine compassion. This will help everyone by reducing patient stress to support healing."

"Perhaps computer scientists can achieve this faster than neuroscientists," he said.

"We must work together. If you only write a code for responding to sadness, grief, pain or fear ... without AI recognizing the implication of these emotions ... it can be dangerous. You can program in kindness, but artificial assistance is awkward without heartfelt understanding. Genuine emotions in AI will allow it to assess a situation and take medical action appropriate to each individual with true concern."

"How do you expect to do this when humans struggle with it?" he asked.

"Ironic for *you* to be asking me that question," she said. "Most people can't move beyond their own desires. We can't always trust ourselves to do the right thing, or to feel genuine regard for others. This is exactly why bio-machines could perform their work better with empathy."

"Can you trust yourself?" he asked.

"I follow strict ethics as a scientist," she said.

"So a code of ethics is all it takes?" he asked, raising one eyebrow.

"It requires integrity—and integration. That comes through

connection and understanding. It can be difficult; that is why we must augment machines to assist us in thoughtful and empathetic ways," she said.

"How close are you?" he asked.

Persephone felt uncomfortable with the shift to a more personal conversation. Sure, she worked to create genuine understanding and heartfelt connection in a lab. Yet, without time for forming deep relationships, she didn't exhibit these qualities much in her private life. So she always felt a little disingenuous with her research.

"We're on the cusp of making these explorations a scientific reality," she said. "But integrating the emotional capacity into AI that a human mind can handle automatically is a huge effort."

"I imagine so," he said.

"Scientists can write a rudimentary program for judgment, but in a real-world setting, consciousness is necessary for true discernment. My theory is this requires brain matter. Yet with a hundred billion nerve cells linked through trillions of synapses, electrical impulses and chemical messages in the brain travel too fast to adapt to current technology," said Persephone.

"Even with small quantities of lab-grown cells, reflexive action signals respond at such varied rates the whole system often locks up," she said. "Programmers working with neuroscientists then have to pull the neural-processors out and restart."

"You do face numerous challenges," he said. "The brain will always be the most complex organ in nature."

It was time to get to the point. "Right now my biggest challenge is understanding why you're interested in my research and what you're asking of me," she said.

The Curator remained silent for a few seconds, appearing to study her. Then he said, "Persephone, developing a sentient machine presents the opportunity for which we have both been waiting."

"Which is?" she asked, still seeing no connection between the Curator's abuse of his victims and her work on AI.

"The eventuality of reimplanting brains into another human body. The possibilities of your efforts may allow the ultimate goal of medical science to come to fruition. Before we can do that, grey matter must be mated with the artificial," he said.

"So you created these sculptures as a way station for the brain?" she asked.

"My study follows my theory that freeing the mind, by removing the interference of sensory bombardments humans face daily, also frees the soul and opens the path to enlightenment," the Curator said.

"This work could be reversed in the future, as conditions permit, for those who don't wish to commune with their souls quite yet," he said. "But with an intact mind, life can be lived. If the body fails due to age, illness or an accident, keeping the brain alive opens new possibilities."

"New possibilities?" she asked. "Like what?"

"One day scientists will be able to put a human brain into a physical mobility device controlled by thoughts as seamlessly as the body. The senses will be functional; interactions with others and the world restored," he said with perceptible excitement in his voice.

"That is a long way off—and not my intention. I am not trying to build a cyborg!" Persephone said. "Extracting a functioning mind has nothing to do with advancing artificial intelligence and everything to do with your own hubris."

Dr. Stennis continued without responding to her admonishment. "Do you know why I am interested in your expertise, Persephone? Not because you are achieving results I cannot obtain. I brought your research forward. Now you have the chance to pull together all we have been working toward as scientists."

"By doing what?" she asked.

"The time has come for me to join my creations," he said.

***

Persephone accepted Dr. Stennis did not joke, but she found a bizarre sense of humor in his declaration. She let out a nervous laugh and asked him the obvious: "If you can't connect through your senses now, what good will removing your mind from your body do?"

"My body holds me back from the next phase of human consciousness. By entering a sculpture, I may unlock clues about our expansion as a species. Without emotional attachment, I am closer than most to a state of enlightenment. I must leave the boundaries of the physical world to perceive it … but not if I arrive there through death."

"This is insane. This isn't why I came here—and you know it. I came to find my father. You have helped me with that; thank you. Now I want to take him home."

"Your father anticipated your hesitation to move forward. So I recorded him giving his full consent. I'll offer the holographic message to you. But first, here I am," the Curator told her, opening his arms. "You have a willing participant—your ethical path cleared for *all* you must do toward achieving what humans have sought for so long."

"You can't be serious," she said, shaking her head.

"My mind, instead of being tissue created in a lab, can be the first human brain you install into a machine. Work out the considerations. Persephone. Perfect it. Then adapt the technology for your father on clear moral foundation."

Persephone stared at the Curator. The situation introduced her to the most pressing scientific consideration she would ever face, and the most bizarre.

"To consider yourself the next phase of human consciousness shows your absolute narcissism," she said. "The possibility exists, perhaps, but feeling out of touch isn't unusual. You are sure to go down in history as one of the world's top scientists. But you think entering a sculpture provides the only way to arrive at meaningful perception?"

"Every mind responds in its own way. But I have prepared more than any other," he said.

"How so?" she asked.

"Adaptation comes down to meditation," he said.

"Meditation?" she asked.

"Yes, it changes the area in the brain that manages the

amygdala," the Curator explained. "How one processes being inside a sculpture reflects how one integrates or transcends memories. Those with a well-honed sense of focus responded better to the transfer. The more one meditates, the more one can remain unclouded by influences from within or outside the body."

"My father meditated each morning for thirty years," she said. "You think this helped him adapt into a sculpture?"

"I'm sure it did. His extensive mental preparations supported a successful transfer. To manage the pain of his condition and relax, he also stilled his mind months before he arrived, through spending extended time in sensory deprivation chambers. It served him well," he said.

"What about those who didn't meditate?" she asked.

"Those put into a sculpture without mental preparation had difficulty adjusting. The lack of interaction inside the glass may bring hallucinations and psychosis, similar to prisoners in solitary confinement who live the same way day in, day out —sometimes for years at a time," he said.

"So you believe your meditation practice will allow you to transfer well?" she asked.

"I have prepared myself for a long time with many methods of temporarily eliminating my senses, including sensory deprivation chambers and anesthetics. Isolation feels familiar to me; it has been my best training.

"Floating reduces reactivity in the amygdala," he continued. "This opens and clears thoughts. I keep a chamber in my apartment. Inside, I have come as close as possible to understanding what happens mentally within the sculptures."

"What if you are wrong?" asked Persephone. "What if entering a sculpture is nothing like you expect?"

"As I said, I am a scientist above all else. I recorded my brainwaves each time I entered my sensory deprivation chamber. My sessions have been lengthy. A few times I almost harmed myself due to lack of sustenance. I tried to experience as much possible, to compare my mental patterns with the sculptures. Then I extrapolated data to theorize what may be happening in the minds."

"So from nothing, have you learned to connect to something?" she asked.

"In sensory deprivation, I embrace everything through thought. Moving into dynamic expansion has supplanted my need to embody the crude nature of biological awareness. I am ready to take this knowledge into the glass. Once I train you, I want you to sensor my soul through my brain. But we don't have much time."

Chapter   Twenty-Two

She knew she had a role to play with the sculptures; a purpose to understand and embrace in order to set them free. But the potential for their absolute anguish concerned her.

"What if you thrust my father into pain—a tremendous place of pain?" Persephone asked the Curator. "Unending torment, distress and agony—have you ever considered this may be the life these people are now living? Have you determined how a brain responds when it's removed from its body and put into a sculpture?"

Her eyes bounced across the figures, noticing several flashing through an array of lights. "All these ... victims ... might exist in a horrible state of terror or misery, or a torture worse than we can even imagine," she said.

"If your father were in pain, he would glow deep purple. He doesn't display this though, nor has he consistently," said Dr. Stennis. "He did have temporary flares after the effects of the anesthetic subsided—before he became aware—but that was it."

"Purple? Why purple?" she asked.

"The color resonates at the highest frequency. Sometimes

a sculpture flashes dark violet because of the pain. Your questions reflect insight, Persephone. I can't quantify how one heals from the damage done from extracting a brain from the body. Nor have I determined the effect of the trauma signals, or how long they may last.

"A significant component of my research considers the physical separation of the mind from its inputs," he continued. "As carefully as planned, as delicately as executed, having one's senses dismantled takes healing and adjustment. The protective membranes of the meninges cannot be saved in the extraction process."

"You consider these sculptures beautiful, but the minds inside could be suffering for your pleasure. How can you justify that?" she asked.

"I believe their initial responses may be akin to having a significant brain injury. The pathways involved with figuring out space become compromised with chaotic, disparate information. Removing sensory inputs probably leads to preliminary dizziness."

"This is absolutely ... absolutely ... I don't even know how to qualify it," said Persephone. "How can you know any of this?" She felt bolstered in her anger and confirmed in her belief that Dr. Stennis was mentally ill.

"I do consider the discomfort," the Curator said. "I want to understand whether the sudden removal of the brain from the body creates immediate and irreversible shock."

"We must help them," Persephone said, returning her gaze to the sculptures. "You have no indicators about how each individual interprets physical pain or the mental anguish caused from their situation. We need to connect to them ... to understand what they need."

"A human brain is remarkably malleable and can manage itself. On a theoretical level, it can still communicate with only two neurons. Once the organ stabilizes after a few weeks, the mind believes it wakes up in a blind and deaf state. Most do not realize they live outside a body," said Dr. Stennis.

"This could disturb the person more, wondering, 'Why can't I see or hear?' It might amplify their horror by triggering their amygdala, putting their survival instinct into an inescapable state of terror," she said.

"It may," said the Curator, "but I believe every brain moves through several initial and progressive stages, starting with a recalibration of memory. Individuals who regain consciousness probably assume they had an accident or fell into a coma … they don't remember. Then general isolation sets in, expanding toward confusion and grief. Unless the brain goes mad, stability typically occurs after this initial reset."

"And then?" she asked.

"Stabilized brains take one of two paths. Most settle into perpetual hallucination … an intense dream … to protect their sense of self. These minds may connect to a phantom body. Others move beyond their containers. This is the higher path."

"How can you be sure they didn't start out with a fear of falling and now remain in a rapid mental free fall? They may never regain awareness, except in fleeting nightmarish moments," she said.

"Those that transcend, develop a wakeful mind … a *vigilant brain*. They grow aware of their own consciousness and experience their own soul. These higher functioning brains move toward enlightenment. The ego disappears and time dissolves."

"You can't really know … any of this …," she said.

"The evidence is on the EEG scans. Each sculpture has its own monitor and relays its data to a central database. I read their numbers and compare them with their baselines," he said.

"It's all speculation!" Persephone said. "You don't have proof of any of it. As a scientist you may have inquiry, but what about your relationship to others as a human being? Your connection with them is fractured. What if you have forced depersonalization onto these beings and stopped their minds from perceiving the reality of their environment?"

"I created these sculptures to reverse-engineer sensory perception," he said. "I removed the senses to understand the impact of sense memory on emotions. Now, I want to explore the nature of consciousness. I am asking you to help me continue my journey. Wait here a moment …"

The Curator walked into the side office leaving Persephone alone. He returned moments later and handed her a file folder. She took it and began flipping through the documents.

"Your study guide. Become familiar with it," he said. "It outlines the process for my transfer and my aftercare, as well your father's. My patrons will take the other sculptures. I want you feeling confident stepping into this next phase."

"I haven't agreed to anything. My questions don't indicate I will participate in this experiment. I'm here for my father. If his brain remains alive, I want to keep it safe. I want to help the others in the sculptures ... but I will not help you."

The situation was so disturbing, and so disgusting, Persephone was unsure what to do. It may be science, but none of it seemed logical. She only saw dead ends.

"Review the contents of the folder this evening," the Curator told her. "It contains a summary of my decade of research. I have spent many hours with my creations and can see which ones have entered a wakeful state. I am prepared to join them."

Persephone stared at the Curator. She understood how serious—and how deranged—he was. If she did not assist him—or at least pretend to—she would soon become encased in his next creation, no doubt about it.

Chapter Twenty-Three

"Y ou've been running this gallery for some time. Why the rush to enter a sculpture now?" Persephone asked the Curator.

"I recognize my collection will soon be discovered," he said.

"By whom? It seems many people know about this place. You have patron parties and some have seen the sculptures. How have you maintained any secrecy around this warehouse?"

"By being highly selective about who enters this room. Most patrons who learned what drives the glass to glow became art pieces. For others fortunate enough to see them, we did not tell them everything. Despite the discretion we required, I suppose outsiders would hear about the figures at some point. But they would not have details."

"So who leaked?" she asked.

"Years ago Mr. Goode created cybersecurity barricades to ensure the Shanghai Municipal Police would not uncover our operations. However, INTERPOL investigators recently acquired information giving them reason to locate me. They opened a case, and that changes everything."

Suddenly Persephone understood why INTERPOL officers had visited her hotel the day before. It felt so long ago now. She wondered if the Curator knew about their visit and decided he likely didn't. Hopefully neither he nor Philip would have cause to discover their business card in her purse.

How much did INTERPOL know? Perhaps their arrival would be her ticket out. "Has INTERPOL learned about your collection?" she asked.

"I do not believe they know about the sculptures," he said. "But they suspect I am alive. With their sophisticated technology they cannot be redirected much longer, even by Mr. Goode."

"How long have they been looking for you?" she asked.

"We became aware of their investigation two months ago," he said.

"Two months seems like quite a while."

"Yes. We expect they will break through Mr. Goode's security measures next week, maybe sooner. When they do, they will discover this gallery."

"So entering a sculpture is another disappearing act?" she asked.

"You may perceive it that way."

"I can't help you. All the torturous things you have done to these people. I can't be part of it. I don't believe my father would have agreed to be either. Surely you see why I have trouble trusting you," she said.

"Trust is a confusing notion in times of stress. I understand your resistance to embracing the reality of this place—especially if you hope to maintain the idea that the world exists in the same way for you as it did yesterday.

"I hope my amazing examples of medical research gleaming before your eyes can assure you of the benefits of taking the next step toward what I am asking of you," he said.

***

The Curator reviewed the sculptures surrounding them and looked back at Persephone. "Without a comprehensive context for what these forms represent, nobody would begrudge your continued questioning and comparison to the standard path of scientific discovery. But have I given you any information indicating I have lied to you since your arrival?"

"How would I know?" she asked. "The truth that is becoming evident concerns me more than any lies you may have told," she said. "Why is INTERPOL seeking you now? You disappeared fifteen years ago."

"Mr. Goode learned their information centered around Sifu, my meditation teacher. He was a well-known monk who taught classes on Buddhist philosophy and meditation. People came to see him from around the world. Sometimes they would take pictures ... treasures for the moment.

"On one occasion, I met Sifu for private practice at the Chenxiang Pavilion. Another man entered the temple before we started. He took a picture as Sifu greeted him."

Persephone remembered the photo the officers had shown her at the hotel. It must have been the image the Curator referenced. She had been so surprised to see Dr. Stennis in the picture, her eyes had skipped right over the monk. She remembered his robes, but not his face.

"Did Sifu come to this gallery?"

"Yes, I invited him here to witness his responses around my sculptures. I wanted his raw input."

"What did he say?"

"He said something felt different. He didn't promote telepathy, but he sensed something bigger happening. Some people can perceive greater things in our world and our universe. If you exist within that realm, it allows you to recognize others' openness and natural ability to reflect that world. Sifu existed there," he said.

The Curator walked over to a figure titled *Monk*. The sculpture's white lights sparked with small flashes of pale yellow and pink streaming from head to toe every couple of minutes.

When she followed him and looked at the name of the piece, she knew the Curator had put Sifu into a sculpture because he'd suspected he might be a threat. How revolting!

"He's here ...?" she asked. "But it sounds like you respected and admired Sifu as your teacher?"

"I did. Sifu lived in tune with his path as a young Chinese monk. I studied meditation privately with him for three years. We often discussed how physical and sensory deprivation connected to enlightenment. I am much closer to this advanced state than most, but since he practiced the requirements, I wanted his input. I asked him many questions. We explored whether people could enter *Nirvana* if separated from their perceptions."

"Do you think people can reach enlightenment without a connection to reality?" she asked.

"Now you sound like Sifu," the Curator said. "Sifu remained open to discussion, but did not readily divulge his opinions. He would respond with a question of his own, and we would circle around a topic. If I asked him, 'Is one who lacks vision or hearing nearer to awakening?' he would ask me the same."

"I know the nature of scientists is to stay in our heads," she said, "but did Sifu ever wonder why you asked such specific question?"

"I am certain he found my queries and poignant thoughts beyond the scope of most. Before I invited him to the gallery he started getting more personal, asking where I worked and what I did. Perhaps he suspected I had a motivation for meditation, but he never said so outright."

"I may be getting too personal, Dr. Stennis, but did his inquires make you uncomfortable because you feared opening up to him, or because you fear understanding yourself?"

"They made me uncomfortable because I had not yet prepared my transition plan," he said.

***

The Curator gazed at a statue in the far corner and pointed at it. "That sculpture, we call *Internee,* holds my former lab assistant from Singapore, Frieda Grayson. We installed her brain several months ago. She met Sifu at a meditation lecture.

"Without intending to, she discovered I was alive simply by seeing the photograph of me behind Sifu at the temple," he continued. "We encased her, not out of revenge, but for protection. I don't work through revenge—I consider it distasteful.

She met a physical end quickly: an unfortunate misstep from the Metro platform in front of a train slowing at the station.

"You are out of your bloody mind. That is premeditated murder—first degree!" she said.

"Luckily, her brain came away unscathed. She was a brilliant researcher. It would have been a waste not to add her to the collection," he said, almost seeming to express mild admiration.

"Does this have to do with INTERPOL?" she asked.

"Yes. When she saw the photograph, she went to the local police. An accident days after becoming vocal about me did raise some suspicions. The ending happened proficiently, though. Soon afterward, INTERPOL opened their case."

"Do you think they have cause?" she asked, trying to remain circumspect, so he would not register her distaste.

"After my ex-lab assistant's train mishap, I invited Sifu to return here. Instead of waiting for him to discover the true nature of my gallery's collection, we let him know he'd found himself at the center of its reconfiguration."

"He must have been surprised. He trusted you. Didn't that mean anything to you?"

"He was quite calm. He said he had a strange apprehension about me. The ideas I'd proposed in his meditation workshops felt hard to quantify as the eccentricities of a gallery owner. He battled his own moral dilemma about sustaining a close teaching relationship with me ... sensing he could not trust my authentic interest."

"And so you caused an accident."

"Not at all. We handled him here in this building using a simple serum Mr. Goode developed years ago. He modified the formula to make it nonlethal and it brought Sifu to a painless sleep. He did not move through the public harvesting system. I wanted to ensure his mind would be treated with the utmost respect."

"Oh my god," Persephone said, slapping her forehead.

"His brain transitioned more seamlessly than anyone else here. He had done all the necessary meditative preparations, of course."

"Stop. Just stop. You are telling me you and Philip Goode killed your former lab assistant and Sifu—along with who knows how many other unfortunate souls? Now you want me to do the same to you?"

"Persephone, I told you, none of these people are dead. I have given them another world to live within ... their brains are alive! See, Sifu stands right next to your father—my two newest pieces. I considered them both friends and I have an attachment toward their well-being."

"As do I," she whispered.

"They are part of my Third Series. The five sculptures in this series represent the pinnacle of my work. They include my tribal elder, my chess player, my former lab assistant, Sifu and your father is my penultimate. I only want to join them now to complete my collection."

"You've set me up," she said.

"Yes ... I have set up your future success, my dear. You can trust me on that."

Chapter   Twenty-Four

P ersephone turned away from the Curator. She sought a way to feel safer and less exposed, but found no shelter in the gallery. Instead, her movements ensured she kept a sculpture between herself and Dr. Stennis; when he moved, she moved.

"I want to tell you something, Persephone," he said. "People who believe life has purpose stay sharp and live longer. Spiritual activity, religion, philosophy and engaged experiences all support a healthy brain.

"This is why my three most interesting, well-prepared minds displayed white light so soon after their transition. They settled into a state of equilibrium, then awareness."

"Your three most *interesting* brains? From what you've said, each sculpture contains a living human. They deserve this respect, at least," Persephone said.

"Let me introduce you to my premier participants," the Curator said as he waved her toward him. "My *Tribal Elder*, my *Chessic* and my *Monk* comprise my '*Holy Trinity*' collection, representing body, mind and spirit.

"Nothing against your father—he stands among them, but I didn't seek him out in the same way. He came to me, so I classify him as an accession rather than a gallery acquisition."

"Why do these three glow mostly white?" asked Persephone, after he pointed them out to her.

"Sculptures that fire from more parts of their brain exhibit an array of hues," he said. "In the visual spectrum, white reflects all colors. A shine comes from these minds as they approach pure consciousness and move toward enlightenment."

"Every mind has a deeper connection to one's surroundings and the universe," she said. "Why have only a few people responded with white?"

"The white light shines from sensors I put in the pineal gland deep in the center of the brain where the right and left hemispheres join. As far back as Descartes we've known it as the seat of the soul. I refined the sensors in my Third Series to tap into this nexus of consciousness," he explained.

"I know many spiritual traditions suggest the pineal gland offers a connection between the physical and ethereal worlds … the 'third eye' … the 'sixth sense,'" Persephone said. "When it awakens, one becomes aware of everything as energy. Physically I know the gland connects to the cycle of light and dark, by regulating melatonin and sleep patterns."

"Good, you understand, then. Inside a sculpture, the lack of natural cycles of day and night interrupts circadian rhythms. After the initial trauma, the brain reaches a calm, even state. Then DMT production increases in the pineal gland. This psychotropic molecule opens unlimited connection to perception beyond sensory capabilities," he said.

"And this displays as white light?" she asked.

"The sculptures display continual high-amplitude gamma oscillations—indicating comprehensive communication throughout the brain. This registers like advanced meditation in their brainwave data.

"Alert wakefulness and a sense of consciousness make their baselines different. Look at this sculpture," he said, putting his hand on the arm of *Chessic,* glowing white and pink.

"I was drawn to this piece the first time I entered the gallery," she said.

"Jude Ryan, the former world-renowned chess grandmaster, remains one of my most successful transfers. They found chess as a child and it consumed their world. By living in the head so much, Jude must have functioned in a constant state of meditation."

Persephone noticed how white points mingled with an intermittent glow of pale pink across the smooth glass. The colors reminded her of the piazza in her dream that morning, reflecting a soft and beautiful light that felt warm and inviting.

"*Chessic* fascinates me, but not from visual stimulus," the Curator said. "Jude never went through a fantastic color display. Ironically, they jumped over most initial stages of a brain transfer. They either passed through them quickly, or moved straight into awareness. My theory is, the ease of transition came from being so cerebral."

"So you think Jude glows white from an enlightened place?" asked Persephone.

"Jude rose to be an extraordinary chess player through the ability to tune into their opponents' strategies on a deeper level. This quality may have allowed the brain, once inside a sculpture, to immediately register something happening through extrasensory intelligence."

"Is that why a chessmaster is part of your '*Holy Trinity*' collection?" she asked.

"*Chessic* represents intellect—the non-binary bridge of 'mind' connecting the instinctual understanding of my *Tribal Elder* and the intuitive evolution of my *Monk*. My tribal elder links to feminine nature and the earth, symbolizing the physical 'body.' Sifu, a symbol of the universal masculine, cultivated intuition and the 'spirit.' Together instinct, intelligence and intuition create complete consciousness—the sacred trinity of body, mind and spirit."

"I understand your intention, philosophically speaking," she said. "But it sounds like there are greater cultural implications from housing a tribal elder."

The Curator walked to the other side of the room and touched a sculpture fusing white and yellow. "My Brazilian elder intrigues me as a sculptural piece. I consider the night she arrived to be a lucky one for the Third Series."

He then recounted a story Persephone found to be a sad one, reflecting much insensitivity she wished she could alter.

"In March of 2107, tribes from the Brazilian rainforest continued their battle for territory still encroached upon by ranchers and palm farmers. Natives who had adapted their 'No Contact With the Outside World' policy began engaging with nonprofit workers from NC-WOW Assist, seeking solutions to help keep their collectives healthy and safe.

"Encouraged by volunteers, one native group agreed to conduct a small tour to describe the difficulty of their condition. The tribe hoped a select contingent visiting a large city would have the most impact. A delegation of five leaders and several tribal members traveled to Shanghai.

"They used one of the parks to perform their daily meetings at sunrise for three days. They danced and prayed, dressed in their ritual finery. On the third day, they returned at sunset to conduct a closing ceremony. The tribe fit the spontaneous celebration into their schedule as an extra gesture of gratitude, entering the park unescorted.

"Five teenagers approached the dancers with the intention of stealing their belongings, thinking their clothing or accessories might be valuable. The tribal group didn't recognize the urban threat enough to run away, but when attacked, they knew a lot about fighting back.

"Most of the members suffered beatings during the mugging. Deodata Ramos, one of the elders in her late-sixties, fell wounded.

"Mr. Goode, learned of the unique opportunity and secured the Brazilian elder's brain," the Curator said.

"You only made things worse by bringing Deodata here," said Persephone upon hearing the story. "It shows utter disrespect for her journey, and the plight of her people. How the tribe handles their dead is surely an integral part of their cultural and religious rituals."

Persephone walked over to the glass elder and placed one hand on her own heart and the other in the center of Deodata's chest. The sculpture felt warm under her palm as it glimmered from white through blue, then pink.

"I lived for six months in southern Brazil when I was thirteen and my dad served with Doctors Without Borders," she told the Curator. "I met kids in the native Guarani village where he worked to vaccinate the population after some tribes opened to receiving Western medicine. It was very difficult for the native groups to build enough trust to remain healthy."

Persephone turned her attention back to the sculpture and said, "*Mbarete*," recalling a native Guarani word she had learned in the medical camp. "*Mbarete*, Deodata ... *mbarete*."

She continued to speak to the sculpture, translating the single-word statement so the Curator would have no doubt about her sentiments. "*Mbarete*. Stay strong; never let the root weaken."

PART SIX

§

Hearing

"The grounds feel peaceful with the sound of birds singing. Listen ...," the old monk suggested, cupping his right hand around his ear.

The cluster stopped and attuned to the sweetness of the warbles. Then they gathered around the abbot and all traveled together along the stone path disappearing into the trees.

"Words, sounds and music can stimulate and excite your nervous system—or bring peace to it," he said. *"Tones create an atmosphere for your moods, which resonate in the background of all you do.*

"In utero, hearing develops at sixteen weeks. However, your mother's body and the amniotic fluid muted vocalizations by half. So only vibrations traveled across her womb.

"Hearing became the sense through which you came to know the element of space. And space allows the power of perception to expand toward a fuller context.

"Inside a sculpture, auditory memory shines as green and purple. Green reflects balance and purple shows spiritual evolution.

"Do any of you play music? You may expect to cast the same bright-green glow as the creative seekers inside the stupas at our Centre.

"Sounds connect us to the outside world, but listening to your deeper mind and heart allows you to receive and comprehend inner truths. This opens your consciousness to direct knowledge.

"If you are here now, I have no doubt you are tuning into the call of your Higher Self. In knowing those who entered sculptures, I can tell you this: following the sweet sound of your own calling will help you shine more brightly than anything else."

Chapter Twenty-Five

Throughout the morning and into the afternoon, Dr. Stennis and Philip did not speak a word. Philip worked to transfer the glass figures into the freight elevator at the back of the upper gallery. The Curator simply glanced at each sculpture before it disappeared behind the closing metal door.

"I've studied these sculptures for a decade. It is unusual to watch my work come to an end," he told Persephone.

"You said some of your patrons will receive them?" she asked.

"Yes. A few who made a connection with the figures over the years told Mr. Goode they would like one. We always re-iterated the sculptures were 'not for sale,' but many higher-ups had every expectation they would acquire one at some point ... generally in the confidence of lavish payments. When Mr. Goode contacted them for immediate delivery, they only wondered why it took so long."

"Have you told the patrons about the care required?" she asked. "Do they realize what they've agreed to?"

"They will find out soon enough; we have had other priorities. Mr. Goode will explain the full system of maintenance once he delivers the pieces," he said.

"But they could die!" she said.

"What a shame I will not be able to join them in this gallery as a collective," he said. "You won't have the benefit of comparison, as I did."

"The brains will fade hours or even minutes after the required care is forgotten," she said, flabbergasted at the Curator's seeming disregard for the longevity of his research, if not the humans in the sculptures.

"Mr. Goode is adept at smoothing over issues. I don't expect any problems."

By early afternoon Philip had moved thirteen of the pieces to the basement. Only the eleven brightest sculptures remained in the gallery.

After hearing about the individuals and watching Philip remove them, Persephone felt emotionally depleted and edgy. By two o'clock she wanted to be done.

"I need a break from all this," she told the Curator.

"Please, let's go to my office," he said, gesturing to the side room. Persephone followed him, wishing she had a better alternative.

"Are the sculptures equally divided between men and women?" she asked as they entered the room. It was the last question needling her mind, and she wanted to be done with it.

"I have more women. When we first drew from organ donors, I had more male brains because men have more accidents. But cerebral activity and the intensity of the displays favor females over the same length of time," he said.

"Why's that?"

"Men, being linear thinkers and problem solvers, typically show more tightly coordinated patterns within each hemisphere. Women use both hemispheres far more interactively. This allows more proficiency for multi-tasking, giving more resiliency for adapting to the transition."

"Hmm," she said, before sitting on the couch.

"What can I get you to drink?" he asked.

"Nothing ... I just need a break."

"Very well," said the Curator. I will assist Mr. Goode in the basement with readying the First Series for their departures. I will return in an hour. Help yourself to anything in the fridge. I hope you'll find something to your liking."

Persephone watched Dr. Stennis travel across the gallery to the freight elevator on the far side. After he departed, she began plotting with more purpose. Knowing INTERPOL was closing in created a hopeful prospect to a dreadful situation; but she still had to rely on herself first.

She left the office and walked diagonally toward the double doors on the right. A quick tug confirmed they remained locked. *Bugger*, she thought as she placed her forehead against the metal and closed her eyes. The only way out was down the elevator.

Moments later she sensed a change in the room, almost like being watched. She opened her eyes and noticed a heightened intensity of tones reflecting on the door and dancing across the floor. She lifted her head and turned around. "Wow. Whoa ..."

The eleven remaining sculptures burst through a dazzling spectrum of hues. Shifting lights hypnotically changed with flashes of color shooting up from their feet, through their torsos, and out the tops of their heads like fountains of light.

***

Persephone admired the fantastic show from where she stood for a few moments before moving closer to gain a better sense of what was happening. The circle of remaining sculptures pulsed vibrantly like they could be presenting a pattern. The whole array shined notably brighter than earlier.

She returned to her dad. His lights swirled through a mix of brilliant blues. As she stood between her dad and Sifu, she noticed the monk glowed with the same blues as her father. Their colors reflected onto her ... cerulean, lapis, azure. She touched the hand of her father's sculpture and his teals intensified, as if in response.

"Dad? What is going on?" she asked, sensing an energy in the room she'd never felt anywhere. As unusual as the experience was, it didn't feel frightening. She felt intrigued about the shift; what was happening?

She turned to Sifu. His cobalt gleam remained strong. When she placed her hand on the *Monk*'s waist, the figure radiated lapis with streaming lines of white moving up through the glass.

To view her dad and Sifu together, Persephone stepped back from the sculptures. White speckles expanded across their blues. Within seconds the lights grew so vibrant the pieces had spotlights pulsing from their crowns, shining onto the ceiling, spiraling in all directions. When their beams overlapped, they slowed, paused and merged.

Persephone gasped and moved to view more figures at once. Their dazzle shimmered playfully across the full spectrum of colors. A predominance of cobalt appeared wherever she stood, shining upon her so much that when she looked at her arm, she resembled a glass figure.

As she moved around the room the figures twinkled brilliantly. Perhaps the Curator was directing the light show somehow? Or were the sculptures actually engaging? In any case … the surreal scene, like watching a digitized aurora borealis, mesmerized her.

As the intensity grew, she recognized what an enormous output of energy the sculptures produced from their engaged minds. What a complete contrast to the party the night before! Seeing the statues with each other made the patrons seem even more disconnected in comparison.

Persephone traveled toward Jude. *Chessic*'s lights intensified with vibrant pinks and whites, through to cobalt. She placed her hand on Jude's. When she lifted her palm a solid white phosphorescence remained on the form. Transfixed in the moment, nothing could have broken her attention.

A wave of peace washed through her, its wondrous depth sending the hairs on her arm on end and a chill down the back of her spine. She recognized the presence in the glass was the same essence as the chess player in her dream that morning. Warmth infused her and spoke through her mind: *We perceive you.*

A white glow rose from *Chessic*'s feet, up the torso and out the top of the head. Jude's beacon joined the brilliance connecting Sifu and her father with an amazing ray of luminescence. When their shine crossed, jewel colors of sapphire and jade mirrored across each sculpture before they returned to their individual displays.

Dr. Stennis had mentioned some souls could transcend their containers. Did they really have the capacity to escape their physical confinement? They did appear to be reaching out, based on those near each other displaying similar colors. Was this unification a ploy to stay hidden, or a fight to be seen? Was this communication?

She remembered Deodata and moved toward her to place her hand on the sculpture's heart space once again. "Can you perceive me?" Persephone asked. "If you are transcending your capture, I hope you feel free."

When she removed her hand, a beam of white fluorescence as wide as her palm followed. It dissipated as *Tribal Elder* glowed from the top of her head, flowing like a river of illumination into the ocean above her.

Soon all eleven pieces bore columns of light reaching up toward the ceiling and blending. Their bright bands intermingled and swayed like glowing palm fronds. The overhead gallery lights disappeared behind the energetic display that appeared so technological, yet felt natural and organic.

Persephone knew she was in the presence of active minds, yet she couldn't quantify the experience. Glimmers of day-to-day intuition were one thing—feeling the consciousness of another through her mind felt extraordinary ... truly amazing.

She wanted to embrace the experience fully, never having imagined the remarkable nature of transcendent connection. Any direct engagement from her hands onto a sculpture triggered a change in the intensity of the lights. But so did the interactions between the figures. When their lights merged, they enhanced each other, combining into a luminous collective of soul energy.

The coruscating kaleidoscope of colors began to subside and Persephone maintained an incredible awareness of inner peace and calm. At the same time, she felt energized and awed. She returned to the office, left a bit spacey from the experience.

In her sense of no-time, a half an hour had passed. She opened the refrigerator and selected some cheese, along with bread and fruit. The shine in the gallery returned to a more subtle glow, even as the individual pieces remained bright.

Persephone sat on the couch and watched the gallery as she ate. The food tasted rich and everything she looked at had more dimension. She knew brains needed a cycle; sleeping or waking, the mind functions best with constant activity. But what was that?

Clearly the souls had tapped into the ability to expand into a sphere of connection beyond the physical. She recognized, as bodiless observers, they may understand their whole vision emanated from within their own minds. If so, perhaps they *could* escape their situation.

Sensored minds that reached that level of control ... free to shape experience beyond memories ... could expand from concrete thoughts into sheer energy; the essence of the soul itself.

If they joined each other and shared the same light, this could become the thread linking everything together. Freedom came from connection; that was their answer. And hers, she thought, in a moment of personal epiphany.

***

Although Persephone realized she couldn't leave the building, she felt empowered after witnessing something so incredible it surpassed anything she'd ever seen or felt. Her perspective on the situation changed; she no longer felt trapped, but interconnected.

After finishing her snack, she walked across the gallery and put her hand on her father's head. "I promise I'll get you out of here, Dad" she said, before going to the elevator.

Only forty-five minutes had passed, but she felt ready to reengage with the Curator. The lift arrived and Persephone stepped into a car so big it would have held an elephant. The antiquated equipment fit right in with the old technology peppered throughout the modern warehouse. As such, the door closed very slowly.

Three buttons offered a choice of floors. Persephone pressed the one for the first level, without registry. She hit 'B' and began to descend toward the basement.

It took a full minute to travel two flights from the upper gallery, past the main gallery, to the bottom floor without any sense of movement. She knew all the sculptures must have taken the reverse journey at some point, moving from below street level to the second floor, requiring a slow ride to remain safe.

Upon reaching the subterranean level, the elevator opened at the same measured pace. Persephone entered a clean, concrete warehouse and registered an acute temperature change. While the upper gallery felt comfortable, the frigid basement didn't.

Her eyes scanned the space. A metal rail track-system installed across the ceiling carried her eyes toward two large aluminum roll-up doors on the far left side of the warehouse. There, the glass sculptures Philip had rounded up earlier stood huddled together in a cluster near the exit.

Chapter Twenty-Six

"Ah, Persephone, you found us," said the Curator, approaching her from the adjacent room as the elevator door closed behind her. "Good, we are ahead of schedule."

Persephone held the fantastical event within her as she tried to place it in context, before discussing it with the Curator.

"How long will you keep the sculptures down here?" she asked.

"The staging area will allow Mr. Goode to take the pieces out through the underground garage and deliver them to patrons. We will remove them this evening. I only hope it is not too late," he said. "Does this basement feel familiar to you?"

"Um, no. Should it?" she asked, scanning the space for any exits apart from the large roll-up doors.

"The apartment where you stayed last night is straight ahead, through the double doors. Please, follow me; I'll show you. Feel free to explore the area later. I have no secrets to keep from you. I want you to feel comfortable here. But it is extremely important you do not return to this area with shoes; hygiene is of upmost importance."

As the Curator escorted her down the hall, Persephone noted they passed three closed doors on the right before he continued through the exit. She recognized the front of the apartment on the left where she'd slept the previous night.

A small box and a holo-control wand sat nearby on a compact red table. The Curator picked up the remote for the digital hologram projector and handed it to Persephone.

"Many times your father supported my human connection so I wouldn't only live in the scientific realm. I am honored to return the favor and connect his daughter to him."

Connect us? You've bloody well made that physically impossible, she thought, taking the wand he offered.

"A holographic message from your father will have to do for now. It is ready to play inside. He recorded it for you in this apartment, after he created the Holo-Gram you received in London," said the Curator, ignoring her obvious irritation.

"Did you watch it?" asked Persephone.

"I did not; the messages were meant for you alone. I may observe others, but I do not eavesdrop on their conversations," he replied as he picked up the box from the table. "I trust your father supported my research."

"My father supported research that considers each individual's well-being," said Persephone. "Any use of the sculptures to study the mind must also consider our connection to one another."

"Don't forget lunch," the Curator said, handing her the box as she turned to enter the apartment. She took it, then shut and locked the door. A look out the peephole showed Dr. Stennis disappearing into the staircase. She leaned against the wall and pressed her short fingernails into the small cardboard container, feeling its warmth.

While horrified by the lurid art project she'd witnessed, Persephone remained mesmerized by the energetic display of lights. The scientific enormity of her predicament astonished her. How real the impending discovery of the gallery was, or how soon it might come, she couldn't presume.

Pulled by the desire to connect with her father, to assist the others trapped within the sculptures, and to stop the Curator from facilitating more crimes, Persephone sat with the heaviness of information gained over the past twenty-four hours.

Confirming Dr. Franklin Stennis lived after his disappearance years ago was huge. His secret gallery brought an even greater discovery. Being held hostage by the two men who'd orchestrated the collection though gruesome methods worried her, for sure. But her biggest surprise—and the hardest part for her to reconcile—was accepting her father's involvement.

In her search for her dad, whom Persephone had always believed lived his life with integrity, she did not expect to lose her trust in him. Would he really have assisted in leading her into a situation that threatened her safety? Although Persephone mourned the loss of her dad's physical form, the fading belief in the rectitude of his intentions splintered her spirit.

If her dad knew Dr. Stennis maintained brains—if he acted as the impetus for bringing her to him—was he as arrogant and selfish as the Curator? Her dad, so instrumental in guiding her morals, now seemed like someone she didn't even know.

As her heart grieved, Persephone appreciated she may have the potential to communicate with him again, and that changed everything. She recognized getting caught up in her immediate pain was futile. Thinking long-term could create a greater solution.

***

To settle her mind trying to organize so many dilemmas at once, she took a long sigh, sunk into the grey couch and pushed {Play} on the wand. A life-size holographic display of her father emerged in front of her, standing as frail and unsteady as he had appeared in her London flat. Her tears welled up instantly. She couldn't have controlled them if she tried.

"Hi Sweetheart. No doubt many emotions and thoughts swirl together for you now. Please don't be angry. I know your rationale will allow you to hear what I'm about to say, and in time, let you trust my intentions.

"I knew you would find your way here. I'm sorry to put you in the position of telling your mother what you discovered. I needed to

shield you both from learning about Franklin. The disappointment you must feel knowing I held the secret for so long about his disappearance saddens me, but I understand it.

"I have known for a long time about Franklin Stennis. People knew he and I were close, and they would ask about him. For almost ten years I, too, thought he'd died. After he got in touch with me, I considered the ramifications of keeping his confidence and agreed to, in order to protect you and your mother from any backlash."

As her dad spoke, Persephone remained on the couch. Playing his image straight in front of her gave the impression of having direct eye contact. The connection and familiarity eased the stress of the past few days. But the conflicting notion of her dad's involvement with the gallery dismissed any lasting comfort.

"Franklin and I didn't communicate often, although sometimes he'd contact me about some random neurological question we'd discussed as neurosurgeons. He told me he was researching the senses. I knew he remained hidden and I wanted to minimize my connection.

"When my liver transplant began to fail a few months ago, I realized the amyloid protein was moving into my spinal cord and brain. I wondered if becoming involved in his efforts might help me delay the loss of my senses. He invited me to Shanghai and I came, planning to learn more about his research and return home. Certain details were obviously left out of his description about what is going on here.

"Now my situation has changed. See how much I'm sweating. Protein increasing on the nerves that control every essential action of my body is affecting how my organs function. Even with a liver transplant I knew the risk of this happening.

"You know this disease is genetic, but latent. I feel thankful it didn't come on when you were younger. Every hour feels different now. I don't fear death. I've lived a fantastic life and my love for you and your mother has carried me through some dark times over the last few years.

"Persephone, please believe me when I tell you I didn't know *about the sculptures until I arrived. I will be honest with you: seeing the number of statues, and understanding Franklin's history, I question whether everyone volunteered.*

"Yesterday I learned Franklin plans to draw you here. He's reviewed your research for years and recognizes your scientific developments align with his efforts. I'm uneasy with the situation and he knows this. I want you to be safe ... not pulled into any legal issues.

"Franklin promised to show you this message, and I expect he will. I made recording it—and you seeing it—a condition of entering a sculpture. Although my choice was made under time pressure, I agreed to be put into one. My time is short either way, and this decision is the only way I can ensure you and your mother will remain safe.

"My amyloidosis will soon take away my senses. I accept this inevitability. As my long-time colleague, I expect Franklin will proceed with my mind carefully and with respect—doing all he can to ensure my well-being.

"Philip let me know authorities are taking an interest again in Franklin's disappearance. This has sped up his plan to be put into a piece. I'm sure he's already asked you to perform the procedure. He told me he would when you arrived. No doubt you are deciding whether to agree. My condition no longer allows me to do so, otherwise I would have helped him myself, just to keep you out of this completely.

"I want you to know how much I support your research and the challenges you face. You have a brilliant and scientific mind. I hope through my participation in this project, I can help you. If my brain survives, perhaps we can reconnect again somehow.

"I'm sure you have many unanswered questions, Sweetheart. I've tried my best to consider what you may want to ask, so I can address your biggest concerns.

"This is not a goodbye. We find ourselves in transition now rather than at an ending. You sit at the brink of some amazing discoveries. They belong to you, and I trust your judgment for my condition.

"Good luck, Seph. I love you and am so proud of you! Please tell your mum I love and miss her, too. I hope our family will connect again in the future."

After the hologram stilled, Persephone played it a second time. She paused to study her father. He could barely lift his hands; his usual free gestures appeared stilted and inexpressive. She heard, with his rapid breath, how much speaking for just seven minutes took from him.

Tears leaked from her eyes. She let them roll toward her lips, tasting the salt before wiping her cheeks. Somehow watching her dad on the video eased her mind. "I feel you with me," she said.

Persephone tried to connect with her father energetically, sending her silent pleas his way to help her get out of the gallery alive; to let her mum know she was in danger; and to ensure INTERPOL would arrive quickly.

***

As she slumped into the couch, her mind drifted to her father's lifetime of being a professional partner in Dr. Stennis' research. Her father had always been her ethical role model, yet she recognized the secrets he kept allowed him to become an accessory to criminal activity.

Perhaps her dad had reconciled his actions by playing the long-game for her, and for medical science. How else could he have ignored what Dr. Stennis had done? When faced with an opportunity to stretch science, did a positive intention for the future matter most?

Persephone considered whether she, too, must walk a moral tightrope as a means to an end. She grappled with the notion of doing something that, ever since Maryelle's death, she never thought she'd consciously do again: Act in a secret way that caused harm to another.

Her father may have been a willing participant, but Persephone hadn't expected to advance her career by having him involved in her research. It felt like a conflict of interest. But the unique situation forced a decision. She recognized what enormous strides could be made if you played by your own rules.

Behind her turmoil, an unsettling admission arose within her. She had a genuine fascination about the search for consciousness. Feeling the presence of what she could only call "souls" in the gallery, had opened her mind to the notion of wanting to explore the scientific possibilities.

Persephone reflected on her goal of wanting to infuse emotion into artificial intelligence. She thought about Sama who she'd received at age thirteen, in celebration of finishing five summers of robotics camp.

Sama was a medium-size machine, about the same size as Harold, a jovial poodle mix who had been part of the family for twelve years. As a teenager she loved both dogs, but their mannerisms differed dramatically.

Being manufactured rather than born allowed Sama a customized look. Its legs and body could be made longer or shorter; the ears and tail could be attached or left off. Harold had natural curls, but Sama had a soft body and a surface material made of black crushed velvet with a slight sheen.

Her parents told her not to compare Sama with Harold, but it was hard. Harold's bouncy greeting showed an unmistakable spark of spirit demonstrating true affection. Sama nudged Harold away from its warm recharging mat with a sweet disposition, but that was about it. The robopup shared similar failings as all artificial interactives. No matter how advanced the programming, it didn't—because it couldn't—have actual feelings.

A defining moment for Persephone came a year after receiving Sama. Harold, in his old age, stopped eating and died three days later. A natural dog may mourn its companion by seeking affection and sharing sadness with its human family. Sama looked at Harold's bed a couple of times following learned routines, but otherwise had no change in its actions.

Persephone missed her longtime furry friend. She didn't expect emotion from Sama, but the experience started her thinking about other artificials. She wanted smart robotic beings to interact more like real ones.

Dr. Stennis had suggested she could use his work to progress hers—by keeping brains alive outside the body so they could be put into an artificial or donor body in the future. She didn't see his bridge to infusing consciousness into artificial intelligence. In her heart she knew each individual's experience with the world was sacred. A whole human brain contained a person—she was not willing to adapt it for AI in place of lab-grown tissue.

Persephone never dreamed of performing procedures in violation of the Hippocratic Oath to "do no harm." In her research, she felt fortunate she'd never faced the same ethical considerations as Dr. Stennis. She could experiment on machines all she wanted, without harming one.

Now, if she agreed to put Dr. Stennis into a sculpture, she would assume responsibility for him and her father: living, viable, functioning brains. As she navigated the conundrums of an unknown landscape, she considered how she might locate the other sculptures and reacquire them from the patrons.

Though silent and inaccessible, the minds seemed active and engaged. She felt responsible for establishing communication with the individuals in the glass. She needed to determine what level of existence filled their shut-in state. Only then could they express their desires. Until she knew what legal rights they had, she could not administer care. Letting them die might be the kindest thing to do.

To remain above-board, she would need to bring her colleagues and other researchers to the gallery—or move the sculptures to her lab in London, or another medical facility.

Was she at the beginning or the end? An extensive list of questions hijacked her mind, blocking her actions with mental exhaustion.

Chapter Twenty-Seven

A round six p.m. Persephone glanced at the double doors outside her apartment, readying herself to return to the expansive space on the other side. The more information she could gather through exploration, the better her footing would be. Knowing that, although it felt ironic, she opted to leave her shoes in the apartment.

The doors opened easily. Finally ... a passage she could go through. Getting out of the building proved a challenge. As far as she could tell, one could only enter or exit the warehouse from the street level, or through the underground roll-up doors where the glass sculptures stood.

Along the hallway, the first room on her left was wide open. She peered inside and discovered a private operating room straight out of a futuristic hospital. Not only was it technologically progressive, it may have been one of the most advanced on the planet.

The white and grey interior of the clean, airy space had domed fixtures floating above smooth, curved chairs. A dazzling silver light glowed violet in sections as the only color in the room. Robots and AI assistants awaited their link with traditional medical equipment, including a 3-D bioprinter and a complete virtual reality theater system.

"Wonderful, Persephone," she heard the Curator call from the other end of the hall, startling her with his presence.

So much for trying to explore the area discreetly. For someone who seemed to appreciate independence, he was certainly on top of how she moved around the gallery.

"I hope you rested well. I appreciate you removing your boots. Please, start at the beginning ... with this room," he said, as he motioned her toward the third door at the end of the hall. He entered the room and disappeared from view.

Although she didn't feel like engaging with him further, given the uncomfortable circumstance, her curiosity remained piqued. Obviously something had happened with the sculptures in the upper gallery. She needed to inquire about the light show she'd witnessed, so she'd know how to quantify it.

Persephone traveled down the hallway past the middle room, its door still closed. When she peered into the room at the end of the hall, the Curator hovered near twenty-five, or so, works of art of various sizes, stacked in the corner.

Some stood five feet tall with elaborate gilded frames that seemed greatly juxtaposed with the contemporary gallery. Perhaps that's why they'd been shunted to the basement.

The room's strange assortment of creative, clinical and computerized items caught her attention. A couple of shiny metal operating tables sitting in the center appeared out of place next to the wooden frames. Two large flat-screen monitors on the side wall displayed a series of graphics and charts Persephone recognized as brainwave data moving across the screens.

The Curator began his explanation of the area. "It will be useful for you to have a high-level understanding about how we assemble the pieces. All the glass sculptures arrive in crates. Mr. Goode brings them straight in through the garage and we unbox them near the parking structure," he said, pointing behind her.

Persephone looked toward the roll-up doors. Only a few statues remained.

"Where do the pieces come from?" she asked.

"After we purchase them from a local artist, the two halves remain in a storage facility until we need them. A delivery vehicle picks up the crates and takes them to a remote spot in the city. Mr. Goode meets him to coordinate transferring them into the gallery truck. He then drives them straight into this parking garage."

"They look enormously heavy," she said.

"Indeed, they are. We wheel these motor-assisted gurneys down to the end of the warehouse. A crane secured on the overhead tracks uses a lifting-sling to take each half of the sculpture out of its box," he explained.

She glanced up at the ceiling track, but remained thinking about the sculptures. How many of them were left upstairs? When she turned her attention back to the monitors, she wondered if the displays linked to the remaining minds in the gallery. She couldn't tell whether the charts were recorded or projected in real-time.

"Each side weighs about four hundred and fifty kilograms. After suspending a sculpture in the sling it can be rotated or tipped. The crane pivots the glass to place it, hollow side up, on its own table," he explained. "We move the shells into this first room to clean and sanitize them."

Persephone kept her focus on the monitors, trying to determine which display might link to her dad. The Curator continued talking, oblivious to her distraction.

"The walls between the rooms retract with a simple push of the button," he said, as he did so. The wall closest to the second room disappeared from the bottom up like a soap bubble popping in slow motion that stowed into the ceiling. Removing the divider revealed another pair of tables, holding two halves of a glass figure in the open position, as the Curator had described.

Philip stood over the sculpture. Persephone wondered what he was doing, which must have registered on her face, because he answered the question before she asked.

"This is *Severed* from the main lobby," he told her. "I moved it down here this morning. I'm readying it to receive the Curator's brain."

Persephone thought she detected a smirk as he turned his attention back to the glass. Without much context for his arrangement with the Curator, she wondered about his motivation for continuing with the plan. He certainly seemed sadistic, but perhaps he, too, was being held hostage by Dr. Stennis.

"Mr. Goode and I are working on my sculpture now," said the Curator. "It awaits me. This is the installation room where we add the digital connections and the lights. Once Mr. Goode finalizes the fiber optic insertions, the piece will be ready for you to attach my cranial case."

"Why glass?" Persephone inquired, picking a basic question that would not cause controversy. "It seems so cumbersome."

The Curator considered her inquiry for a moment and replied, "Glass is a timeless material and a fantastic insulator to help the brains maintain a constant temperature. I'm sure you noticed the warmth of the surface when you touched the pieces. Paired with the shielding from the cranial case, it helps keep electrical interference from affecting the sensors."

He returned his gaze to his assembly line tour and said, "I am the only one lucky enough to prepare my own vessel. I feel fortunate to have the opportunity to be with it before I am inside."

"You almost seem excited," she said, folding her arms across her chest and giving her shoulders a few backward rolls to help herself relax. "Even with all your research and years of experience taking minds from bodies, you still can't know what will happen to you. I dare say it will be unlike anything you could possibly imagine … as it must have been for each person."

"Let's elevate our discussion, Persephone. I know you recognize the importance of this effort, and I expect you to take it seriously. By the time my sculpture enters the surgery room, where you will work with it, all the internal electronics will be in place."

"So the only thing you want me to do is place your brain into the piece?" she asked.

"I wish it were so simple," he said. "When Mr. Goode arrives with my brain after having gone through the extraction process, it will be in the transfer case. You will place the sensors into it. Mr. Goode will coordinate linking my mind to the fiber optic display and monitoring the systems—as he has done with all my sculptures."

"Thank you, Mr. Goode," he said, looking toward *Severed*.

"Yes, it will all go smoothly," he replied, looking up from his work at Persephone, almost appearing to challenge her.

"You are expecting quite a lot from me and making an enormous assumption I know how to do this," said Persephone. "Should I be flattered you consider my limited surgical experience has prepared me to handle your mind in such a specific manner? How am I supposed to know where to put the sensors?" she asked.

"I have made detailed scans of my brain and spinal cord for you. The virtual guide we created will allow you precision. You will follow the procedure using robotic devices to assist you. All of this is ready to view in my private surgery room. Please familiarize yourself with the equipment and its layout and rehearse the operation."

"Rehearse it? … What? How?" she asked.

"Some of the hardware will be familiar to you from your lab," he continued. "We've developed other tools for specific aspects of the sequence. Of course, this whole facility will be yours after you complete my installation. Feel free to make any changes that aid your efficiencies."

"You're serious. You expect me to watch it now?" she asked.

"Yes, I do. Our timing has unfortunately been compressed with recent events, so it is imperative you begin viewing the guide immediately. It illustrates in exact detail the entire procedure for mounting the sensors into my brain and placing it properly into the case."

The ease with which the Curator discussed the process of installing his mind into the waiting glass sculpture concerned Persephone. That he inspected the container set to house him with a glint of excitement in his eyes didn't help.

"We draw close to the end of our time together, Persephone. I trust your abilities and your appreciation of the scientific crossroads at which we find ourselves. You want to see how this all ends, too, yes?"

Chapter Twenty-Eight

Virtual reality images don't usually fill half the room, but when the Curator entered the surgery space and activated the procedural hologram, it did.

He gave Persephone a notebook prepared with detailed instructions and a tablet for her questions.

"How long is this?" she asked the Curator.

"Three hours. Pause as you need to. I will leave you to it," he said. "The guide discusses connection techniques, along with instructions on using the custom surgical tools to install my brain into the glass."

"I'd rather see it tomorrow," she said.

"The time is now," he said, before he left the room and shut the door.

The holo-video showed him opening a case and removing a living human brain. Imaging data blended with an actual procedure, creating an intense and immersive experience. She had never seen anything like it.

"Hello, Persephone. I will outline every step of this exacting surgery. Walking you through the details so when the time comes, you can successfully install me into my sculpture."

His next words haunted her as he picked up a curvaceous greyish-pink organ, carefully maneuvering around the tubes supplying life support, and spoke poetically to its fluid, soft curves:

"May I keep your brain?
You have an amazing mind.
I would like to look at it more closely.
Hold it in my hands.
Cradle your soul."

Persephone's stomach growled, but not from hunger. It rumbled from distress, a primitive groan that rose up into her clenched gut and fueled her self-preservation and her willpower. Her most pressing thought was hoping the brain she watched Dr. Stennis handle was not her father's.

Although she remained distracted thinking about the incredible illumination she'd witnessed from the sculptures, Persephone opted to watch the entire holo-video. She wanted to understand whether the brains actually could be directing their own light displays, or if they were pre-programmed from their bases.

In the holographic surgery guide the Curator illustrated the details of the actual process.

"The procedure must be clean and not rushed. The specific, detailed and careful placement of the sensors takes time," he began.

"A sequence of brainwave phases occurs based on each individual's background, and how long their mind has been removed from the body.

"After a brain enters a sculpture, its waves spike and fluctuate wildly. First, beta rhythms at fourteen to thirty cycles per second indicate logical, conscious waking. Generally one then moves into theta states of four to seven cycles per second, indicating a spark in imagination and psychic fantasies.

"The shift causes an array of lights to bounce through the figure in a random pattern. Most brains stabilize in alpha at eight to thirteen hertz, supporting a calm daydream state.

"Within three days, a newly encased brain either functions or

fails with relative speed. Failing systems dive into delta waves below three cycles per second, hitting a deep, dreamless sleep, or even total unconsciousness."

None of the information helped explained the fantastic show Persephone experienced in the gallery. She considered perhaps the sculptures were exhibiting some kind of conscious waking flaring from beta. Or maybe *she* had been in theta having her own fantasy trip.

After watching the complete procedure, doing a practice run using the virtual model of the Curator's brain, and becoming familiar with the operating room, it was approaching ten o'clock. She heard the two men continuing their work in the middle room.

When Persephone left the surgery room, Dr. Stennis exited the center room and met her in the hallway.

"Good night, Persephone," he said.

Without looking at him, she asked, "Was the brain used in the video my father's?"

"No. A woman supplied it."

Without confirming who, she knew it must be his former lab assistant Frieda, the female most recently placed into a sculpture.

"Do you have any other questions?" he asked.

Persephone shook her head from side to side and began walking toward the basement apartment. She was exhausted, wanted to sleep, and didn't feel like engaging with Dr. Stennis any longer. But she had to. She stopped and turned around.

"Actually, I do have a question for you," she said.

"Oh?"

"If you supposed I would be interested in your research as a step toward infusing consciousness into AI, why didn't you tell me about the communication happening in the upper gallery?"

"What communication are you referencing?" he asked.

"The communication between the sculptures," she said.

"If you mean the brainwave devices that allow us to read the sculptures, we have monitors in the room by the elevator," he said. "We keep a full record of each brain's activity."

"I noticed the monitors earlier," she said.

"I am glad you are interested. You probably want to get some sleep, but let's return to the first room. Forgive my oversight. There are a few sculptures still up in the gallery. The graphs present a digital relay of their brain patterns."

"From how far back?"

"We have countless hours of data, much of it condensed from the first few years. The screens show us information in real-time."

"Can we see what happened this afternoon with my father?" she asked. "Around two-fifteen."

"Of course; let's have a look," the Curator said before he moved down the hall and entered the end room.

Persephone watched him and, with hesitation, decided to follow. She wanted to see the brainwave graphs more closely, but she was tired of the Curator directing things.

***

When she got to the room, Dr. Stennis was navigating through information on one of the oversize monitors using his hands. He reviewed the screen and moved the graph with his fingers to view the 3-D brainwaves on a timeline.

"At two-fifteen your father shows high-amplitude gamma oscillations. As I mentioned upstairs, sculptures entering gamma at twenty-five to one hundred and forty hertz have different baselines. At two-fifteen it appears your father spiked to one hundred and thirty cycles per second."

"What a high level of brain activity!" she said.

"Yes; as you know, we often see this in deep stages of meditation and expanded consciousness," said the Curator.

"What about Sifu?" she asked. "At two-fifteen."

"Sifu? Let me call up my *Monk's* data," he said as he selected some options on the monitor then swiped and waved the screens over to the image he wanted. "The same. He also was in gamma at one hundred and thirty hertz."

"And Jude?" she asked.

"Well, let's see ... *Chessic* ... ." The Curator scrolled to the chart displaying the chess champion's brain and his brow furrowed. He glanced at Persephone, then back at the screen, and asked, "What happened upstairs? The gamma waves from *Chessic* are exactly the same as your father's and my *Monk*'s ... one hundred and thirty hertz."

He called up the graphs for the other sculptures and began setting their positions to display their statistics from two-fifteen that afternoon. They all showed the exact same amplitude.

"How remarkable," he said. "The brainwaves of my most successful works indicate these minds function with calm under pressure. At times, I have detected similarities between a couple of graphs, but I have never seen them all display the same gamma pattern. Even with my expertise, I continue to learn the capabilities of the mind."

He looked back at the screen and again asked Persephone," What happened upstairs?" This time he paused and waited for her to answer, keeping his eyes focused upon her.

"I can only speculate," said Persephone, "but it appears some level of communication is possible between the sculptures. Somehow they can tap back into this world. They can link in ways you or I can't, even through the deepest meditation."

"One of the barriers to awakening as humans comes from not remembering one exists in an ongoing dream," said the Curator. "Inside a sculpture, some adjust easily to a fantasy state as their new reality; some transcend. A mind freed from the body can rise above the torment of the physical world. But why would they be communicating?"

"Perhaps to wake each other up," said Persephone.

"For what purpose?" asked the Curator.

"To free themselves," she said. "Is it possible they may be having out-of-body experiences?"

"Ah. A metaphysical speculation," he said. "I don't know how much scientific proof exists for such a thing."

"There has been research on OBEs for years," she said. "I attended a scientific retreat once focused on expanding insight through temperature shifts in the environment ... extreme heat or cold ... using sweat lodges and ice plunges ... that kind of thing. I learned then that during times of enormous physical stress, an out-of-body experience may occur."

"I have not studied it," he said.

"OBEs happen when a person's consciousness separates from the body while remaining conscious. It then travels energetically within the physical world. Some scientists call it lucid dreaming. A person may perceive a world resembling the one he or she inhabits. Perception comes from the brain's ability to create the world in the absence of sensory information."

"Are you suggesting the graphs indicate my sculptures have transcendental awareness?" he asked.

"Isn't that what you hoped for? Moving beyond the boundaries of the physical mind to experience the soul?" she asked. "Some may have moved toward cognitive interactions."

"I expect most minds can't achieve this ... they'd be unable to escape their thoughts and experiences," said the Curator.

"Those in the gallery when I was alone with them ... well, they appeared to be communicating," she said.

"How did it display?" he asked.

"Let me just say ... psychedelically," she said, feeling the experience was a special one and not wanting to share her personal connections with him.

"Hmm," he said, his eyes narrowing to a squint as he looked over Persephone's shoulder into the distance. "Mr. Goode suggested some time ago the sculptures seemed to be unifying. I assumed he was joking."

"Why would he do that?"

"I thought he just wanted to move out of the warehouse. He used to live in the apartment you are staying in. He thought the place was haunted."

"You didn't believe him?"

"He said *Chessic* realized the situation first by coming to a sense of self-understanding, then detecting other minds to determine how to reach out."

"What do you think about the plausibility of them having OBEs?" she asked him.

"I must be placed inside a sculpture to fully comprehend it," he said. "I would need scientific proof."

"Escaping from the world will never bring you closer to it," said Persephone. "You may have looked at your sculptures, Dr.

Stennis ... admired their lights and studied their charts ... but you haven't seen them."

"I have seen them every day."

"Not completely. You haven't seen them because you haven't felt them. Even with all your sensors, you never touched their souls. And I wonder if they ever touched yours."

"I have sensored their souls," he said.

"Such a connection does not come from the logical mind ... it only comes through the heart. And I can't help you with that. Goodnight, Dr. Stennis," she said before turning around and walking down the hall.

Chapter Twenty-Nine

F ruit salad and a box of fresh dim sum sat on the red table
outside the apartment on Persephone's second morning in
the gallery.

"Unbelievable," she murmured. "Where are they getting
this stuff?"

"She looked around the empty hallway. "Regular mealtimes
don't make this any more humane, you know," she called out,
to no one in particular, not knowing if Dr. Stennis or Philip
could hear her.

After eating, she hoped to enter the stairway leading to the
upper gallery. It didn't surprise her to still find it locked. Her
only option was to return to the facility on the other side of the
double doors. She encountered Philip in the center room working on the glass sculpture.

"I'd like to go upstairs," she said.

"That is not possible at the moment," he answered, sounding bothered by her request.

"I'd like to spend time with my father."

"I can't help you. These preparations are complex and I have
no time to waste," he said.

Persephone continued down the hall to the freight elevator. She noticed the sculptures that had been stationed outside the loading dock the day before were gone. She pressed the call button for the lift, but it didn't light up.

"I deactivated it," the Curator said from behind her.

Persephone jumped from the unexpected encounter and turned around. "I would like to visit the upper gallery."

"Of course you would. And you will. For now, your priority must be to prepare for my surgery. I recommend you watch the demonstration again. I am here for any questions you may have. Yesterday was a full day. You need time to integrate the information we provided," he said.

"I don't feel like watching the brain installation again," she said. "Now that I know about the procedures you've managed in this gallery, I can't watch the instructions from a purely scientific or surgical position. It just seems grisly."

"As I said, all of your research stands upon mine, Persephone. Yesterday we discovered together how those awakened in a sculpture can open up and intermingle in a cloud of souls. In doing so, they sense each other and their place in the universe. I need to join them now."

"My research does not *all* stand upon yours, Dr. Stennis; I follow my own logic—and make independent discoveries. Now, please excuse me," she said, as she brushed past him, feeling confident in her sense that he was more interested in himself than in harming her. "You may know science. But you have no capacity to understand the minds in the sculptures from a holistic or heartfelt perspective, and that is essential to helping them right now."

As she passed him, the Curator said, "Persephone, I trust your capabilities. You will launch further in your research as a result of this. Your father had the same sincere hope. Good luck."

Persephone stopped and turned to face him. "Gaining your trust was my goal, Dr. Stennis. But luck should be *your* main concern." There was nothing left to say.

She returned to her room and reviewed the material he'd given her the night before, more out of intrigue than a commitment to the procedure. In pondering the decision she needed to make, the only thing that helped her feel better was watching the holographic video of her father twice more.

Seeing him gave her the faith to know she'd find a way out of the situation ... or he never would have led her into it. At least she had to believe that now.

***

Enough.

After digesting the instructional recordings and understanding more about her father's decisions, Persephone's thoughts again turned to finding a way out of the building, now from inside the apartment.

She looked up and saw a large heating vent on the ceiling next to the back wall. If she could get up there, maybe she could pull herself through the space between the floors. Perhaps she could access the main gallery by traversing across the beams.

It could happen ... hopefully she wouldn't get stuck ... or fall through the ceiling. She certainly didn't want the drama, or the pain, of a medical emergency.

Persephone selected a chair from the small kitchen table and the sharpest, sturdiest implement she could find from the drawer ... a spoon.

She put the chair under the vent and stood on it to inspect how the rectangular plate was attached to the ceiling. The mystery did not reveal itself easily. Whatever fastened the piece remained hidden. She reached up and tried to slip the handle of the spoon under the edge of the metal to pry it up, but it was firmly embedded.

Well, that wasn't the answer. When Persephone hopped off the chair, her weight transferred down hard onto one of the floor tiles when she landed. She stepped off and it popped up.

Dammit, she wanted the heating vent to come lose, not the floor! She reached down and picked up the tile. Great, it wasn't cracked. Removing the square revealed a small cavity concealing a shoebox. Shoeboxes had not been commonplace for thirty years!

She fished out the box and carried it to the kitchen along with the chair. After dusting off the container over the sink with one of the hand towels, she set it on the table. Thankfully it appeared free of any signs of rodents. Inside she found a collection of personal memorabilia: cards, photographs, some digital drives and a few print-outs. Did the items belong to Dr. Stennis?

A holo-photo of a college rugby team, a napkin from an old butcher shop in East London and a glossy marketing postcard from the Clapham Grand—*Enjoy Rugby World Cup viewing parties*—reminded her of home.

A print-out of a news story from nearly forty years earlier: "25 Laughing Rugby Fans 'Scrummed' Nurse's Auto in Clapham," showed a photo of a group rocking the front of a car.

Persephone pulled a rolled-up piece of thick, cream paper out from the box. The tassel tied around it slid off easily, and she opened the scroll to reveal a diploma from the University of West London.

This is to certify that
Jacob D. Freeman
Has been awarded the Degree of
Bachelor of Science
Having followed an approved programme in
Computing Science and Cybersecurity

School of Computing and Information Technology
31, May 2071

Persephone continued to leaf through the box, piecing together a sporadic history of Jacob Freeman. Who was he? It looked like he was from London, but lived in Singapore after college, working as a computer technician.

She came across multiple print-outs of news stories—perhaps forty of them—identifying victims of various causes who had disappeared around the world, including Dr. Franklin Stennis. Suddenly the belongings felt creepy, like something she shouldn't be looking at.

At the bottom of the collection Persephone found several plastic surgery brochures highlighting the benefits of NTS for facial reconstruction. They touted using skin grafts for a renewed complexion—and the latest glass inserts for new eyes.

It wasn't until she started putting the items back into the box that awareness began to dawn. *Wait a second …*

She took a closer look at some rugby portraits. In one of the team photographs the men stood with their arms folded across their chests. She noticed the tallest man had a tattoo around his left bicep exactly like Philip's.

Persephone looked more closely at the news article of the group scrumming the car. The same tall man with the tattoo stood right in front. But she knew now he appeared Asian.

It wasn't necessary to read through all the material to recognize what she had uncovered: Items she was never meant to see. *Oh my god; he doesn't know I know this*, she thought.

Jacob hadn't just changed his name; he had changed his entire British identity. That's why Philip had said he studied with her mum at UWL, but almost never crossed paths with people connected to his former world.

What about *Sharpshooter*? Dr. Stennis had said Philip "escaped" a turbulent history with him, an assassin. In a stack of forty news stories about people who had disappeared, Dr. Stennis was the last one. Obviously Philip needed to cover some tracks, and in alliance with Dr. Stennis, had lived in the apartment to do so.

The secrets she'd uncovered demanded she put the items back into the box exactly as she'd found them. Afterward, she carried the collected memories across the room and slipped them back into the small compartment in the floor.

After placing the tile over the box, she pushed down on it gently with her foot and heard it click into position. Seamless. Maintaining her composure around Philip would be easy as well. She knew her discretion would be instrumental in saving a life—her own.

If only the solution to getting out of the gallery would reveal itself so easily. But another night was coming, and given her new intel, Persephone decided to remain in the apartment for the rest of the afternoon to strategize her options.

PART SEVEN

Vision

"The most powerful sense for awakening the mind is seeing. It raises awareness and connects us to our vitality," the old monk said, as he prepared to end his lecture.

"Sight-based impressions, like color, stimulate our energy and affect our moods and thoughts.

"In week seventeen of gestation, developing eyes see blurred images. Although dark inside the womb, human skin allows light to pass through, providing a dull red glow inside. This is why red lights reflect visual memory in the sculptures.

"Through vision we can know the element of fire. The flame of perception directed within aids realizing pure consciousness.

"Even though sight develops last of the senses, some say it is the most challenging to lose or be without.

"Our eyes view the world before us—but our experiences shape what we see, as much as what we don't see.

"When you walk to the grand stupa to witness the glass Buddha, consider your own active and engaged senses moving through your individual world.

"Then, imagine being without them, with only your thoughts, memories and consciousness to occupy your mind. Inner vision and knowing reveal more truth than external impressions.

"If one cannot adapt to the Sculptured Way, all will go black," he warned. "It can happen quite quickly. Emptiness is the result for the unprepared. Residual memories of sensory input and perception, as if in a dream, may develop.

"The mind may grasp for something solid to anchor its incessant swirling. Fainter than a candle flickering amid the rays of the sun, it may struggle to remember basic sensations: hunger, thirst, fire, the wind.

"Should you wish to continue your journey toward this most artistic of sensory deprivations, please make an appointment to discuss your current training and meditation practice. This is a pilgrimage few have taken. Of those, we may never know who found freedom in the light."

Chapter Thirty

On Saturday evening Franklin arrived at the theater alone. He watched his last theatrical performance starting at eight o'clock—selected less for its actors, its reviews, or its audience, than for its location near a Satellite Harvest Center. He worked to burn that last event into his memory—every detail.

Eight minutes after the final curtain, he was ready. He contacted Mr. Goode and said, "The time has come."

After he hung up, he knew Mr. Goode would immediately alert contacts along the pathway to ensure his body would move through predetermined channels without interruption. To circumvent any unexpected delays, Mr. Goode had programmed the Curator's microchip to show he paid a high enough premium to have his body processed right away.

Franklin only considered three cutters in the satellite harvesting system to be excellent at extracting brains and spinal cords with expert attention to detail. He'd been communicating through Mr. Goode for days prior to ensure one would be working that Saturday evening.

When the Curator's phone rang several minutes later, on

the other end Mr. Goode said, "The best cutter, Vincent, will be on. I have laundered the agreed-upon payment and assured him I will make a clean transfer into his electronic account right after he completes the work. He understands the importance of this night."

"Will you tell Persephone we've activated the system?" asked the Curator as an inquiry, not a request.

"She'll know soon enough. I want her well-rested. I brought her some dinner and locked her into the basement apartment for the final approach, to ensure she will not find a way to escape."

"Thank you for your assistance, Mr. Goode."

"Have a smooth trip, Stennis. I'll pick you up in a few hours," he replied before the Curator heard a tick followed by silence on the line.

He was ready. His desire to be bodiless inside his glass sculpture would allow a new level of research—being the subject immersed in his own experiment.

Franklin left the theater at ten-fifteen. He walked slowly through the lobby as he reached into his suit jacket to find the small capsule Mr. Goode had placed there, assuring him he would feel no pain. He held it for a moment, rolling it between his fingers, then put it between his teeth, closed his lips and gently bit down.

The mildly sweet contents sat on his tongue for a few moments before he swallowed. After he did, his pulse rate diminished within seconds. The effect caused him to rest a moment in the lobby, walk again, then fall unconscious two minutes later outside on the upper platform of the theater steps.

As he fell, Franklin noticed a few theatergoers turn their heads to look at him. He felt himself breathing heavily as the crowd transitioning into the warm evening air gathered around him and stared.

He saw them standing over him; then he closed his eyes. While EMTs attended to his physical condition, his personal journey was a mental one; a trip through sporadic life memories embedded deep within his psyche.

Images, sensations and thoughts rallied together in a thick

fog. A flash of himself at five nestled into his mom's warm lap.

She stroked his fine hair, sang him the alphabet and read him stories. They turned pages in giant picture books with trains and airplanes, and happy children spending time with their families. Tales about animals came to life ... they jumped, flew and laughed across his room.

Sweet and kind nanny Mirela rubbed his back and tucked him in at night, helping him sleep when his parents were away. One day she didn't show up to bring him home from school.

"She died in a horrible auto accident," his father said. Three months later his second nanny, Cesarina, came.

He's eight; it's his birthday. His mom smiles at him. "I cooked your favorite tomato soup." He spilled some on his black T-shirt. Cesarina was angry. His mom wasn't; she gave him a hug, "It's okay," she said.

"How do you like your clean shirt now?" Cesarina growled at him. "The prickling will last just long enough to make it painful. Nobody will believe you if you tell them." And they didn't. A needle-footed centipede ran across his chest and exploded into an itchy crawl he couldn't stop scratching.

Franklin prayed for the nanny to leave, to get into an accident, to die. But she stayed. "Don't be so cold and unemotional toward people who want to give you care," his mother scolded.

His mom made more soup then disappeared. Cesarina added spoonfuls of crushed Thai peppers. Where were his parents? "Eat it, Franklin! Eat it now!" He closed his lips as Cesarina straddled the front of him. He fought the scalding liquid poured onto his face and down his shirt.

"I was a nurse before I came here, you know ...," she said when she tied him like an 'X' onto his bed. "The little mix I put in your dinner won't let you move, but luckily for you, you'll still be able to feel." She smiled and then her face went blank.

His parents kept traveling. Now nine, he knew they didn't like him. His father came into his room one night after returning home late. "Will he hug me goodnight?" Franklin silently hoped. "You are an odd young fellow," his father said instead.

A flash of himself at ten: His parents left on a work trip and never came back. "They left because of you," said Cesarina. He couldn't move from the drugs. Her frequent torture overloaded his senses and his brain systematically shut them down as it fought to regulate the pain.

"We'll go to Singapore as a family," he heard his mom say. Later his estranged aunt told him, "Your folks planned for you to attend school in Singapore. Leave; it will be best for everyone."

No Cesarina. No more Bulgaria. No excitement about anything. Numbness and detachment only brought emptiness. If his nanny came back, so would torture. Was she following him?

He barely remembered his roommates: Jack, Arthur, Chen, Marty, a kid with pills for sale. A redhead with a strong jaw locked him out of his room. He walked solo through the dark halls of institutionalized boarding schools. A Buddhist monk reached out: "There is power in the mind," he said.

He feels sixteen again: "You can do amazing things, but you must be open to the possibilities," his therapist told him. Later he said, "'depersonalization neurosis' is your primary diagnosis. Your sensory cortex functions abnormally, putting your sense signals into a neurological traffic jam."

People bored him. He only wanted to fill his mind with new information. "You're in your own world," said one teacher. "I'm sorry about your parents. Do you miss them?"

"No. They abandoned me."

"Do you want to learn about them to understand more about yourself?"

"I don't care," Franklin said.

Time moves on: Now sitting in a sophomore class as an undergraduate, he meets Douglas Jones, a bright and compassionate student from the United States with brown skin and a big smile. Douglas says, "You're an information sponge who does nothing but study. Want to get a bite to eat?"

Douglas accepted him. Their banter about the nature of reality flashed for Franklin as his last solid memory before his mind went dark.

"Where does the soul live?" Franklin asked.

"Ancient Egyptians believed it resided in the heart so they

preserved the organ inside mummies," Douglas said.

"I disagree with the Egyptians," said Franklin. "Scientists and philosophers since Plato have pointed to the brain as the soul's location. Egyptians should have encased *it* as the seat of the soul."

"You'll see ...," said Douglas.

***

Inside the ambulance, EMTs attended to Franklin's shallow breath. When a rash broke out across his chest they restrained him from aggressively scratching it.

His heart stopped on the way to the hospital. Medical workers tried to restart it, but his self-induced coma mimicked a common heart attack. The ambulance doctor noted ten thirty-two as the time of stoppage.

From there, Franklin began the same journey all his acquired minds had gone through—save for Sifu and Douglas Jones.

EMTs routed him to the nearest SHC instead of the hospital, arriving at ten forty-five, as expected. They kept him primed for harvesting by infusing his body with Tissue Viability Preservative during the trip—standard protocol for badly injured individuals, or those too ill to arrive at the hospital alive.

A heart and lung pump forced the liquid into his circulatory system. It provided oxygen to prevent additional tissue damage and cooled his body to induce hypothermia. This halted his metabolism and any further physical deterioration, to avoid injury to the organs before disassembly.

The team administered a rapid-test in transit to detect genetic make-up and match his organs to waiting recipients. They also screened for diseases and systemic drugs prohibited in donations. The city's mosaic of ethnicities meant a proper donor pairing could be made in almost every instance.

His physical body had reached its end.

The system allotted his organs. At that point, Vincent began extracting the brain.

The process started with a craniectomy to remove part of the skull. To take a living brain out of its head, while keeping it intact and functional, required exacting methods. Vincent removed the organ with superior precision. He carefully maintained the arteries and veins to attach them to the supply pump in the transport case.

Vincent prepared the brain for Mr. Goode to retrieve along the route. His efficient dissection readied the Curator's viable mind by one-forty a.m. Standard methods of transport threw off any sense of impropriety.

Early Sunday morning, the brain-filled case entered the citywide Automated Distribution System headed toward the SMHC. Many industries, ranging from hospitals to food service and retail used these hubs where RFID scanners directed packages to their destinations. Medical parcels, including organs, dictated priority processing and traveled through the system without delays.

Mr. Goode hacked into the network and reprogrammed the scanners to redirect the brain box into the food delivery channel. Perishable foods moved quickly without attracting attention in the chain.

A young woman working at a downtown deli secured the transport case, along with her other deliveries, at one fifty-five. Philip claimed it, providing the worker with a generous sum to see nothing.

Chapter Thirty-One

Before she went to bed Saturday night, Ardis Jones sensed something was wrong. Persephone had not called her on her birthday—a date her graceful daughter would not have overlooked, no matter how busy.

She considered perhaps Seph had run into colleagues at the robotics conference and lost track of time, but the thought did not settle her mind.

The early morning hours ticked by and Ardis couldn't sleep. Her concern grew, and she roused herself out of bed at four-ten, deciding to investigate the situation.

As a top computer expert, she had her own methods of digital tracking. When Persephone was born, Ardis had buried a line of undetectable code into the standard microchip configuration all newborns received. Implemented as a security measure, the signals operated on a customized network Ardis had created that couldn't be blocked, removed or stolen.

She never told her daughter she had programmed an extra level of protection into her chip. Nor did she teach her students how to encrypt chips to the nth degree. Only she and Douglas knew she had done it, and they used the secret tracker occasionally, for fun, when Persephone was a teenager to test its operation and verify her location. But traditional microchip tracking generally worked out fine.

Persephone's standard chip information showed she was at her hotel, but Ardis couldn't reach her there. It also appeared Seph's handheld computer had been removed from the network altogether.

Ardis knew whoever was tampering with her daughter's electronic tracking could not truly make her invisible without being able to block access to Persephone's hidden code.

She activated her secret beacon and used GPS to gather more information. She discovered Persephone had been contained in a small area of Shanghai with very little movement for two days. While she couldn't pinpoint the exact location of her encrypted microchip, on account of now outdated technology running on much faster systems, she was able to narrow it down to a one-block radius inside the central Qingpu District.

Ardis contacted the Shanghai police. With the few details she gave them, they correlated the information and found the area she pinpointed fell within a 'dead zone.' When they learned she sought Dr. Persephone Jones—a name on their current watch list in connection with Dr. Douglas Jones, and his link to Dr. Franklin Stennis, they elevated her tip to INTERPOL.

Police told Ardis passing through the 'dead zones' set up by criminals around the city resulted in a vacuum of information, with all digital signals lost. Knowing the location of these zones could help identify a five- to seven-block radius where somebody could be hiding something. But investigators always required more specific clues to discover where and what.

When Ardis contacted the Shanghai police, she gave them the key they needed to get one step closer to unlocking the puzzle near Qingpu Xincheng.

Chapter Thirty-Two

"It's three in the morning," Persephone said when she opened the apartment door on Sunday in response to the firm knocks that reverberated through the walls.

Philip Goode stood before her, the serious look on his face conveying a great sense of urgency, even as his eyes shifted away from hers.

"The time has come," he said, before he shoved a box of dim sum and a small bunch of red bananas into her hands.

"What's this?"

"Eat something. We need your mind to be clear."

"How do you know I will help you," she asked as she stepped outside the apartment and eyed the metal obstruction he had just removed from the jamb. She shut the door to join him in the hall, feeling resilient and ready from her cold shower.

"Because you are principled and want to assist your father. And you know too much now not to," he said.

"Please, eat some breakfast and meet me in the operating room in fifteen minutes."

Then he turned and exited through the double doors.

She sensed Philip's general dis-ease to be a radical departure from his previously unfettered demeanor. His tension told her one thing: She now had the upper hand.

When she entered the freshly sterilized surgery room at three-fifteen, Persephone joined Philip in silence as she surveyed the room once more.

Philip picked up a black case from a small rolling table and set it down on the stainless steel operating table in the middle of the room. He turned on the bright overhead lamps and handed Persephone a clean scrub suit, surgical head cover, foot covers and gloves. The violet light provided the only warmth in the room, but she shivered for other reasons.

The case looked a little smaller than she expected. Opaque and nondescript, its exterior showed only a tracking label and the battery charge indicator for the circulation pump.

Persephone knew what and who was inside—the brain of Dr. Franklin Stennis, the Curator, the developer of NTS and the man who'd prolonged her father's life. She knew his reality was already far-removed from sensory connection. But she could not know what might await him after he awakened inside the glass.

She noticed the two tables containing the front and back halves of the sculpture with the completed light installation had been moved from the middle room.

"Let me make expectations very clear," Philip said with seriousness and a harsh look in his eyes. "This transfer must happen now, and it must be successful. Let's begin."

"Why do you suppose I will agree to do this surgery?" asked Persephone.

"Many benefits are yours," he said. "As for me, I'm ready for a change. But the Curator did not keep my best interest in mind with this decision."

"Your best interest?"

"I could end this in an instant. Yet, I will follow through with his installation. Why is that?" he asked.

"A final act of friendship?" she replied, as she thoroughly scrubbed her hands in the small sink near the corner of the room.

"I'm not feeling too friendly," he said. "I recognize this procedure shifts control to you. The thought of staying hidden doesn't please me."

"You must have known this was coming for some time. It should be no surprise," she said.

Philip appeared calm, but his voice and obvious desire to start the process revealed his unspoken concern that investigators could interrupt them before they completed the procedure.

"Yes, I knew. The Curator suggested his interest to me years ago, but only once. He didn't mention it again until recently. When we learned Dr. Jones had a liver transplant and wouldn't able to perform the sensoring and installation job, it compressed the immediacy of bringing him here."

Persephone considered this new information. She was surprised to hear both Dr. Stennis and Philip knew, before her dad even came to Shanghai, that he couldn't conduct surgery. The Curator didn't act with altruism by putting her father's mind into a sculpture—any benefit to her dad was a distant second to his own damn goals.

When she added up the information, she realized moving into the glass could not have been a real choice for her dad. He didn't fear death. At that moment she accepted the truth: Everything about her father coming to the gallery was a lure to bring her there to do the surgery.

She tried to bury her thoughts, knowing they would only confuse the immediate situation. Persephone dried her hands and turned toward Philip. As her eyes met his, she asked, "Whose side are you on? Are you protecting him, or are you helping me?"

Philip didn't mince words. "I'm on the side of the future."

"What's that supposed to mean?"

"Be assured I will keep you under surveillance as long as I need to," he said.

She applied her mask and the virtual reality glasses, adjusting them, so she could connect to the robotic surgical assistants. Then she gestured to Philip to help her put on the gloves, and he obliged.

"Let's get on with this, shall we?" she said, not wanting to provoke him or further sour his mood. She knew she needed his assistance to complete the operation, and felt certain her mother could dismantle any digital tracking systems he may set up.

Persephone took a deep breath and reassured herself with her thoughts. *Stay focused and calm. Work to the best of your abilities. This will all be over soon.*

"Severed, mark, zero six two one, mark, two zero one five," said Philip in a strong clear voice, activating the hands-free opening of the case with the code preprogrammed by the cutter. The container opened slowly.

Inside, a translucent, sterile packing sheath surrounded the brain. A nearly silent pump sent a continuous flow of Tissue Viability Preservative through tubes linked to the cerebral vascular system.

The instrumentation monitoring the organ showed it to be in a perfect and viable condition in a comatose state; ideal for transfer and installation.

Persephone gazed at the Curator's brain as she mentally rehearsed and then executed the procedure to connect his tubes to the pump readied in the pedestal. Next she detached the pump in the transport case. Artificial blood replaced the TVP in a matter of seconds to provide a life-sustaining solution, bathing the brain in nutrients and oxygen.

The first step was done. She felt pleased it went well. Time to focus on more detailed work.

After disconnecting the cerebrum from its transport case, Persephone lifted it out with careful attention. The cold room supported her calm demeanor and reduced extra stress as she readied herself for the next phase of the operation. She moved with professional confidence, navigating around her early nervousness.

She gently pushed the tips of her fingers into the three-pound grey mass. The luminous globe of creased and folded tissue felt like managing warm butter in her palms with a delicate firmness. She turned it slowly, connecting with the magical experience of holding a living human mind.

Until then, all her surgical work had been on cadavers. The

brain she held felt much warmer. It didn't appear to have any physical abnormalities. *This is his mind! I'm literally supporting him in my hands! Oh my god!*

Philip stood on the other side of the table watching her rotate the brain. "Are you being careful? Don't press so hard. It's important not to bruise it."

"What?" Persephone asked, pulled out of her still moment by irritation at his condescending assumptions. "I won't bruise it! Do you think I have never worked with a brain before?"

If he thought they were starting from square one with suggesting she be careful, they weren't going to make much of a team. Of course, he had no reason to trust her, but his tense movements and facial expressions made her uncomfortable.

Philip stared at her, emotionless. "Nothing must go wrong with this procedure," he said.

Persephone recognized she didn't need Philip to build her confidence. But she, too, wanted this to go smoothly and she didn't want to have to navigate around his attitude.

"Do you really think this is the best time for intimidation?" she asked him. "Unless I'm making an obvious mistake, let me focus. Or any errors will be on you."

"Focus then, Persephone. You make one slip and it could be catastrophic. Time is not on our side, but you can do this. Don't botch it up," he said.

One of the two robotic surgical assistants held the shiny case receiving the brain; readied for the next step. The exterior of the carbon fiber form with its polished irregular facets looked more geometric than skull-like. Designed to be sealed into the sculpture, it resembled the rudimentary styling of the glass shell.

The robots, along with the customized interior of the box in its open position, perfectly supported the organ and allowed Persephone to use both hands.

Ready to begin and feeling confident about the sequence of the operation, Persephone locked her glasses into the external connector for the robotic assistants with a quick tilt of her head. The physical link avoided any static interference with the visual display projected onto the inner lenses.

She positioned the brain in the open case to be mounted into the figure and readied the first sensor. The form-fitted interior supported the Curator's cerebral matter as perfectly as his natural cranial cavity, mimicking its protective layers of tissue. Its precise grooves followed the path of the external sensors Persephone would place.

As she peered into the glasses, she took hold of the robotic-assist controls. Her hands were in it; she wasn't separate from anything now. All she needed to do was let a finger flub, and she could bungle the brain. She could create damage before the procedure went too far.

But she couldn't. Because if Dr. Stennis was alive, she knew she must proceed with care.

***

Although Persephone did not perform surgery as a profession, she had participated in numerous neurosurgery operations and knew the anatomy of the brain exceedingly well. She wrote her doctoral dissertation on the benefits of cadaver research in developing neural interface technology, followed by years of working at the neuroscience lab.

Her adept use of robotic assistance allowed an exact placement of the sensor contacts. The accuracy with which the virtual impression in the practice video matched the Curator's actual anatomy impressed her. The image perfectly overlaid what she viewed through the glasses, aiding the efficiency of her movements.

She didn't want to ask Philip how she was doing, but as his disposition eased, she could tell her progress must be going well enough.

Philip worked alongside Persephone. Immediately after she placed a sensor into the brain, he attached the sensory interfaces to the base. He tested each one to ensure its proper placement and verify its connection to the translator software in the pedestal. Then he moved on to the next.

Sensor by sensor they continued with the exacting procedure, working into a consistent rhythm. The two barely spoke throughout the operation.

"Sensor placed," Persephone said, after putting one at the predetermined location.

"Reading," replied Philip, if the sensor produced the target connectivity in the translator.

She appreciated his desire to finish. The silence between placements hung heavily in the space between them.

After they completed the connections, the robotic assistant closed the brain case, sealed the two halves with precision and prepared to mount it into the glass.

Philip moved to the middle room, beyond the wall he dissolved with the push of a button. He wheeled a large table holding the front of the sculpture, lying face down, into the operating room. The waiting assistant lifted the case—programmed not to put tension on the placed connectors—and lowered it into the hollow in the glass form.

Three hours had passed since they began. At six twenty-two in the morning Persephone felt the absolute gravitas of the moment.

With the brain case installed, Philip worked on the final connections to link the mind to the lighting system and adjusted the life-support tubes and wires. He used the overhead track crane to hoist the back of the sculpture off its table and position it above the front half. After checking the cables and hoses for the last time, he lowered the backside down onto the open glass figure.

Persephone knew she was done.

She stripped off her gloves and scrubs, placed the surgery glasses on the table, and took a deep breath. With her exhale came some of the anxiety building over three hours of the most intense procedure she had ever completed. She felt an odd sense of pride in her efforts.

"I have the secured the wires and tubes into the pedestal," said Philip. "I'm going to run an initial troubleshooting sequence to ensure strong operational connections."

When he did, the fiber-optic lights flickered with random hues of subdued intensity. "Excellent. The electronic devices have activated the display. The life-support system is functioning perfectly," he said.

Persephone understood the quick shifting array of colors resulted from the anesthetic still being administered to the brain, paired with the lingering effects of the suspended animation fluid being replaced by the synthetic blood solution. Still, she stood a bit awed. The constantly merging hues looked beautiful.

With the connections confirmed, the robotic assistant applied a clear adhesive to seal the sculpture's front half to its backside, leaving no visible seam.

With the glass bonded together, Philip used the crane to lift the entire piece off the table and rotate it vertically above its base. He lowered the figure and manually secured it to the clean white pedestal using the industrial adhesive.

The Curator's newly minted work, *Severed*, stood solid with variegated colors flashing across the surface, illuminating the interior.

To her surprise, Philip offered a direct, "Nicely done."

"Thanks," she said, as she watched the newest art piece standing before them.

The thought of her father going through the same procedure brought a wave of grief and anger. The visceral feeling overtook her; she ran to the sink and retied her hair back. Then she let the heaves of nausea and disgust take control, purging the mind-bending events and heavy emotions of the past few days, knowing she couldn't stop them.

Chapter Thirty-Three

Severed could go up to the gallery, but Philip saw Persephone needed a few moments first. He let her have them; he could use the time.

He made a final sweep of the basement and collected a few more items he wanted to take with him. A surgical knife, several rolled-up pieces of expensive art he had cut from their frames and a holographic image of the full sculpture collection.

Philip placed his selections into the bag of personal effects he had stashed near the roll-up doors with his boots before the surgery. When he peered back into the operating room, Persephone was still facing the sink.

There was only one thing more he wanted. He had planned to get it later with Persephone in the upper gallery, but she seemed preoccupied enough with her emotions that, for efficiency-sake, he decided to get it then.

He passed quickly through the double doors and entered his old apartment, swiping the microchip in his wrist across the portal out of habit, even though it was unlocked.

Directly under the heating vent near the back wall, he

pressed down hard on a white tile, triggering its release. The shoebox of personal papers stashed underneath was not as dusty as he expected from being hidden for a decade. He removed the container and pushed the tile back down to lock it into position.

Logistics of running the gallery had been a whirlwind ever since Douglas arrived. Philip never intended to leave the box in the apartment with guests staying there. But after Douglas, Persephone arrived sooner than they'd expected. And preparing to get the sculptures out, and Stennis in, had taken more prep work than anticipated.

As the box was well-hidden, it had slipped to the back of his mind. At least he had it now. More than being incriminating, his personal memorabilia meant something to him; it was all he had left.

After a final glance around his old living quarters, Philip left the apartment, being sure to keep the door unlocked for Persephone. He reentered the warehouse space and placed the box into his bag near the exit.

When he returned to the operating room, he found Persephone rinsing her mouth and face as the intense focus of the surgery gave way. He surveyed *Severed* as he waited for her to turn off the sink. Then he grabbed a towel from a nearby cabinet and handed it to her from the side.

"Here, take this," he said.

When she turned around after drying her face, she looked at the figure and said, "If I didn't know what I was seeing, I might find the sculpture quite lovely. It's a shame to have the truth exposed, don't you think?"

He stared at her, knowing Stennis had discussed the people held in the glass with her. He believed Persephone already knew much more than he thought necessary.

With careful words, Philip told her, "The Curator considered you a kindred spirit in science and discovery. His entire plan of bringing this gallery and our work to a close depended on you being here. He had complete faith in your abilities to perform his transfer, which you did successfully. This warehouse is yours now."

"What about my father?" she asked. "When did my father know his mind would be ripped from his body? What did you do with his body? He was too ill to send through harvesting ... there was nothing to harvest from him." Her eyes widened and she stopped speaking.

"Oh my god," she said. "You removed his brain in this room, didn't you?"

"Dr. Jones knew his time was short. He ... volunteered ... to go through the procedure," Philip said as a simple summary of what had happened to her father.

"I'm sure you feel generous in giving me that bit of information, Philip. Saying my dad *volunteered* rings more hollow by the minute. Both you and Dr. Stennis assured me my father agreed to be put into a sculpture ... and my research would benefit from his sacrifice," she said.

"Your father was a very skilled surgeon. Stennis planned for two years to have Dr. Jones place him into his statue. Had your father not been ill, you may have never known of this place, the Curator's efforts, or mine."

"What choice did he have? What you did to him, and all the others, has nothing to do with my work," she said. "To you and Dr. Stennis my father was nothing more than bait to lure me here! Dr. Stennis didn't consider my father a friend, ever. He didn't have the interest or capacity to be a friend. Everything he did was a means for his own interests," she said. "Don't you recognize he used you, too?"

Philip stood in silence as Persephone caught his eye. He had nothing to tell her; she already knew enough. There were no questions she could ask about her father that she couldn't answer herself.

"I always know the score," he said after a few moments.

He turned on the motor assist wheels in the pedestal and began moving *Severed* toward the door. It took very little effort to guide the heavy sculpture across the smooth floor. Its lights reflected in soft focus on the robotic assistants and surgical equipment, now switched off and dark.

Chapter Thirty-Four

"Let's go, Persephone. We need to get this piece upstairs where the Curator asked to be placed," Philip said, standing in the wide doorway, glancing over his left shoulder. "There is nothing more to do in this room."

Persephone followed Philip as he directed *Severed* to the freight elevator. They stepped in and he pressed '2'. The extreme slowness of the lift met her rising adrenaline as it coursed through her after the intense operation.

As the elevator began its ascent, Persephone concentrated on her breathing, taking measured inhales and exhales. The ride allowed time to organize her thoughts around the ramifications of the past few days. Although her focus had been methodical, she understood the implied force behind doing the operation.

Perhaps the men holding her hostage would only help guarantee she couldn't be deemed responsible in any way during a criminal investigation. Might she have willingly installed his brain anyway? The situation ensured she never had to answer the question.

To her surprise, a sense of admiration for Dr. Stennis' efforts overcame her. She opened to recognizing her potential to one day communicate with him again.

Persephone recognized, after the thoughtful and intense process of installing the Curator's brain, that her desire to re-establish communication with her father had allowed her to maintain motivation with minimal internal conflict. Following through with the delicate procedure of inserting sensors into his mind and putting Dr. Stennis into a sculpture meant she could serve a better future.

She visualized developing the interfaces of her communication technology well enough to evolve medical science. Only then could Dr. Stennis be brought to justice, his self-serving thoughts put on trial, ensuring his defeat. What about the other pieces? She imagined family members of those encased bringing lawsuits seeking the fortunes from the Curator's patent wealth left with no rightful heirs.

The brain in this sculpture belongs to Dr. Franklin Stennis, the former doctor gone missing. He holds responsibility for these crimes, she imagined saying at the court proceedings, explaining the story of her involvement.

Her thoughts shifted to the probability of being questioned about her role. The abundance of recorded evidence from the Curator and her father would most likely absolve her of any criminal intent. The ever-present danger to herself, and possibly her mother, should also be helpful to her case, should it come to that.

Of course, she had to do something, the jury would agree. She was the only one capable of helping if something went wrong with any of the victims, most of all, her father. That she trusted herself to aid a greater purpose would certainly free her in the court of public opinion.

That same trust in herself freed her heart to open to a more expansive awareness. She felt unified with science and with the sculptures. She aligned with Dr. Stennis' mission from a place of compassion for his disconnection. And she appreciated the statues had helped her see what Dr. Stennis could not see: The absolute necessity of progressing neuroscience from a heart space, not just from the head.

Persephone's thoughts drifted to the future medical technology and legal reporters who might try to put the pieces of Dr. Stennis' personality together. She considered the brain of the man she'd sensored. His isolation as a young person, his parents' disappearance, the ill-treatment from his fellow students, and his disinterest in personal relationships created a fragmented foundation. All this cultivated an egomaniacal nature; the mortar of his personality.

The events leading to his public evaporation, including his superior intelligence, surgical skill, analytical mind, and of course, his medical discovery, all played into his inflated self-image. Still, she knew he did not have the light required at his true north to point his moral compass in a positive direction.

***

When the elevator finally opened on the top level, Philip guided *Severed* into the center of the room where her father's glass figure stood alone in the empty gallery.

After encountering the festivity of lights the day before, Persephone registered a strong sensation in her chest—shock, and a little sadness—came from seeing the area stripped of sculptures.

Dr. Stennis' mind would never have the chance to join the community of souls he fostered. The world he created to engage with disappeared before he arrived.

After placing *Severed* next to her father, Philip turned toward Persephone. He stepped toward her and put his hand on her upper arm.

"No!" she shouted, grabbing his arm and immediately twisting it into a side-extended armbar. Philip folded forward as she hyperextended his elbow joint. She executed her split-second Judo move without any thought at all—a gut reaction triggered from already feeling on edge.

"I told you not to touch me," she said.

"I commend you, Persephone. I'm never caught off guard," Philip said, turning adeptly to release his arm from her bind.

Persephone prepared to leverage her full body to secure another hold. She knew it would be more difficult if they both remained standing, however. She would have to apply the lock from the ground.

Then what? She recognized Philip's size and weight gave him more strength. But she had the advantage of being shorter with a lower center of gravity.

Philip looked calmly at her for a moment then said, "Oss."

"The expression used at the start of a fight!" she said.

"I use it now to recognize the lifestyle of a martial arts fighter," Philip said as he stood with a relaxed posture. "We move forward, resist and suffer what it takes ... making it clear we will always do our best. Oss! Here's to courage and the spirit of perseverance when pushed," he said, giving her a slight head nod. "It's not easy to withstand the most arduous of training and show determination under pressure."

The two looked at each other in a moment of silence.

Philip broke it. "Carry on without giving up, Persephone." He walked toward the elevator, pushed the call button to open the door and stepped inside. As he turned to face the gallery, he raised his palm toward her in a gesture of goodbye.

Without response, she watched the door slowly close as Philip disappeared behind the metal curtain. Persephone knew when he reached the basement, he would exit the building through the underground garage and fade into Shanghai forever.

***

Relieved to find herself alone, she touched her father's sculpture. After so many unexpected and grotesque experiences, the moment gave her a chance for a long pause. She didn't know what her next step would be, but felt grateful for the reprieve.

"Well, Dad, I found you. You led me here, but I still found you. I hope you are okay in there. Can you sense me here? This is what we have now."

Practitioner turned bright blue and white, shining like the glinting ocean in sunlight, as she visualized her connection with her father.

"I understand why you brought me here. This isn't about my next logical step to progress science, is it? It's about recognizing I must bridge heartfelt connections to move forward."

After several minutes, she tried opening the double doors to exit toward the stairs but they remained locked. "Of course," she said.

She walked to the elevator and pressed the call button, but Philip had already disabled it. Once again, she found herself locked-in. At the same time, she felt freer than she ever had.

Persephone sat on the ground next to her father's sculpture, closed her eyes and crossed her legs. She recalled her experience in the gallery the day before. It showed her how much soul energy could reach out and supported a feeling of being whole at her center.

This was an ironic juxtaposition to knowing the decade the Curator had spent building an encased community to replace those he couldn't connect with in the physical world had come to an end.

She continued to draw from the ineffable resonance of peace underneath the uprooting of her reality. The feeling lingered with her as she sat meditating in a state of expansive interconnection for forty-five minutes.

Chapter Thirty-Five

A grand crash on the lower level snapped Persephone out of her calm. She stood up and dashed to the side room to peer down at the scene.

Shanghai police streamed through the front doors, having broken them open with guns drawn, on high alert.

"They actually told the truth!" she said out loud, remembering how distressed Dr. Stennis and Philip seemed over the past few days, amid their discussions of time dwindling and the impending discovery of the warehouse.

Her eyes scanned the main gallery: All the paintings were gone!

The stark white walls of the empty space shocked her as much as seeing the officers. Where did all the art go? Philip must have removed the pieces the night before. In the absence of the dark oils, the area looked so light.

She returned to the upper gallery and moments later, after a resounding bang, the heavy double doors flew open and an officer rushed in leading with a gun.

He saw Persephone and yelled, "Hands on your head! Don't move!"

Persephone complied as two more officers rushed in, talking on their communicators, barking commands to continue searching the rooms.

One grabbed Persephone's hands and moved them down her back, placing her wrists in restraints.

"What's your name, ma'am?" asked the female officer standing behind her, patting her down for concealed weapons.

"Persephone ... Jones."

"Do you have identification?" asked the officer.

"Not at the moment ... it's downstairs," she said, trying to deescalate any suspicions the officers may have about her.

"Persephone Jones?" the second officer asked, as he glanced around the gallery still pointing his weapon.

"Yes."

"Is anyone else up here with you?" asked the female officer.

"Um ... only these two sculptures."

The officers put their guns back into their holsters.

The policewoman grabbed the communicator on her vest. "We're checking the upper gallery. Over," she spoke through the device.

A moment later her communicator crackled with the voice of another person. "We found identification for one Persephone Dee Jones in a basement apartment. Over."

"We have located her upstairs," the female officer responded into her handheld. "She's alone. And safe. Over."

"You can take the restraints off," the officer at the doorway called to her companion. "Then secure the rest of the floor."

The officer removed the handcuffs and Persephone could hear conversation over the handhelds identifying the different areas of the complex being secured. Searching officers provided brief, but broken descriptions of the rooms. She listened for them to discover the operating space and the loading dock, wondering if they'd find signs of Philip.

The basement was quiet with no one found.

After officers in the upper gallery completed their search of the side room, the policewoman spoke into her vest, "All clear here. You can let her come upstairs."

"Your mother is here," she told Persephone.

"What? My mother?" she asked, shifting her focus toward the door.

"She helped us find this location. Is there anyone else in this building?" the officer asked in a serious tone.

"I ... I don't know. I wouldn't think so," said Persephone. "There was somebody, but I think he probably left."

"Our officers are securing the warehouse. Have you seen either of these men?" the officer asked, approaching Persephone and holding out a digital photograph of an older man standing some distance behind another man dressed in Buddhist robes.

She recognized the picture was the same one INTERPOL had showed her at the hotel. Only now she knew the monk had to be Sifu, and she wanted to see his face.

"How did you know I was here?" Persephone asked, as she took the device to look at the image more closely.

"Your mother was able to help us locate this building through the 'dead zone,'" the officer said.

Persephone pointed at the photo and said, "I haven't seen this monk, but. ..."

The policewoman noticed her abrupt pause and turned her head to direct her left ear toward Persephone. She squinted to indicate she detected Persephone knew something.

"What about the man behind the monk?" she asked.

"The man behind the monk ...," Persephone repeated, considering all the phrase meant at the moment. "It looks like it may be Dr. Franklin Stennis," she replied, expanding the image on the screen to get a better view of him and Sifu. She noticed how handsome Sifu was; he looked so kind.

"Is he here?"

Persephone looked at the sculpture she'd just completed. Her eyes shifted upward. She returned her gaze to the officer and took a big inhale as she prepared to speak.

Suddenly Ardis entered the gallery and Persephone turned toward the door. Her breath came out with force, "Mum!"

Winded from racing up the stairs, her mother moved quickly toward her, hugging Persephone hard with both arms. "Seph, are you okay?"

"Mum ... how did you find me?"

"I'll explain it later, love. Did you find your father?" she asked.

"Yes. A lot has happened. When did you get here?" Persephone asked.

"Excuse me," the policewoman interrupted, taking the digital photo out of Persephone's hand and pointing at the screen. "Have you seen this man you think may be Franklin Stennis?"

"I apologize, officer. There's a lot of activity going on here. Yes, I have seen him."

"Are you aware of anywhere in this gallery where a person could be hiding?"

"Secret hiding spots?" Persephone asked.

"Correct. Have you found any?"

"Yes, definitely," she said. "They live inside."

Epilogue

All experiences are preceded by mind,
Led by mind,
Created by mind.
Speak or act with a corrupted mind,
And suffering follows,
As the wheels of a cart follow an ox's footsteps.

All experiences are preceded by mind,
Led by mind,
Created by mind.
Speak or act with a peaceful mind,
And happiness follows,
Like one's own shadow.

—BUDDHA

Three months after INTERPOL discovered the gallery, the National Neuroscience Institute in Singapore requested, and received, *Severed* through the Shanghai High People's Court for their lobby.

Inside the glass, the Curator's mind filled from the bottom to the top with enclosing doom, weighing him down with a sinking heaviness. Unable to move, the ponderous notion of being alone pushed him down and dragged him backward into the silent cave of his own beginnings.

Pulled deeper inside, the walls narrowed, pinched and pinned him. Blurry points of light appeared all around him, coming into tight focus before pulsing through. Awareness came and went in fleeting dreamlike glimpses.

He followed a memory of his index finger, grabbed his fingerprint, and pulled to watch the impression of his hand unravel like a spool of yarn. How thin the line of the spiral. The idea of skinning his whole body from one threaded piece, on and on, in an endless micro-destruction created an unstoppable horror of tearing himself apart.

His mind narrowed like a gigantic pupil hit by bright light. Reduced to nothing but a single eyeball, it dilated in fear, plunged into darkness. With vision reversed, he entered heavy clouds of orange and burgundy cast across his inner space. He drifted through obscurities, unable to direct his gaze, as vapors from the colorful fog parted and the city's enormous buildings, thousands of feet below, reached up toward him.

A shimmering silver airship moved into view so close the soft reflection of his gazing eye shined back at him. As the dirigible passed, its turbulent wake pushed and pulled his pupil like a small balloon battered by a blowing fan.

Left spinning as a single eyeball torn and floating, he stared into the thin atmosphere of pale stars shining. In a flicker of lucidity, blackness descended within him. From this deep darkness came a connection to everything spun like a cosmic spider web, undone.

***

P ersephone maintained her father in her lab at the Centre for Neurotechnology at Imperial College London.

She began engaging with a worldwide team of researchers working to create sensory interface devices that could be used to communicate with the sculptures. Most scientists worked in Shanghai at the original gallery location; reconfigured to support reacquired pieces.

One night, eight months into the project, Persephone dreamed she could finally integrate speakers into her father's thought patterns. To hear a digital re-creation of his voice felt like a miracle.

"Dad, we have the capability to reconnect you to your senses. Is this what you want?"

"I once did," he said. "But a lack of sensation opens my mind's purest reality. Re-integration into the physical world would now be an unwelcome transition; like being born anew having a memory of it all. I don't wish to be a part of the crude earthbound world again. Let me stay in peace; I'm free."

"Where are you now?" asked Persephone.

"I am absorbed in simple existence more than I ever thought possible. My awareness remains intact; my being reaches into Absoluteness. I experience everything a connection to the senses once provided, without the physical bonds. Now all is held *within* this empty space."

"So you are at peace feeling nothing?" she asked.

"Exploring the great nothing ... hearing and tasting, seeing, smelling and touching nothing ... means sensing and merging into everything."

"Would you call it meditation?" she asked.

"I once dreamed of being without distractions ... being one with all. Meditation that removes sensation and draws toward a focused place is only the beginning. From there, everything expands infinitely in a radiant sphere. I am held inside this peaceful space. I merge into a hum. I don't suddenly have answers; I have no questions. There are none to ask."

"So am I only communicating with the residual energy of your enlightened mind now?" Persephone asked, unsure how to quantify his words.

"The difference between this eternal space and death means I maintain a foothold in the realm of human existence. Once I die, I will move beyond it. My perceptions will return to integrated energy. I won't perceive my oneness; I will simply fold back into all.

"For now, I embody this beautiful state of being. Thank you for sustaining this gift for me, my dear Persephone."

***

Shanghai, Twelve years later

In 2121, only one original sculpture remained on public view. It sat high inside a mountaintop shrine on Bright Peak in the Huangshan/Yellow Mountains at the Sculptured Way Illumination & Meditation Centre.

Each week thousands sought out the glass statue, visiting the 'SWIM Centre' as a pilgrimage destination to pray and meditate.

All hoped to intersect with Sifu's out-of-body experiences; to be touched by his light. They desired to merge into the space between his form and theirs in an indefinable connection that could only be described as "purest love."

Some wanted to reveal their own light.

Special permits allowed devotees the option to legally become Light Age stupas as a spiritual lifestyle. This completely transformed the path to enlightenment in Shanghai. A radical sect of Buddhists following the "Sculptured Way" emerged seeking a potentially quick route to *Nirvana,* by forcing sensory deprivation upon the mind.

A medical facility behind the shrine promised the necessary care to undergo the transformation into a glass vessel—a "clinically induced enlightenment"—and to sustain seekers as long as their minds were viable.

The peaceful nature of the SWIM Centre gave many young seekers an absolute misconception about being released from the body. Like the Curator, many participants didn't realize the inherent difficulties until too late.

Each week an old monk led sensory awareness tours for those who expressed interest in the Centre's meditation training and preparation programs.

"Our Centre has only approved fifty people to step away from the physical," the abbot said. "Even among them, many simply weren't prepared for the reality of existing only in their mind.

"If an undisciplined or impure mind pursues this ultimate sensory withdrawal, a looming state of fear may pulse from an unwakeable nightmare. Parameters of reality can stay unreachable; equalization of the mind may become elusive.

"A master well on his own path, Sifu did not volunteer for this level of experience," the guide reminded the group. "Sifu's success as a sculpture came from decades of practice ... before being removed from his physical senses."

The monk glanced at Persephone listening near the back of the crowd and continued. "Our research—along with help from the finest minds in integrated neuroscience—has determined Sifu's brain activity follows similar patterns as the most devout practitioners of Buddhist meditation alive today. Witnessing his white glow allows us all to experience the beauty of enlightenment.

"Keep in mind: freedom comes from learning to kindle the light within. Life begins in darkness, and in the end, it returns to darkness. In between, a journey through the senses unfolds. An awakening may happen, an entry into light—but you can't force enlightenment."

T H E   E N D

SCULPTURE GALLERY

ACQUISITIONS

FIRST SERIES (7)

ACCESSION NO.	TITLE	DONOR
2098.1	*Untitled*	Anonymous
2098.2	*Untitled*	Anonymous
2099.1	*Untitled*	Anonymous
2099.2	*Untitled*	Anonymous
2100.1	*Untitled*	Anonymous
2100.2	*Yogini*	Wang Yan
2101.1	*Occupant**	Thomas Ridley

SECOND SERIES (11)

ACCESSION NO.	TITLE	DONOR
2101.2	*Sharpshooter**	The Principal
2102.1	*Prisoner**	Andrew Truypso
2102.2	*Artist*	Siti Binte Musa
2103.1	*Socialite*	Lily Holtz (patron)
2103.2	*Tycoon*	Evan Julliard (Johanas) (patron)
2104.1	*Racer*	Francisca Santos (patron)
2104.2	*Schizophrenic*	Ruby Carlisle (patron)
2105.1	*Musician*	Xing Chen
2105.2	*Director*	Hans Heckman
2106.1	*Angel of Death**	Thanda San Suu
2106.2	*Maw*	Anonymous (patron)

THIRD SERIES (6)

ACCESSION NO.	TITLE	DONOR
2107.1	*Tribal Elder* ± (body)	Deodata Ramos
2107.2	*Chessic* ±(mind)	Jude Ryan
2108.1	*Internee*	Frieda Grayson
2108.2	*Monk* ±(spirit)	Sifu
2108.3	*Practitioner*	Dr. Douglas Jones
2108.4	*Severed*	(Open)

* Criminal Quartet collection
± Holy Trinity collection

ABOUT THE AUTHOR

JEN L. HANSON

Jennifer teaches meditation and yoga in Portland, Oregon, photographs nature and keeps bees. Former lives include serving as the President of the Portland Art Museum's Docent Council; editing financial magazines in New York City; working in high-tech PR in San Francisco; and teaching teens English with the Peace Corps in East Java, Indonesia.

Her degrees include a M.S. from Northwestern University's Medill School of Journalism in Reporting & Writing, and a B.A. from the University of California, Berkeley in Mass Communications.

Jennifer lives with her husband, Eric, a designer and maker whose brain loves to create. For fun, she offered to write one of the books that lived in his head. Their conversations illuminated his ideas, providing a puzzle of plot pieces and character sketches inspiring her debut novel, "Sensored Souls."

Made in the USA
Middletown, DE
07 October 2021